Marriage of the Smila-Hoffmans

Also by Maryann D'Agincourt

Journal of Eva Morelli

All Most

Glimpses of Gauguin

Printz

Shade and Light

August

Marriage of the Smila-Hoffmans

Maryann D'Agincourt

PP

Portmay Press
New York

 This is a work of fiction. Names, characters, businesses, places, events, and incidents are either the products of the author's imagination or used in a fictitious manner. Any resemblance to actual persons, living or dead, or actual events is purely coincidental.

Shade and Light was originally published in slightly different form by Portmay Press in 2018.

August was originally published in slightly different form by Portmay Press in 2021.

Cover image: *Thistles*, 1883/89, John Singer Sargent, public domain image via the Art Institute of Chicago.

Cover design by Emily Albarillo

Printed in the United States of America

ISBN 978-1-7360536-7-6 (pb)
ISBN 979-8-9860337-1-6 (hc)
ISBN 978-1-7360536-8-3 (ebook)

Library of Congress Control Number: 2022906496

Names: D'Agincourt, Maryann, author.
Title: Marriage of the Smila-Hoffmans / Maryann D'Agincourt.
Description: New York : Portmay Press, [2022]
Identifiers: ISBN: 978-1-7360536-7-6 (paperback) | 978-1-7360536-8-3 (eBook) | LCCN: 2022906496
Subjects: LCSH: World War, 1939-1945--Fiction. | Artists--Psychological aspects--Fiction. | Fathers and daughters--Fiction. | Families--Fiction. | LCGFT: Historical fiction.
Classification: LCC: PS3604.A332544 M37 2022 | DDC: 813/.6--dc23

PP
Portmay Press
244 Madison Avenue
New York, NY 10016
www.portmaypress.com

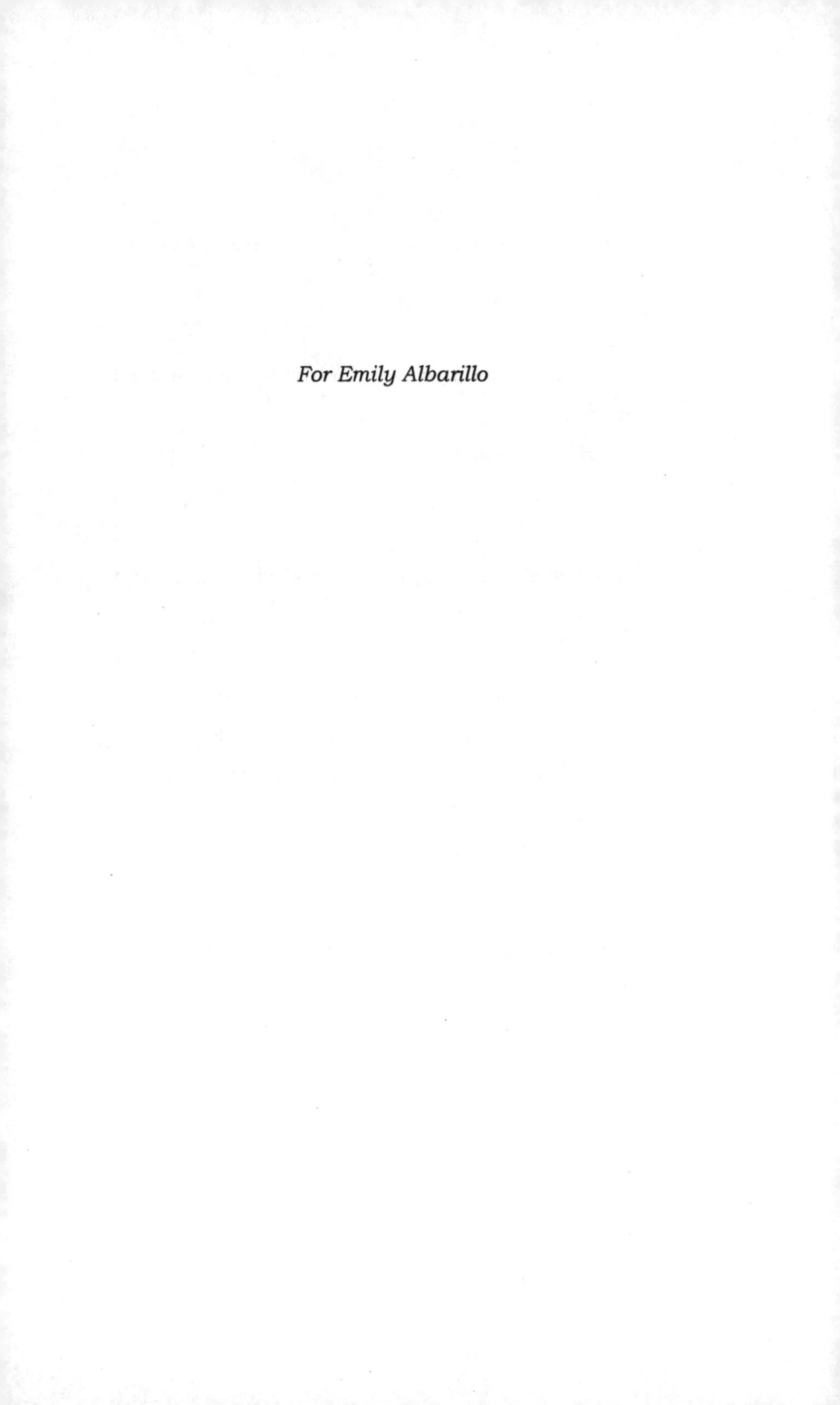

For Emily Albarillo

Marriage: A word which should be pronounced "mirage."
—Herbert Spencer

"Impressionism" was the name given to a certain form of observation when Monet, not content with using his eyes to see what things were or what they looked like as everybody had done before him, turned his attention to noting what took place on his own retina (as an oculist would test his own vision).
—John Singer Sargent

Contents

Prologue

Trieste, 1941

A breeze off the Adriatic tousles Henri Smila's fine brown hair, his cheeks slacken, his firm visage appearing less severe; turning away from his view of the sea, he looks toward the wide piazza facing the harbor. His sense of discipline, intellectual and physical, is evident in his presence—shoulders raised tightly, his eyes sharp, alert. In his hand is a plaid cap, which he now fits onto his head, adjusting the brim at a precise angle. Although his inherent lightheartedness has been subdued for the past year, there is a suggestion of it in the slight curl of his lips, yet it does not extend to his gaze as it would have in the past. More decisive than patient, his passions embedded, he's both in hate and in love. His hate is a drumbeat pounding into the depths of his being; his love is rumbling, profound, like a Beethoven sonata. Fixedly he's awaiting his future.

In the strong noon light Johanna makes her way past the throng of people in the square; crossing the piazza, she strides toward Henri, vaguely aware of the seagulls flying above the harbor. Catching the slight change in Henri's demeanor, she is filled with hope. But within moments she forces herself to face reality: this is not a joyous time, this war will hammer our happiness, bend it out of shape, deform it, she fears.

Henri has asked to meet her by the harbor after her singing lesson. They have been married for a month and he has encouraged her to proceed with her plans for a career in opera as if she were a single woman, as if they lived in a time of peace. Apprehensive now, she doesn't know why he has asked her to meet him. If there is something important he needs to say, he could speak to her in their apartment.

In the time that she has known Henri, he has never been completely carefree or relaxed and because of this she is uncertain of him, of his proclivities, of how serious he is in his solid opposition to fascism. When she is alone and uncertain of his whereabouts, she'll wonder if he is more committed to his political philosophy than he is to her, to their marriage. He is ten years older than she is, highly intelligent.

Her strong confidence in herself is evident as she approaches her husband, her shoulders thrust back, accenting her pronounced chest and slim legs. But it is her sensitive and poignant expression that is most telling; it is what causes her to appear more experienced than her years. She was born this way, she'll say.

Her parents have spoiled both Johanna and her younger sister, have taught them to accept only the best. Her husband is different from her family—her parents ignore politics, they live in a cocoon, but Henri doesn't, he never will. There is an edge to him, and then there are his moments of lightness, which have been less and less in evidence these past few weeks. Though they have not discussed it and probably never will to any extent, she has gleaned that he's been attending political meetings after work. She suspects he and his colleagues are contemplating risky activities, which if detected would result in their imprisonment or worse.

As she draws closer, approaching him, Henri smiles, his expression relaxing even more. "Why, Henri? Why have you asked me to come to the harbor?" she asks. Her full voice carries a pulse of anxiety.

"I needed to see you before I return to work," he says unabashedly. She smiles deeply, aware that he aches for her presence as much as she does for his. But she knows there is more on his mind, more than he is willing to share. She reminds herself again of his political sentiments and where they could lead, and she experiences a darkness within.

He is determined that Johanna not see his concern; he knows this may be slightly disingenuous on his part but she is the only person who is able to distract him from his worries. She is vivacious in a mature way. It is not the day to tell her where they soon may be forced to go.

Again and again he questions himself. Is he more compelled by the actions he and his colleagues are considering, or is he more enthralled with Johanna? He never could have foreseen that it would come to a choice—political ideals or love—that one would need to take precedence. Do you stay and fight, or walk away to the comforts of marriage and eschew your beliefs? To be successful at both would be impossible at such a time, and in times of war because of lurking dangers, even marriage provides few comforts. As he embraces her, he is riddled with conflict. Tightly closing his eyes he recalls her clear, operatic singing; he envisions her nearly beatific expression, her spontaneous breaths, and then the release of her voice. Yet once he opens his eyes, he looks upward and studies in detail the cawing gulls crossing the harbor.

Shade and Light

One

Encounters

Jonas Hoffman's parents met in 1941, in front of the Ethel Barrymore, two months before the attack on Pearl Harbor. Moonlight flowed down Forty-Seventh Street, burnishing the lettering on the marquee. From opposite directions they each approached the theater.

On the trip to New York, Jonas's mother, Cora, then twenty years old, had been accompanied by her younger sister Rina. As the Arenzi family lived in close proximity to Boston, the sisters had taken the train from South Station to Grand Central to see the musical *Best Foot Forward.* David, Jonas's father, was alone; a few hours earlier a customer in his family's hardware store had offered him a free ticket to the play. Because of the vigorous wind that October evening and the future Mr. and Mrs. Hoffman's attempts, heads lowered, to dodge the next anticipated gust, along with the disparity in their heights, they collided. Then, after collecting themselves, they each profusely apologized, while Rina, her shoulders sloping, waited near the door of the theater. When the play was over, Cora Arenzi and David Hoffman spoke again.

A concise version of the encounter was told to an eight-year-old Jonas on a Sunday afternoon in late 1953. He sat slouched in a large, soft armchair across from the vacant brick fireplace in his aunts' living room, the November rain pelting the windowpane. With a bored and dubious expression crossing his narrow face he toyed with the plastic figures of horses and cows Rina would present to him whenever he and his mother visited.

Fraternal twins, Rina and Belinda were five years younger and four inches taller than his mother—Rina had blond hair she wore upswept in a chignon, later it would be a French twist; Belinda's dark fine locks fell unstyled to her waist. In contrast, his mother's chestnut brown hair was cut short and tucked behind her ears. Whenever a young Jonas would come upon Cora sleeping, he'd gingerly touch her hair; enticed by her beatific expression, he'd rub a few strands between his fingers, moved by how soft and wispy it felt.

While her two sisters smoked incessantly, Cora refused to touch a cigarette. Moments before they had come into the room, he had noticed a trail of cigarette smoke wafting from the kitchen, followed by the low and pressured voices of his mother and aunts.

Jonas's heart pounded; he sensed something of consequence was about to happen. He tightly clutched the white plastic horse in his right hand. When he looked up, Aunt Belinda was approaching. Her lips pursed, she knelt before his chair, her long hair grazing the armrest. Although she was the one Arenzi sister who had not been in New York that October evening twelve years before, she had been chosen to speak because, of the three, she was best able to contain her emotions, and her speech was most to the point. She leaned in close, and as she spoke, he felt the pressure of her forefinger on his wrist. He was uneasy: no one but his mother had acknowledged his father's existence—it was a forbidden topic, he'd gleaned—and whenever Cora had done so she had spoken in a soft and somber tone about David's passing years before.

As he had never known his father, the young Jonas had no desire to learn how his parents had met. His sharp sense of color was what he would often refer to to help him interpret what he viewed as an intrusive and murky adult world. Half listening to his aunt's words, he became absorbed by his mother's royal blue skirt, the curvy hem, and how the material swung as she paced by the window, her arms akimbo, the shade half-drawn, the lower pane splattered with rain. Next, and with the same intense focus, he studied Aunt Belinda's purple V-neck sweater, his gaze lingering on the two cigarettes she had tucked inside her bra. Lastly, he fixed his eyes on Aunt Rina, standing in the far corner of the room, wearing a pale gray dress, soft and diaphanous, her face slightly flushed. It then came to him—he imagined his mother as a blue arc darting forward, Belinda a hovering and fierce purple wind, Rina a floating moon, and his father a large moving shadow.

After Belinda finished speaking, she rose, her mouth now relaxed, and caught his gaze. In the same direct way, she asked if he'd like ice cream. Within seconds, his aunts and mother had gone back into the kitchen; Jonas soon followed.

What he would most remember about that day would be the persistent sound of rain against the windowpane, the curve in the hem of his mother's skirt, and the cigarettes crushed between Belinda's breasts. He would carry no particular memory of Rina because she was and always would be the same to him—warm and elusive. It would be years before it would dawn on him that the intervention had occurred because his mother and aunts had been concerned—as of that day he had not asked any one of them about his father. For he had remained silent and still whenever his mother had spoken of David.

Over the years that followed, the circumstances of his father's death would become more and more clear to him. From conversations he had had with his mother at different stages in his life, he had pieced together that his father had died toward the end of World War II, two months after he had married his mother and five months prior to Jonas's birth. His father, during his training as a medic, had developed a mysterious infection a few days before he'd been scheduled to be sent overseas. He passed away three days later. It was difficult to imagine a strong, vibrant young man, as Jonas believed his father had been, becoming suddenly very ill. In his photos David Hoffman appears tall, robust. In most of the pictures his father's pose is identical, his hands pressing against his hips, his elbows spreading out to the sides. If he had lived, Jonas imagined him striking the same pose if he'd done something his father approved of or if he'd done something that had displeased him—his father's chest more expansive in the former case and more concave in the latter. The only photo Jonas had seen of his father not posing with hands on hips was his wedding picture. When Jonas was about fourteen, he deduced that in this photo he was already growing inside of his mother and, with both angst and gratification, he realized it would be the only picture of the three of them together.

On those snowy weekends of his childhood his mother would appear less grounded, more ethereal, more similar in demeanor to Rina. In the small, wood-paneled den, Jonas would stand close to her and study how languorously yet precisely she'd iron a dress of hers or a shirt of his. Or in the kitchen he'd sit on a stool and observe her stirring flour and eggs together, her hips gently swaying. She'd speak about his father in a low full voice. "He was kind and sensitive," she'd say, her warm and intelligent brown eyes reflecting concern. Then, while collecting her thoughts, she'd momentarily raise the object in her hand—either a wooden spoon or an iron—before continuing. "Because of his kindness, his sensitivity, his family had to a certain degree underestimated him. They were New Yorkers—their ancestors had come to America years and years ago, one hundred or more, I think. They'd been hoping for an ambitious son. But he was happy." And then she would smile, her lips closed, in that quick and thoughtful way of hers.

This had led to a recurring image of his father dressed in beige, lazily lying in a hammock with his eyes shut, and yet Jonas felt uneasy viewing him in this way. He believed he had done so because he had found the meaning behind his mother's words obscure: "to a certain degree," "underestimated," "ambitious," "New Yorkers." He was convinced there was more to what she was saying than he comprehended or she wanted revealed.

After a year or so of such conversations with his mother, which began when Jonas was about ten years old, he turned to his aunts for clarification. He did so on the day his class discussed their fathers' work. When it came to what he presumed was his turn, Jonas stood up, his heart beating frantically; he said, "World War II, he died." Everyone in the class turned to look at him in awe. Although they all knew his father had passed away during the war, they appeared to have a newfound respect for him now that he had boldly acknowledged it.

His teacher, a frenzied woman with dark unkempt hair and pointy glasses, looked confused for a moment; she had had no intention of calling on Jonas. She blushed and said, her voice weakening, "Thank you, Jonas. Your father was a hero." Reflexively Jonas smiled with hesitant pride, gazing back at the other students—he liked the word "hero"; it erased the image that previously had come to mind—no longer would he view his father as lethargic and unfocused, but energetic and larger than life—heroic.

After school was dismissed he made his way to his aunts' home. It was a warm day in mid-June, and he found Aunt Rina sitting outside on the front steps, her palms grazing the concrete, a cigarette burning between two fingers, her long legs crossed, an open book overturned next to her. She was looking off into the distance. Jonas knew she enjoyed conversing with Mr. O'Malley, who lived across the street, and assumed she was staring at his home, a red brick ranch with flagstone steps, hoping he would come over and strike up a conversation. She wore more makeup than usual, her eyeliner going beyond her eyes, giving her a theatrical look.

As Jonas approached, he waved his hand. He knew she at first had not noticed him coming up the walk.

Her tone easy, she said, "Handsome, you nearly scared me." He was encouraged, for he relished the sound of Aunt Rina's hushed voice.

"Are you waiting for him?" he asked, turning to look in the direction of the house across the street.

"I'm waiting for you, Jonas," she said defensively, her eyes on him. "How was your day?"

Her eyes peered into his; he felt a deep sense of comfort. Hastily she turned to snuff out her cigarette, and then cupped his chin in her hand, her long fingers enfolding his face, gazing at him in that penetrating yet elusive way of hers.

When she released his chin, he sat next to her and placed his homework folder down beside him, his hands pressed against the step. He stretched out his legs and crossed his ankles. The sun in his eyes, he squinted and told her what happened in school that day. Occasionally a car passed by. The sound of a lawn mower in the distance afforded him a sense of privacy. From time to time his gaze would stray across the street to see if Mr. O'Malley, who was a few inches shorter than his aunt, had come out of his home.

"Did you know him well?" he asked, feeling the words stick in his throat. It was the first time he had asked her about his father.

"Of course I knew David," she said with a distant look in her eyes. "He was shy and sweet and I thought Cora was lucky to have met someone like him."

"Was he a hero?"

Her eyes saddened, her voice even lower now, she answered, "Yes, he was a hero, he was heroic, he'd been that way since the day we met him." Brightening some, she continued, "Your mother and father were an attractive couple—sophisticated."

No longer fixated on the house across the street, her eyes wore a hurt expression.

Seven months later, on a cold, wintry day, he asked Belinda about his father. It was a snowy day in early January and school had been canceled, but it was not stormy enough for his mother or Rina not to go into work. Jonas spent the day with Belinda, who was free on Mondays. Once finished with her chores, phone calls, and shopping—usually by the middle of the afternoon—she'd sit down with Jonas and read aloud from a novel by Mark Twain or Charles Dickens or James Fenimore Cooper. Her body hunched over, she'd enunciate with pinpoint accuracy, which Jonas often found more intriguing than the story.

On that day she held a copy of *A Tale of Two Cities* in her hand and was about to open it to the page she'd left off reading a few days before. Touching her arm, Jonas asked, his voice stoic, if she had known David. She paused and sat still, her fine dark hair sprawled across her narrow back. Turning to him, she met his gaze and spoke frankly: "Your father was a fine man, Jonas—kind, considerate, and truthful. He was an individual—well-read and intelligent. Your mother was content with him. They were a happy couple." Then she opened the book, lowered her head, and began to read in her precise way. Although her eyes were steady and fixed on the page, he noticed a lone tear trickle unevenly down her cheek.

Jonas harbored two visions of what his parents had been like as a couple, gleaned from his mother's textured words about his father, and from what he had learned from Rina and Belinda. And then there was his own independent impression—what he had come to understand about his father from the grainy photograph he kept beneath his mattress. His father had been eighteen years old when the picture was taken. He is standing with two other men of his age in front of what appears to be a hardware store. Jonas thought he could make out the name "Hoffman" on the sign. He would pull the photograph out, hold it close to the light, and assiduously study it in bed each night.

One vision he had of his parents was of the two of them living in a big city with many skyscrapers, walking down a crowded street, holding hands, his mother's set expression emanating with passion and determination. His father's demeanor was quiet and humble as they passed through the crowd, nothing about them ruffled, their expressions not changing, a halo of contentment surrounding them amidst the throngs of people and light rain.

The other image he held of his parents was of them at an elaborate party, admired by people, involved in separate conversations, dressed elegantly, his father heroic-looking and debonair, his mother wearing makeup, dressed in a fitted red and gold shimmering gown, her shoes matching the colors of her dress, the heels narrow and high. They confidently conversed with others, and when those they happened to be speaking with didn't notice, they would steal a long and passionate glance at each other.

Given his doubting nature, Jonas lightly questioned his imaginings. Ultimately it did not matter to him whether or not they were true. In such instances he was not a stickler for veracity. He chose to conjure his parents in these ways because such thoughts buoyed him.

Jonas grew to view marriage as a complex mystery. His perspective was the natural consequence of having experienced his parents' union only within the realm of his imagination, one that filled his young mind with gauzy images of heroes and halos, rainy days and sophisticated parties. Whenever any one of those images began to fade, he would turn to the dictionary. With the heavy Webster in hand that his mother kept lying horizontally on the lowest shelf of the kitchen bookcase, he would climb into bed, his heart racing, and scroll his flashlight across the tiny printed definition in an attempt to seek out the true meaning of the word "marriage." Yet invariably it remained a dry and elusive concept for him.

He would sustain that viewpoint for many years not only because of the unions of those in his general purview, but because of his natural dubiety. Imbued with primarily an artistic temperament and not necessarily a psychological one, in the case of marriage he could not penetrate what was happening beneath the surface of any relationship—all appeared to seesaw unnervingly from banality to excitement. And he, Jonas Hoffman, was the skeptical albeit determined onlooker observing the ups and downs of every union he witnessed.

In his twenties, Jonas would come to know Jenny Smila, a seemingly shy woman of eighteen. He'd often wonder if her shyness was a mask of sorts, not a simple black or white plastic one, but a colorful and intricate papier-mâché mask decorated with rich fabrics and jewels, one that could be found in shops along the narrow cobblestone streets of Venice. It was a mask she wore with much subtlety and ease as if indeed it were a simple plastic one, an item that at her discretion she could gracefully slip on and off.

For Jonas, part of her allure had been how she'd hold her head to the side, her ear in proximity to her right shoulder as if she were at a museum studying from a particular angle a complicated and dense painting. While walking or speaking with another person, she'd lower her head as if to avoid what she'd see when she looked up and met the doting gaze of her companion. Yet whenever she did make eye contact, she was surprisingly frank in her assessment, her gray-brown eyes sparkling with candor and at those times seemingly not shy at all. But her frankness was short-lived. For whenever the recipient of her candor returned it in kind she would immediately lower her gaze as if needing to hide what she had been intending to reveal. Jonas knew this well, as he was often that recipient. This led him to conclude that she hoped to scrutinize another's psyche, but did not want her own to be penetrated.

Not only was she evasive about her height, in her tendency to lower her head, but also about her slimness; she wore loose-fitting clothes, neutral colors, mostly pants and skirts with silky blouses.

Although he may have been the first man she had found compelling, there was nothing about her demeanor to suggest inexperience. She was composed—less romantic and more practical than her appearance indicated. And despite her shyness, which he naturally questioned, she was not naïve, nor was she cynical.

Because of her overprotective mother and strict father, both of whom had been born in Trieste of mixed ancestry—her mother, Austrian and Italian, and her father, Austrian and Flemish—Jonas soon realized Jenny carried with her European sensibilities and protocol. He noted how she had arranged it so that her friends interacted as little as possible with her parents, particularly with her mother. For if they were too much exposed to Mr. and Mrs. Smila, Jonas had gathered, Jenny believed it would brand her in the eyes of her peers as overly dutiful and perhaps passive. If her nature were different, Jonas supposed, she would have been a more rebellious eighteen-year-old. But rebellion was not her inclination. Instead she was tenacious, unlike anyone he had known.

Although he had come to know Jenny when she was eighteen, Jonas first had become aware of her four years earlier. Following his graduation from college he had returned home to learn that a new family had moved into the house next door. It was 1968 and he was twenty-three—because of his dreamy and skeptical nature, which at six had revealed itself as hesitancy, his mother had kept him home an extra year; she had decided he would not be mature enough to start school for another year.

Their neighborhood consisted of a row of ranch-style homes with back lawns that more often than not were overgrown. His mother had informed him about the Smilas the morning after his return. Her words were soft and persistent; she didn't want to discuss the alternative, which was his future. He had been an art major, and had no job prospects in sight. She feared he would be drafted and sent to Vietnam.

It was a hazy morning and over breakfast his mother spoke in a detailed and respectful way about the new family in the house next door, the Smilas, creating a shadow as she pressed her finger against the yellow-and-white checked tablecloth. Jonas assumed this was the same manner she would use with her customers in her position as bank manager, a role she had worked diligently to achieve.

Soon the sun broke through the mist, and a breeze flowed in through the open window, lifting the half-drawn shade. The soft light illuminated the coffeepot on the stove, the percolator at the top of it now still, and the side of the refrigerator, a dark gold color. The shade gently slapped back against the windowpane.

"Jonas," she said, giving him a quick and endearing smile. She had named him Jonas because she'd come across the name in one of the novels she had read. She had a predilection for westerns—she'd read or watch one on television or at the movies, with her glasses on and a solemn expression crossing her face, as if soon afterward she intended to write an analytical essay.

"Jonas," she said again, her smile more abrupt. "The Smilas are from Trieste, though their daughter, Jenny, an only child like yourself, was born here." It gave her an added confidence, he thought, that the Smilas presumably were interested in staying in America, which was important to her as a daughter of immigrants. "I spoke to Mrs. Smila—Johanna is her first name. She is an experienced and knowledgeable woman; she and her husband, both of mixed ancestry, first and foremost view themselves as Europeans," Cora said, pressing her finger again on the table for emphasis. Jonas studied her deep brown eyes. There was something in her expression, particularly in her gaze, he had not before noticed—both steady and questioning, her lashes blinking more than usual, her mouth slightly open when she paused in her words, and he wondered what she really thought of Johanna Smila. He wasn't certain if in truth she loathed her, as he knew his mother would never acknowledge not liking anyone, or whether it was because Johanna Smila had piqued his mother's curiosity as very few people had done before.

After speaking with his mother, Jonas stepped out into the backyard. The sun shone brightly; it was unseasonably warm for a late spring day. His mother recently had had the lawn mowed. He went over to the lounge chair that she had parked in the middle of their small yard to sun herself.

He lay back in the chair and closed his eyes. It was difficult to fathom that he would not be returning to college. Memories from his days at school crossed his mind like a series of colorful fireworks on a sultry summer night—sparkly and fleeting. Then he thought about his conversation with his mother. He knew how worried she was about him, and he could not blame her. He realized her talking to him about the new neighbors had been her attempt at diverting herself from her concerns; it pained him that she worried about his future. Still, he gathered, to a certain extent she was impressed with Johanna Smila.

He opened his eyes and slowly looked to the side, glimpsing a young woman in the adjacent yard. He surmised she was Jenny Smila. His mother had mentioned that she was fourteen, but she looked younger. On a ledge close to the sloping roof of the garage she sat alone in a pool of shade. Her naturally curly hair was in a long, loose braid, her cheekbones high and defined, half-catching the light. In her hand was a tennis ball, which from time to time she'd bounce with surprising force and gusto against a dry patch of earth. While her throwing motion was awkward, her expression was surprisingly placid, reminding him of the young woman in Botticelli's *Primavera*. His thoughts now turned to his junior year spent in Italy and France, traipsing through museums, drinking lots of wine, and his affair with an insouciant French woman named Claudine who sold postcards of the paintings at the Louvre. When he came out of his reverie, he looked over again at Jenny and saw that she continued to pound the ball against the ground as if in doing so she was willing grass to grow. Reluctantly he was intrigued.

Two weeks later, he received a call from a college friend who had moved to San Francisco about a possible job in an art gallery. His mother, who had always encouraged his interest in art, was elated to hear about the possibility of his working in a gallery. She paid for his plane ticket; two days later he boarded a flight to the West Coast.

Two

Summer

Outside her bedroom window the sky was gray; faint shafts of light fell tepidly over the sill. Jenny Smila closed her eyes and imagined the sun rising beyond the mist.

It was early April of 1972, her eighteenth birthday. How alone she was, she understood, grasping the blanket and pulling it close to her neck. She lifted her head and between the opening in the drapes she peered out at the still naked trees, the branches shaking from a sudden, brief wind.

Although she was born in Hartford, Connecticut, her parents, Europeans, were dismissive about her birthright. Their indifference to her American nature heightened her sense of alienation, more so than her not having a brother or sister. For no matter how often she'd visit the birthplace of her mother and father, she was keenly aware she was not from or of Trieste. Her disassociation from this city was not a choice she had made, but her reality. Yet she was not disheartened. To the contrary, she was filled with a subdued yet fluttering anticipation about her future, knowing she was strong. She was hopeful. And soon, she would be free.

Rapid knocks, a succession of them, on her bedroom door, before it creaked open. Within seconds her mother, cheeks flushed, appeared on the threshold, holding a tray; on it were two cups in her favorite china pattern, royal blue flowers on a white background, along with shiny silverware. As Jenny watched her mother approach she noticed Johanna's steps were hesitant at first, then swift, the cups and spoons rattling.

Her mother sat on the edge of the bed and placed the tray between them. Her mauve-colored silk robe revealed her ample cleavage and deepened her complexion and oval-shaped green eyes. She smiled and leaned forward as if about to relay a secret. Her voice sounding hoarse, she said she was not certain what the weather would be like that day; New England weather was unpredictable. She drank her coffee black and, after a few sips, added in her practical voice, gesticulating with her soft, round hand, that in one way or another it would be a beautiful day because it was Jenny's birthday. Jenny thought her mother appeared only mildly effervescent, her eyelids puffy; she gathered Johanna had not slept well. For her movements were muted, less spontaneous than usual, her gaze more fleeting. Jenny understood it was because she, her only child, was eighteen, an adult, and because of it Johanna felt older. Though deeply fond of her mother, Jenny knew she did not love her enough—she felt restrained.

Between sips of coffee, Johanna chatted about what they would do that day. Jenny listened with guarded interest, considering how it must feel to be a mother of an eighteen-year-old, the mother of an only child. But she did not ponder this for long—she was not in her mother's position and might never be; she fully intended to have more than one child or no children at all. She had planned her future as far ahead as she could see. On some days her view was clear and expansive and on others quite cloudy. But clouds had never hampered her. She smiled at her mother and, knowing her as Jenny did, she believed Johanna sensed her daughter's concern. Her mother was reassured, her enthusiasm no longer dampened by fears of time passing too quickly. Johanna again was living in the present. Suddenly she placed her cup down on the tray and brought one hand to the side of her face. She hoped she had not burnt the toast, she announced. As Jenny watched, Johanna hastily left the room, neglecting to close the bedroom door. Jenny looked past the tray and empty cups, and out the window; the clouds had dispersed. Light flowed in through the opening in the apricot-colored drapes, and she felt a mingling of concern and hope.

After school that day, Jenny and her mother drove into Boston. Their destination was Maurice's shop on Newbury Street, where Jenny would be instructed to choose any outfit she liked, no matter the expense. It was much cooler now. Johanna turned up the heat in the car. Although her mother's movements in general were expansive and unrestricted, when she drove, Jenny noticed how Johanna would push herself forward in the seat and clutch the steering wheel with both hands, as if, no matter the weather or traffic, she was driving though a dense fog, surrounded by a myriad of cars.

Maurice's was their favorite clothing store in Boston; they had shopped there ever since they had moved from Hartford. They would go twice a year—on Jenny's birthday and, in early November, on Johanna's.

A bell tingled as they stepped inside the shop; they were promptly greeted by Maurice, the owner, a middle-aged man of average height with a crown of thick dark hair, muted by a slight graying around his temples.

"Good day, Madame, Mademoiselle. I have not seen you in a few months, yes?" he stated impatiently. He motioned with his hand to a spiral staircase. Although Johanna wore high heels, she lithely climbed the steps, not holding on to the banister. With a forced elegance, she turned her head to acknowledge Maurice, who trailed behind her. It was Jenny's eighteenth birthday, she said, and she hoped to see her in something more adult, no longer the loose-fitting clothes Jenny insisted on wearing. She was a woman now.

"Madame, your daughter has been a woman for a few years," he answered curtly. Jenny's throat tightened; she felt constricted by Maurice's words, but then intrigued.

At the top of the stairway they stepped onto a plush white rug, which always surprised Jenny; it extended to the circular area on the right where there was a semi-circle of full-length mirrors. Opposite the mirrors was a beige leather sofa and next to it a wide matching armchair. Between the sofa and the arm-chair was an antique wooden table; on it stood a vase of fresh white lilies.

Maurice disappeared, and Jenny and her mother sat on the sofa. Johanna rested one arm across the curved top and crossed her legs, her pocketbook at her feet; smiling anxiously, she drummed her fingers over the arm rest.

Maurice returned with an armful of dresses nearly covering his face. Bluntly, he instructed Jenny to stand in the center of the room, before the mirrors. She felt her flat shoes pressing into the soft, rich carpeting. When she caught her image, she noticed her expression was startled. She had been thinking of their small, untidy home, the chipped linoleum on the kitchen floor and worn carpeting in the dining room, believing her parents should be spending their money on more practical items. She had been told by her mother that they bought her an expensive outfit once a year because they wanted her to be confident, but more often than not, she was embarrassed by their largesse.

Most of the dresses Maurice held up were straight and form-fitting. It was his practice to first show a dress to her mother, and then he'd turn to Jenny. Johanna would intently eye each one he presented, making comments such as not the right color for Jenny, not the right style, it would make her look too thin. Jenny would nod in response to each of her comments, hoping for a dress that was similar to her preferred style.

As she tried each one on, Jenny relished the feel of the material clinging to her body, experiencing a growing sense of physical well-being.

Maurice had given her mother a little bell to summon him once she had changed and they were ready for his next appraisal. He was always quick and eager to point out how well a dress looked on Jenny or if it didn't suit her at all.

As they dined that night at a restaurant on Beacon Hill, Jenny studied her parents beneath the light of the chandelier; she was filled with a high regard for them as well as a slight suspicion. Her father was dressed in his finest suit, black with tiny gray lines. She thought her mother looked unnervingly beautiful in a kelly green dress with a low-cut neckline. Her auburn hair was swept up off her face, highlighting her high cheekbones and exotic green eyes. She wore a gold necklace with a square flat emerald stone. Johanna's mother had given it to her for her eighteenth birthday—Trieste, 1942, the war, Jenny thought—no matter how diligently she tried, she could not imagine her mother as an eighteen-year-old, and neither could she fathom how it was to live in the midst of a world war at that age. To her it was as if the war had occurred in another century, in another universe. For her parents never spoke of those years.

Jenny wore the dress her mother had purchased at Maurice's shop that afternoon. It was silk, sleeveless, black and white, low cut in the front, even lower in the back, and fitted to her form. Her hair had been especially curly that day so she had arranged it in a French braid wrapped around her head.

Her mother leaned forward and patted Jenny's hand, and in a tone loud enough for anyone nearby to hear, told her she looked very beautiful. Jenny was anxious; what was most on her mind was the homework she had not finished, that was due tomorrow. As if reading her thoughts, Johanna told her not to worry about her schoolwork, that she must enjoy her birthday—it comes only once a year. Jenny, disconcerted, thought of their small home with the broken garage door and how once the spring progressed the grass in the backyard would be overgrown until her father was in the frame of mind to mow it. But readily she admitted to herself how much she was drawn to the luxury of the restaurant, the gold-framed mirrors, the glittering chandelier in the foyer and the smaller replicas scattered about the dining room. Yet again it struck her that they should not be there. This was not their reality; it would have been better for her to be home studying. But when she saw the delight written across the faces of her parents, she knew she must respect that this was what they desired.

Her father raised his wine glass and made a toast in her honor, saying that she had never appeared more elegant, that in less than six months' time she would be in college, away from them, that she was an adult now, that he respected her academic success. She lowered her eyes, overcome by his graciousness and his confidence in her. He had never been one to exaggerate or compliment her gratuitously. She wanted this moment to last forever. She did not know how to express her appreciation. Slowly she raised her eyes and gazed directly at him. "Thank you, Father," she said, and looked over at her mother, thanking her as well.

"Jenny, do not be so humble and demure, my darling. You do not need to thank us—don't you see, this is our way of thanking you for your poise, intelligence, and beauty," her mother said, gesticulating with one hand, holding on to her glass with the other. Johanna then motioned for the waiter to pour more wine into their glasses. Jenny noticed a drop of moisture above Johanna's lips. Her mother was anxious, Jenny understood, and her heart beat more quickly. She looked over at her father; he was smiling.

"Is something wrong, Jenny?" he asked. There was an uncharacteristic twinkle in his eyes. He was usually firm and serious, underscored by his narrow and erect frame. She saw he had put on the gold cuff links his father had given to him. There was a story she was not quite certain of regarding her grandfather hiding from the Germans during the war and those cuff links. Since neither of her parents spoke of the war, she had heard this story referred to in passing by a friend of her father's when they had been visiting Trieste a few summers before. His wearing the cuff links that night startled Jenny. She was beginning to believe there was something more to this evening, something she was not aware of. She felt a chill run up and down her bare arms.

"Are you cold, darling?" She felt her mother's moist hand over hers. Although Johanna's gaze was direct, Jenny noted her slight distress, perhaps even a trace of duplicity in her bearing. And she recalled her mother not telling her five or six years before that her great-grandmother had died. One day Jenny had come home from school and had found her mother in tears. Her heart pounding, she had asked her why she was sad, and her mother had looked at her in the same elusive way as she had now. What was she hiding this evening? Why was her father elated? She longed for his usual subdued self. She thought again of her kind great-grandmother, Nina—Jenny had not learned of her death until a year later; the information had come from her father as they were planning their next trip to Europe. He thought Johanna had told her by then. Were there other times when her mother had been evasive? She now wondered if she did not know the truth about a myriad of things. Different circumstances crossed her mind. She looked over at her mother, who was checking her watch.

The waiter came over to pour more wine into their glasses. Jenny felt dizzy. Although she had not had much to eat, she had been easily drinking the delicate wine.

When her mother looked up from her watch, alarm crossed her face. She met her husband's gaze. He shrugged. He was enjoying his meal and soon asked for the dessert menu. Johanna frowned and said, "It is nearly ten o'clock. Jenny has school tomorrow. She needs her rest. And you have to open the store early. You need your rest too."

Again, her father shrugged—his nonchalance was atypical, blurring the image Jenny carried of him as a once exacting engineer who had immigrated to the United States to work as a shoe salesman.

When they left the restaurant and ventured out into the Boston night, Jenny gleaned that the three of them, for varying reasons, were unsettled.

Over the two months that followed, Jenny noticed her mother becoming more and more restive. Johanna would often go next door to speak with Cora. Hoffman, a widow, whose only son—Jonas—worked in an art gallery in San Francisco. He had not been home in four years. Jenny was told that Cora had gone out to San Francisco on several occasions to visit him; sometimes she was accompanied by one or both of her two sisters. Jenny believed she might have seen Jonas once. Soon after their move from Hartford, Jenny had noticed a man reclining in the lounge chair in Cora Hoffman's backyard. But at best it was a hazy memory. She liked to look at the photos of him that his mother had hung on her sitting room wall. The picture that most aroused her curiosity was the photo of Jonas at sixteen, lying languidly in the grass, his arms crossing his face, as if shading himself from the rays of the sun, a scattering of wild daisies surrounding him.

Whenever they visited Cora, Johanna would talk of Trieste society, as well as how diligently she had trained to become an opera singer. While her mother spoke, Jenny would focus on

Cora, her rapt expression, the energy she exuded, her overall posture of optimism, and how Mrs. Hoffman's questioning and sensitive eyes closely watched her mother.

Because of Cora Hoffman's presence in their life, for Jenny, the name Hoffman had become synonymous with America—spirited, forward-looking—in a way Smila never would. For she would forever align the name Smila with their days in Hartford, where Jenny as a child would observe other adults, visitors she did not know, in their living room, many smoking heavily, speaking a foreign language, their expressions fraught with angst and a wary hope.

On an afternoon in late June, Jenny went out to the chaise longue. From her seat, she watched the sun slip behind the clouds. In her hands was Roth's *Goodbye, Columbus.* Most of her friends had read it when the movie version had come out a few years earlier. Her mother had insisted Jenny wait to read it at least until she graduated from high school. Johanna herself had not read the book, and had announced unequivocally she would never do so; she preferred European authors. "American authors favor action; European authors write deep, complex novels, novels that touch the soul. You are an American," she admonished her daughter. "Naturally you are inclined to read American books."

Jenny now lowered her head and read with abandon, her eyes running across the page. Drawn into the novel, she was not aware of how much time had passed. Slowly she heard voices, a conversation in the next yard. There was a slight breeze; the words floated in her direction. She did not look up from her book. She recognized the quick and round tone of Cora Hoffman's voice. Her words were low, but clear. She soon gathered that Jonas would be home on the first of July, and that he'd be spending the summer at a gallery on Newbury Street that was affiliated with the one in San Francisco where he'd been working.

"Cora, the truth is you don't want Jonas to meet Harold—I don't understand why you are so squeamish about their meeting." Jenny assumed it was one of Cora's sisters speaking.

Mrs. Hoffman answered, "I think it is because he never knew his father and I can only imagine what illusions he must harbor about him—probably even he doesn't realize how much he idolizes David."

"You were terribly in love with David."

Cora was silent for a few minutes. "This is about Jonas, Belinda," she answered abruptly. "I can't think of the past—it isn't good, it isn't helpful."

"Jonas is an adult, twenty-seven; he will not be surprised about Harold, and he won't become preoccupied with thoughts of David's absence in his life. You have protected him, Cora. You are not respecting him, his maturity."

Mrs. Hoffman's voice now was so low, Jenny could no longer hear her. Had she become suddenly aware of Jenny's presence? She didn't look up from her book and imagined Mrs. Hoffman motioning to her companion that she, Jenny, was in the next yard. Soon she heard a screen door squeak open, and then shut. Immediately Jenny looked up from her book; they had gone inside.

That evening after dinner, Jenny accompanied her mother to Cora Hoffman's house. As they walked through the front door, Jenny recalled she hadn't been there in more than a year. The foyer looked smaller, the furniture in the sitting room more crowded together than she remembered. There was a pleasant aroma of lilacs from a thick burning candle on top of the television set.

Johanna leaned forward in her seat, resting her hand on her daughter's knee, and said, "Jenny needs to find a more sophisticated and intellectual group of friends now that she will be going to college."

Cora nodded in agreement. "You never know what anyone truly believes, where anyone really stands nowadays." Jenny and her mother glanced at each other, not knowing what Cora meant. Then Mrs. Hoffman, her cheeks slightly reddening, rose reflexively from her chair and went into the kitchen to make coffee.

When she returned and handed them each a cup, the muted evening light caressing her form, she told them her son Jonas would be home for the summer, working in an art gallery on Newbury Street. Jenny studied Cora Hoffman, her short brown hair, her longish neck, her heart-shaped lips, and it dawned on her that she was not simply a middle-aged, long-suffering widow who worked in a bank. Her respect for her grew. Next to Cora her mother did not seem as approachable or real.

~

According to Johanna, Cora Hoffman's son had been home for ten days, but Jenny had not yet caught a glimpse of him. He had become somewhat of an enigma for her; she was more and more uncertain whether or not the man she had seen in the lounge chair four years earlier had been Jonas. Lately she had been having dreams of a man in a black cape, whose face was shaded by a low-brimmed hat. Jonas? she'd ask, tugging at the cape in her dream. But when she tugged too hard he fell facedown and shattered as if all along he had been a glass statue.

During the day her mother, her expression pointed, would urge her to walk to the beach, which was about a mile and a half from their home. Jenny noticed her father was more distracted than usual—he'd leave early every morning and then come home from the shoe store without saying very much. He would become absorbed in reading the newspaper or watching a baseball game on the small black-and-white television set, his foot tapping the floor, a thin burning cigar in the ashtray on the table next to him.

From time to time it struck Jenny that her parents might consider returning to Trieste. She could see the disaffection in their expressions, the sense of loss they wore so easily. She knew some of their close friends had gone back.

Toward the end of the second week of July, Jenny decided to take her mother's advice and walk to the beach. It was not too warm; a slight breeze caressed her arms. When she turned to look back at her home she saw that her mother was at the window and instead of drawing away so that Jenny might not catch her watching, Johanna waved in an encouraging way, prodding her forward. Jenny smiled half-heartedly, though she did hasten her step. After walking far enough so that her mother could no longer see her, Jenny slowed down again. But soon she was crossing the busy main street.

The beach was crowded. She went to the area across from a restaurant where she and her parents would sunbathe whenever they came to the beach. She looked for a space to sit on the low cement wall that bordered the sand and the sidewalk; the ocean was about fifty yards away. It was soothing to watch the waves come in and break at the water's edge. People were sprawled out on towels or in lounge chairs across the sand, and some children carried plastic buckets filled with either water or sand.

She wore her bathing suit beneath her clothes. After she found an empty spot on the wall, she removed her sleeveless blouse and sat in her shorts and the top of her two-piece bathing suit. Soon she lay down, using her blouse as a pillow. Her knees raised, she closed her eyes and listened to the crashing waves and the cawing seagulls. As she inhaled the smell of the ocean, a fine wind fingered her hair. After a while, she opened her eyes and noticed a shadow at her feet. When she looked up, she saw a man in shorts and a T-shirt sitting close to her, his long legs dangling, his toes hidden in the sand. She half raised herself, her elbows supporting her, scraping against the concrete. He looked over, his eyes steely and distant. He had blond-brown hair with slight curls that made him appear as if he were wearing a wreath on his head. He caught her gaze, and waved as if saluting her, then quickly, easily, he said her name.

His name was Eric Stram. He was thirty-eight years old. His body was long and narrow, his laugh, short and sharp. Jenny gathered that her mother had telephoned him to say she'd be at the beach that day and where to find her. He told her that Johanna, a friend of his parents, had sent him a photo of her about six months before.

She was flattered by his attention, his interest. He was not unattractive, yet she did not want to rush her life along. Like her parents, Eric was from Trieste. He was born in 1934; Johanna had been ten years old.

When her mother came into her room the next morning with a coffee mug in hand, Jenny sat up in bed. Taking the cup from her mother, she bluntly announced that Eric was much too old for her, that she did not want to rush her life along.

"His parents helped my family," Johanna responded, stopping herself from saying more. Then she said sharply, "Don't tell me about rushing your life along, you were not in Europe in the thirties and forties—we did not have a choice but to rush our lives along." She walked over to Jenny's bedroom window and, with one swift motion, pushed aside the drapes. Jenny drank more coffee from the mug. Her mother turned and said, "Jenny, you don't know what it is to struggle."

When Jenny met her gaze, Johanna looked away. Jenny

wondered what she was not telling her. With guarded respect she answered, "I understand, Mother, but your struggles belong to the past; the past is not the present."

"Don't be naïve, Jenny," Johanna said caustically. As her mother moved toward the door, Jenny said curtly that she would let Eric know she would go to dinner with him the next evening. In her mother's uplifted chin and trembling lips, Jenny read how conflicted she was.

It was too warm to walk to the beach. Jenny took her book—she was now reading Lawrence's *Women in Love*—and went to the chaise longue in the backyard. She began to read but became drowsy from the sun; her eyes soon closed. She did not know how much time had passed when she heard someone call out her name. She opened her eyes and realized it was Jonas, recognizing him from the photos she had seen on the walls in Cora Hoffman's home. He stood at the low gate that separated the Smilas' yard from the Hoffmans'. She sat up and removed her sunglasses. With one hand she shaded her eyes from the sun.

"That is, I assume you are Jenny," he said. He was older than she was but not as old as Eric. His mannerisms were more like someone of her age. His tone, slightly comedic, or was it more ironic, enticed her. He told her he had the day off, that he was Jonas, Cora Hoffman's son. "She's told me about you," he said. Jenny had not yet spoken. She continued to study his face, which looked more scrunched up because of his mustache, and lightly cynical, yet his body had a looseness about it that defied his skepticism. In a way, she had known him—or, more accurately, known of him—for four years. Without a second thought, she got up and went over to him; her feet were bare and the hot tar near the gate stung them. Her bathing suit was slightly dislodged. He held a sketch pad in his hand. They shook hands, and she avoided his penetrating gaze. He was an inch taller than she was. She asked him if he was an artist. "More of a dilettante," he said and smiled.

She asked to see what he was sketching. He held the pad on top of the gate, and she saw that he had been drawing the back of his home, and then off to the side she noticed he had added her in the chaise longue. It was only a small part of his sketch. She smiled. "Very nice," she said.

He shrugged. "Hope you don't mind I have included you. If you like, I could take you out."

"It's okay," she answered. Then he put the pad down on the grass. They talked for a while about his work in the art gallery, and that she did not have a job. He asked her if she'd like to go to a movie that night—as friends, as neighbors. It's not a date, he assured her. She told him that she was already going with her friends—would he like to come along? She was caught off guard when he said yes. A breeze crossed through their yards. Before she knew it, she was back in the chair and he had disappeared inside his home. She could not determine whether or not she was pleased about his coming that night.

The next day Jenny believed her mother was apprehensive about her date with Eric that evening. Johanna paced in front of the dining room table, her cheeks flushed. Afternoon light streamed through the dining room window. Johanna stopped pacing and crossed her arms, her sturdy wrists illuminated by the sun. She sighed, then recommended Jenny wear the dress she and her father had bought for her eighteenth birthday. Then her mother rested her hands on the table and lowered her head. "Be kind to him," she said in a low, intense voice.

A few hours later, after she had showered, she heard a knock on her bedroom door. Her mother rushed in. Her expression forlorn, she told Jenny that Eric had called to cancel dinner because of an important and unexpected business meeting. Jenny was both relieved and annoyed.

She carried a heavy black suitcase to her father's car. The trunk was open; she put the luggage inside, then slammed shut the lid, her forehead damp from the heat. She would be leaving for college the next day. Jenny did not wonder what lay ahead of her, but instead her thoughts turned to the past few months. She realized it would have been a more fruitful summer if she had had a job and had been able to spend more time with people closer to her age. Not having had a job had distanced her more than she liked from her high school friends, and now that August was nearly over she felt a sense of loss for what could have been.

The previous night she had said good-bye to Jonas. He would flying back to San Francisco that day; he may now be on the plane, she thought. He had been a good friend that summer. He had listened to what she had had to say about Eric, and her mother's insistence that she be kind to him. He seemed to acknowledge and agree, though with an unmistakable hesitancy, that Eric—the worldly Eric, they called him—was too old for her. He said he found it interesting that she had kept her friends from knowing her parents and she smiled, but didn't add anything to his comment.

As it turned out, Eric had been quite busy with his work that summer. She had had dinner with him only twice. Neither time had they touched, other than to shake hands. They conversed as if they were brother and sister. Her mother sensed that nothing of significance had happened between them, and Jenny was aware of Johanna's disappointment.

Her favorite part of the summer had been going down to Jonas's basement, where he had set up an art studio. She found his paintings hazy, not fully developed, but that is what she most liked about them, about him—he had so much more to go; observing his confidence rising as he cautiously improved had elated her.

The previous night she and Jonas had walked to the beach. Sitting on the concrete wall, their legs dangling, they had watched the waves lapping the shore. Steeling herself, her heart pounding, she asked him if he was planning to kiss her goodbye. "I will do so only if you ask with a smile; you look so serious, Jenny," he answered. They laughed and then kissed, and although it was not a very long kiss it was much more intense than she had expected.

Without speaking, they slowly walked in the direction of

their street. The night was warm and the light from the moon reflected over the sidewalk before them, their shadows in stark contrast. When they arrived at her home, Jonas walked with her to the front door and said, his voice low, his expression doubtful, "Friends, we are just friends, Jenny." Closely she watched as he backed away from her. Then as he climbed the front steps of his house, his form was more and more illuminated by the light shining from the front porch. Suddenly he stopped and waved to her. By the time she raised her hand, he had disappeared inside his home.

Three

San Francisco

There had been a light rain that morning, splashing the hydrangeas Cora had planted months before, but by the time they left for the airport it was mid-afternoon, and it had turned into a steamy and still late August day. The roads now dry, they drove in near silence, mostly music from the now-disbanded Beatles playing on the car radio, interspersed from time to time with news flashes. Jonas, reflecting on the past summer, tuned out the latest world events. And because of her quietude, the way she loosely guided the steering wheel with one hand, her elbow resting where the window had been rolled down, her lips closed, he supposed Cora was doing the same.

Silently he acknowledged that the tension between them the past two months had been a result of their inability to reveal to each other who they had become. It struck him how eager he was to be free of her presence, not because he didn't love her, but because she was an incessant reminder to him of his fatherless existence.

After embracing, and as Jonas was about to board the plane, he turned to look back at her. Meeting his gaze, Cora lifted her hand and waved with assurance. It was her attempt to convey her support of him, her trust that he would go forward with his life as best he could, but most importantly without any hindrance from her. Again he turned away, but immediately he stole one last look, a quick glance she did not notice. Her arms were folded, her eyes steady and attentive, her chin lifted as if she were bracing herself for her life without him at home. Surely she would be able to meet more often with Harold, Jonas sharply thought—Harold, whom he had not met and whose existence his mother had refused to acknowledge. And so his leaving was as much a gain for her as it would be a loss.

As he walked down the aisle to his seat, he thought about how he had longed to ask if she perceived his father in him at all. One evening in mid-July they had dined out together; she had taken the day off from work, and her mood was more mellow than usual. She had looked up from the menu she was holding, smiling, and had begun to ask what he wanted to eat but stopped suddenly, her eyes startled, and said, "The expression on your face, Jonas, you remind me of someone, how serious you seem, but I can't recall who it is." She shrugged and then peered down again at the menu. Yet as she grasped it, he saw her hand shake for a moment and he knew she was thinking of

David, his father. There were other times—he could not recall the exact details of where they were or what they had been doing—all he remembered was he was unable to ask the question he most needed an answer to. He knew it was because he did not possess the courage to ask. His heart would pound fiercely whenever he considered doing so.

In the past she had mentioned his father in broad terms; she'd say, her voice soft, precise, "Your father liked to go to the movies—you know I like westerns, but he preferred Hitchcock," or she'd tell Jonas that David's favorite sport had been basketball. Or that he was tall, and serious, but sometimes when she least expected it he'd tell her a very funny joke. She'd speak of David's personality in general, never allowing Jonas to learn who his father was: what he had hoped for, what he had most feared, what he had been most passionate about.

He ruefully acknowledged that what had prevented him from asking more about his father was that he had become senselessly preoccupied with what he had found more pressing at the time—namely, her relationship with Harold.

As the pilot backed up the plane and prepared to taxi down the runway, Jonas looked out the small window, his eyes resting on his mother, who stood inside behind the expansive airport window, her face pressed against the glass. From that wavy distance her brown eyes in his mind appeared more sad than focused, her posture more relaxed than erect. It was a mood and bearing he had not witnessed in her that summer. Instead she had been mostly alert and forthright in her actions and words.

He felt a twinge of guilt, wondering if despite her independent nature, and her relationship with the mysterious Harold, she might need her son to be close for reasons Jonas understood were beyond him.

They had not lived together for that long of a period in years. And so that summer there had been times when they'd been irritated with each other and those first annoyances had been the beginnings of a subtle but undeniable tension between them. He was aware of how much it bothered her when he went out with his friends from high school for the night and didn't call to let her know he wouldn't be home until the next day. But this provided him with a sense of independence—he no longer was simply her son, no longer guided by her sense of right and wrong—and so he had felt justified. For he had been severely disappointed that she had refused to tell him about Harold. If she had been frank about it, as she was about most things, he would have been supportive of the relationship and wished her well.

It had taken him nearly a month to realize she was involved in a serious relationship. Whenever she was about to leave, she'd tell him she would be going to a movie or shopping with a friend or one of her sisters. One evening when he'd been home for over three weeks, Belinda had called to speak with his mother, and he had answered promptly that she was at the movies. Hastily Belinda had said, "Ah, yes." Before he had had a chance to say more she had hung up the phone. He waited up for his mother. He sat alone with the lights off in front of the television. When she came in at midnight, he instinctively jumped up and asked where she had been. Yawning, she said sleepily that she had gone to a movie with her sisters.

"You weren't with Belinda. She called, asking for you," he said, speaking with the edginess of a suspicious husband.

Though weary, she studied him for a moment, her gaze impassive, and said flatly, "I was with Rina." Closely he watched as she turned away, her compact and defiant form moving toward her bedroom door; she opened it, then disappeared inside. Soon he heard the click of the lock. He stood there, faintly reassured. He believed her; he had not ever known her to lie to him.

A week later, a Friday morning, before they each left for work, he told her he'd be spending the night in Boston with friends from San Francisco who were visiting for the weekend. She nodded, but there was no change in her expression. When he got to the gallery, one of his friends called from Chicago to say that the three of them would come the following weekend instead; they wanted to spend more time there, go to a Cubs game. He had not driven the car he was renting for the summer to work that day because it would have been costly and difficult to find overnight parking.

He took the subway home. When he walked into the house, his mother was not there. After he made himself a quick peanut butter sandwich, he went to the basement to work on a painting he'd begun the previous weekend. An hour or two later, he heard the front door open and shut. Then he heard his mother's voice, followed by a distinctly masculine one Jonas did not recognize. He was stunned; his heart beat more quickly. The muted interplay of their voices suggested a deep intimacy. He guessed his mother had been so preoccupied with him that she had not noticed the light on in the basement when they had come up the front walkway. Soon he heard their footsteps in the kitchen, their voices closer and more clear than they'd been at first. Jonas stood in the middle of the basement, a brush in his raised hand; it was a stifling night and he felt moisture from the heat running down his face. He was torn between his desire to hear their words, yet hoping not to. "You never completely acknowledge you love me or care for me. Why should I introduce you to my son?" His heart skipped a beat at his mother's sharp tone. "You are disillusioned about love, Harold, that is your problem."

"And you aren't?"

"No, I loved my husband, but I lost him long ago. I try to remember David, but it is difficult. My memories of him are not lasting. He has become more like a character I have read about in a book. Sometimes I think he never existed."

Then there was silence. Jonas imagined his mother bowing her head and covering her face with her hands. And he soon heard them walk out of the kitchen and down the hallway. He had only heard Harold speak those three words—his voice tired, as if he had had a few glasses of beer.

Defiant and angry, Jonas spent an uncomfortable and sleepless night on a dusty old sofa.

At six o'clock the next morning, a Saturday, he tiptoed up the stairs and left the house through the kitchen door. Hastily he walked the three blocks to the main street. It was a drizzly and misty morning, the temperature had dropped some, and he was relieved that the coffee shop was open. To help pass the time he had brought a small sketch pad with him and a piece of charcoal. Between gulps of coffee he attempted to draw the likeness of the waitress behind the counter as well as any customers who came into the shop. But his sketches were more like caricatures and eventually, out of frustration, he placed the pad facedown on the table and ordered another cup of coffee. When he swiveled round on his seat he noticed at the takeout counter a slim man of average height with dark hair combed to the side, in his mid-fifties. Maybe it was his imagination, but he thought it was the same tired male voice of the night before, and he wondered if it was Harold. He picked up his sketch pad and started to draw him but, deeply conflicted, he soon gave up. Yet whenever he pondered Harold and his mother's relationship, an image of this man would come to mind.

A week later he attempted to bring up the subject of Harold. It was a sunny Sunday morning, and he and his mother were sitting on the back porch drinking coffee and savoring the beginning of what would be a warm summer day. His mother pointed out the hydrangeas, blooming a periwinkle blue color. Then she turned to him, sunlight heightening the thoughtful expression in her eyes, and she asked, studiously, about his work at the gallery. Jonas knew she relished hearing him describe the customers who came into the gallery, how they would decide on what to buy and how he would help them choose a painting. On this day she was inquiring about a particular client she had seen at the gallery when she had visited Jonas in San Francisco a few years before. She had noticed him when she had come in one day to take Jonas out to lunch. The customer had mainly liked to collect lithographs. She remembered him because she thought he'd looked overly tired, but had not allowed his weariness to hamper his interest in the works Jonas was showing him. Jonas told her that he had passed away a year before and his wife had remarried soon afterward. Then he turned to his mother and said nonchalantly that it would be nice if she could get married again, she was still relatively young. But she looked back at him in a stunned way. "Jonas, I don't want to marry again." Abruptly, she got up and opened the kitchen door to go inside.

Following her in, he said, "I hope you aren't saying this for my sake. I am hoping you will remarry. In fact, I want you to marry again." He sat across from her at the table; she was looking over the surface of it as if something was missing. And then she got up and took a pitcher of iced coffee out of the refrigerator.

Her back to him, she said, "The answer is still the same, Jonas. I don't want to marry again." When she sat down and poured the iced coffee into a tall glass, she gave him a brief and tired smile.

And so on that late August day as he studied his mother standing at the airport window, he regretted he had not had the chance to meet Harold. Grudgingly he understood she needed and deserved privacy.

~

Once he arrived in San Francisco Jonas was pleased to have returned to the Bay Area. In his apartment, he thrust open the windows to survey the city, but his view was limited; he caught sight of his neighbor's kitten staring at him from the opposite pane, her tiny paw on the glass.

After ten days or so he began to feel disoriented. Unexpected images of his mother, her expression set, as he tried to provoke her into admitting that one day she might want to marry again. And he'd often muse over one of the paintings he had been working on and had left in the basement. It was a painting of a seagull flying low above the waves. There was something lacking in it—a sense of the bird's strength, he thought. But Jenny had said it had potential. She had liked to linger in the basement and study his paintings. She seemed absorbed by his work, which had puzzled him, as his paintings were far from what he wanted them to be. "Jonas," she'd say, "I like that you don't flaunt color. You are reserved with color and I find it interesting—it is your style, your uniqueness." He told her it was because his paintings were at an early stage—he still had a long way to go. Most of his life he'd had an intense sense of color, and he silently wondered if working at the gallery had dampened it.

He soon realized how disgruntled he had become about his work in the gallery. While on Newbury Street, it had occurred to him that he might have lost his ability to sell. At first he had attributed it to the fact that it wasn't as robust of a market as the one in San Francisco. But after the first few months he wasn't selling as much in San Francisco as he had in the past. He was less enthusiastic when explaining the story behind a painting or a painter and how the work had landed in the gallery. In fact, he thought he sounded rather bland and almost discouraging. Jonas gradually realized it was because what he really wanted was not to sell art, but instead to sketch and paint.

While in Boston, he'd had only an inkling of a desire to establish himself as a painter. The only person he had discussed it with had been his aunt Rina, who worked not far from the gallery. She would meet him for lunch on Newbury Street, usually at a restaurant nearby specializing in crepes that she liked to go to. They'd often sit outside. She enjoyed telling him about her fiancé, Dan. He was from Connecticut and she had met him about a year before on the train to New York. He had boarded at Stamford; and she had been on the train coming in from Boston. She was now in her mid-forties. During one of their lunches, between inhalations of her cigarette, she said Dan was a year younger than she was and had never been married before because he had cared for his sister's family after her husband had died. "He has a big heart, like your father." And she had smiled in her warm way, her lips closed, her eyes penetrating his.

It had been difficult for Jonas to accept that Rina was engaged. From time to time she'd have a faraway look in her eyes, as she had had in the past, but at those times, he knew she was physically present. Now she was not as fully with him as before.

One extremely warm day in early August they had gone inside for lunch; it was too hot to sit out on the restaurant patio.

Jonas lowered his voice and confided in her about his growing interest in becoming a painter. Mildly surprised, her eyes widening, Rina bowed her head and snuffed out her cigarette. He knew by the way she pressed her lips together, her brow furrowed, that she was deciding what she thought about it. When she finished extinguishing the cigarette, she looked up at him, her eyes caring and elusive, and said in a hushed voice, "Yes, Jonas. For heaven's sake—let yourself go."

After lunch, he walked toward the gallery, and by the time he went inside Rina's words had slipped from his mind.

In addition to his mother having a lover and his aunt Rina's engagement, another surprise for him the summer he returned to the East Coast had been that his mother had developed a strong relationship with Jenny's mother, Johanna Smila. His mother had never had many friends; she had relied socially on her sisters and their network of acquaintances. But he should have realized his mother's interest had been piqued by Johanna when she had spoken of her with uncharacteristic intensity four years earlier. Yet during the summer of his return he had not seen much of Johanna—running into her a few times as she was leaving his home and as he was coming in or going out. Although they had become close, whenever his mother mentioned Johanna to him she did so with disbelief and frustration, usually because of what Johanna had revealed to her in their most recent conversation. They were only a few years apart in age, his mother had told him, and his guess was their friendship continued and to a certain degree grew because his mother connected with her on some obscure level. He knew in a practical sense his mother doubted for the most part whatever Johanna said about her past life, and that, like a persistent sheriff, Cora deduced that at some point the truth about Johanna would be revealed.

One day Jonas asked if she thought Jenny was similar to her mother—she had just described to him with a certain amount of frustration what Johanna had said about her childhood in Trieste, and how she could not quite piece together why Johanna's family had been given a sapphire bracelet by a foreign dignitary visiting the city. At that point Jonas had been to the movies and to the beach on the weekend with Jenny only a few times. It was shortly before he brought her to his art studio in the basement. His mother, who had resumed reading an article from one of the various magazines she'd neatly arranged on top of the coffee table, turned to him and paused to collect her thoughts, then said in an abstracted way, her mind obviously more compelled now by the article she had been reading, that Jenny was quiet and not at all like her mother—she holds things in more. You know how Johanna exaggerates. Jenny isn't inclined to make things better or worse than they are. She sees what she sees and that is that. And his mother bowed her head and continued to read the magazine. He wasn't certain if she had been talking more about herself than about Jenny. Nonetheless her words about Jenny intrigued him and so soon after that conversation he had invited Jenny to see his studio in the basement.

He had noticed that with her friends Jenny seemed like one of the crowd, one eighteen-year-old indistinguishable from the next eighteen-year-old. He felt like the protective older brother whenever they asked his advice or wanted to know his opinion about the war in Vietnam. He'd refrain from talking about the war; although it was a different war, he would conflate mention of any war with his father's passing.

In San Francisco, he easily re-established himself with his friends and cleaned up his apartment; it was small and on a narrow street. He bought a print of Monet's *Charing Cross Bridge* and a large mirror to open up the space. But his heart was not in his attempts to improve his apartment—he thought more and more of the studio he had set up in his mother's basement as well as the paintings he had not finished. He recalled Rina's words. Then he thought of Jenny in the studio. She had become part of the scene in his imagination; he had mentally sketched her in the background just as he had drawn her off to the side in the chaise longue the day they first spoke at the gate separating their backyards.

One breezy late October afternoon, Frank, the owner of the gallery, approached Jonas and said he'd like to take him out for a drink. The sky was a vibrant blue, and as they walked up Powell Street, Jenny's words about his reserved use of color crossed his mind. At that moment he promised himself he would paint the sky the very same vibrant blue when he returned home and completed the painting of the seagull. They went to a hotel bar located on the top floor. They ordered drinks, then looked out at the bay. Frank asked Jonas if there was something on his mind, if something was bothering him, some personal problem. "Ever since you returned from the East Coast, Jonas, you haven't been yourself, you seem less enthusiastic, less engaged, and others have noticed it as well," he said, looking away. Jonas shrugged, answering that nothing specifically was bothering him, but he agreed, he had lost his enthusiasm. Frank, turning to him, appeared surprised by Jonas's honesty. Looking out at the bay again, both of them were silent. Then Jonas said maybe it would be best if he resigned, maybe he was no longer very good at selling art, maybe he'd better try something else. He did like to paint, after all.

Jonas remained in San Francisco until the following May. He supported himself by working as a waiter and found a more affordable apartment where he set up a space in the alcove to paint. Still not pleased with his work, he would often think of Jenny's comment about his use of color. No matter how diligently he worked with color, he felt his paintings appeared more and more reticent. For he wasn't able to let himself go as Rina had encouraged.

He refrained from telling his mother he had left the gallery, waiting until the end of the year to do so. He sensed she was uneasy with his decision, yet she calmly asked what he wanted to do next. And when he told her he wanted to paint, she seemed to accept it, though she added that it might be better for him to do so closer to home—after all, he had set up a studio in the basement. He could work odd jobs just as easily in Boston and could save money by living at home. Wouldn't he then be able to spend more time developing his craft? Jonas listened intently to her words, knowing she was and always would be both practical and accepting. He was never certain if she was this way because he was fatherless or because she was naturally flexible.

Another reason he had stayed in San Francisco was because he had become involved in a relationship with a woman named Miranda. Older than he was, she was very much part of the anti-war protests. Although he liked to hear her thoughts about the war, he stayed away from the protests himself. The war reminded him too much of his father's short existence—his sense of conflict only having grown.

He had met Miranda at a bus stop six weeks before he left the gallery. Usually he had walked to work, but it was a little cooler that day and he had neglected to put on a jacket. They were the only two waiting for the bus. She wore sunglasses, but when she took them off, which she did from time to time, her expression was soft yet unflinching—reminding him of Klimt's *Portrait of Gertrud Loew*. When the bus finally came, they climbed on. There were only two adjoining seats available; they sat next to each other. Soon the bus was stuck in traffic, and Jonas regretted not having walked. He would be late, and that day he was responsible for opening the gallery. Out of anxiety and restlessness, he began to tap his foot. Miranda turned to him and said, her voice clear and fine, "Please stop." He did as she requested, but was annoyed. Then she again removed her sunglasses and smiled warmly at him. He saw there were little lines surrounding her eyes and he thought she might be about five years older than he was. They went out to dinner that night. She insisted on treating him and said he could pay the next time.

At dinner Miranda spoke in an intense and pointed way about the anti-war movement and her involvement with it over the past few years. He told her he respected her ideals. Then he explained about his father's death. She looked at him across the table, her eyes warm and muddy, and smiled just as she had in the bus; again she reminded him of the Klimt painting.

Their relationship lasted until the first of January. Although she ostensibly seemed to understand his resistance to protesting, and how it related to his memories of growing up without a father, ultimately she needed him to share the experience with her.

One day they met directly after she had returned from a march. The sign she carried said, "Love is so much more than war; for it creates life." She seemed more elated than usual, more invigorated. Her usual pale complexion was now a deep pink and her eyes were bright with anticipation. Over a candlelight dinner Jonas had assiduously prepared, she raised her wine glass and told him it disturbed her that he refused to take part in the protests. Her words pained him; they were a reminder to him of how much the past was restraining him.

After his experience with Miranda, he threw himself more and more into painting. His work as a waiter was an afterthought; he'd go from table to table in a state of dissociation. Painting had become his reality. After a few months, and as May was approaching, he called his mother to let her know he would leave San Francisco in the next few weeks.

He perceived that although she was excited about his coming home, she was concerned as well. "I'm interested in hearing your plans, how you will manage to become an artist, a very good one," she said, her tone subdued. He imagined she was mentally calculating how she would rearrange her time with her lover, but then he lightly added that he knew about her relationship with Harold. There was silence at the other end of the phone. And then she continued to talk as if he hadn't revealed anything. But he thought he'd heard her sigh. At the end of the conversation she said candidly, "We can each go on with our lives now."

She had not come out to visit him that spring, and before his call he had wondered if she had planned to put it off until early autumn. She had often mentioned during her trips to San Francisco that she imagined it would very beautiful in September or October. She had neglected to say why she would not be coming that spring—she had not said anything at all. It had been as if she had forgotten about her yearly trip. Knowing her and the way she lived an ordered life, it seemed out of character that she had not mentioned it to him. Maybe it was because she had sensed he would be coming home soon. Or she hadn't planned a trip because of Harold's schedule.

He wasn't certain how long he would stay in the Boston area—he had thoughts of moving to New York once he was more settled in with his work. All he knew was he had no intention of moving west again. California was where he had failed, he concluded.

Once home, he spent most of each day in the basement studio he had set up the previous summer. Because he had saved money while working at the gallery in San Francisco, and because the tips he'd earned as a waiter had been plentiful, he was able to contribute money to day-to-day expenses. He was pleased he was not a financial burden on his mother. If he went out, he went to museums to study works of other artists—all he wanted was to learn. He was so focused, he did not call his old friends. He thought only of painting.

At the museum he'd stand in front of a Matisse and try to imagine what the painter was thinking and seeing when he drew a particular line, used a specific color. He studied other artists as well, but Matisse was the one he was most drawn to.

His mother apparently was not concerned that he did not have a steady job—he thought she was happy to see him every morning. He knew after a certain amount of time elapsed she would encourage him to go out into the world again and away from the cocoon of her basement. For now she was patient.

In late May—Jonas had been home for about three weeks—he ran into Jenny at the drugstore on the main street. She had just completed her first year of college and couldn't have been home for long because, despite his monk-like existence, he would surely have bumped into her sooner. She didn't seem overjoyed to see him. She was wearing glasses and her hair was pulled back in a ponytail. She had changed from her year away, he thought. She stood more erectly now, no more head to the side. "Hi, Jonas," she said quite coolly, though her eyes were warm. He was reassured that her feelings toward him had not changed. "Are you home for a visit?" she asked evenly. He realized that although he'd been home for a few weeks, his mother must not have told Johanna. As they walked together in the direction of their respective homes, he explained to her about his decision to become a painter and how he was hoping to go to New York in a year or so. He wanted to be part of the nucleus of the art world, he said and smiled.

She looked at him doubtfully and answered, "I am very happy to hear you are painting full time, Jonas, but New York is not far away. You could go there now if you really wanted to, once a month at the least." In saying this he knew she had discerned his hesitation, his doubts.

A scowl crossed his face; he answered defiantly, "I am not quite ready, Jenny." She smiled, seemingly pleased with his honesty.

She then told him about her first year of college, how she had been puzzled by certain things and not very surprised about others. She thought the atmosphere would have been more intellectual, more philosophical. But instead the discourse between students had been more pragmatic and it had taken her a while to conform. It was clear as she spoke, he thought, that she had already made the adjustment. He imagined her sitting in various coffee shops with her classmates, especially on cold Saturday afternoons, sipping coffee or hot chocolate, dressed in a heavy sweater, hoping to have a discussion about something they'd read in class, trying to break in and mention a novel or essay they had recently studied. But instead her classmates had preferred to talk about the practical side of their relationships with their boyfriends, or possible approaches to a profitable career.

Jenny didn't mention anything about the worldly Eric, nor did she mention a new boyfriend, and so he didn't pursue it.

The previous summer his mother had warned him not to get too close to Jenny—she was too young for him, and Eric, although he was older, might be good for her. She believed in most instances, love was a choice, a personal one. But this was a special case, because although Johanna never spoke directly of it, Cora believed Eric's family had helped Jenny's mother and father during the war and they were indebted to them. "It's a European story," Cora had said, leaning forward. "As an American I can't quite understand it, but I respect Johanna's experience; it must have been devastating to have been in Europe during the war." Jonas had not responded; he had let his mother talk. And now, as they walked, he refrained from mentioning either Eric or Miranda. Jenny would not have understood his relationship with Miranda; she would have expected him to have expressed more sadness, more pain—he was neither melancholy from the experience, nor had he been deeply hurt in any way. On the whole his memories of Miranda were warm and sensuous. His conflicted understanding of war, on one hand, and her poignant stridency for peace, on the other, had never interfered with their physical relationship.

He asked Jenny what her plans were for the summer, wondering if they could meet occasionally; perhaps she'd take a look at his work if she had any free time. He liked her perspective and recalled how much he had considered it while he was in San Francisco.

Jenny was reluctant to talk about her plans. All she said was that her family had decided against going to Europe this summer, but would go the next year instead. She sounded very serious, as if something else was on her mind. Then she said she'd be returning to the college soon—she attended school just outside of Philadelphia—and she would be working there for the summer; it was a clerical job, in the admissions office. He was disappointed and annoyed.

"You are sad, Jonas," she said suddenly, perceptively. He shrugged and pointed across the busy main street at the movie theater—a man in blue jeans, leaning on a ladder, was putting up letters on the marquee. A new movie would be playing that night.

They stopped walking and stared up at the marquee, cars passing before them; they watched as the man held on to the ladder with one hand and adjusted the letters with the other. "*The Day of the Jackal*," Jonas soon read. "Would you like to go?"

She turned to him and frowned, a light wind blew a loose hair across her face. "Not tonight, Jonas," she said dismissively, brushing back the strand of hair.

Four

Day and Night

Ten days before, she had arrived at the station outside of Philadelphia. Early afternoon light had fallen brightly over a bouquet of daffodils left on a bench, spilling across a narrow strip of the platform and down to the tracks. The air was heavy and cool; warm sun was the only expression of spring that day. A sharp breeze pierced her cotton sweater, ruffling the collar of her blouse. Jenny shivered, turned away, and went inside the station. At the ticket counter she bowed her head and asked the woman behind the glass if the train to Boston had been delayed. "It's running thirty minutes late," she answered, her voice a monotone, her dark eyes flashing. Jenny made her way toward a chair close to the exit.

Across from her sat a couple in their early seventies, she surmised, wearing similar blue corduroy jackets. They smiled at her, their expressions mild and complacent. Jenny overheard some of their conversation and gathered they would be visiting their daughter and her family in a midsize city some miles south of Boston. Their voices calm, they apparently were not inconvenienced by the delay. But Jenny was. Impatience was something she had learned over the past year. Living away from the protection of her parents, she had come to understand it was the only way for someone like herself, an only child on her own, to hold her head above water.

In three weeks she would return to the very same train station and then would spend the summer taking classes in addition to working as a clerk in the admissions office. If she did so again the following summer, she would be able to graduate earlier than her class. It was a plan that had been in place for the last few months.

The thought of visiting her parents for even these few weeks filled her with apprehension. As she'd been preoccupied with finishing her first year of college, having just passed in her last paper the prior evening, she had not thought about the upcoming three weeks until then. She envisioned her mother bringing her morning coffee, the sun shining through the bedroom window, spotting the rattling cups and tray. Once seated on her bed, between sips of coffee, Johanna would ask in her sporadic but demanding way about her daughter's personal life. Then there was Jenny's father, his unrelenting respect for her, for her mother, for everyone he encountered, leaving for work every morning, proud yet forever humbled by the turn his life had taken.

~

The prior nine months had passed slowly, but there had been days when she had been jolted by the thought that midterms were a week away or the end of the semester was right around the corner. In those instances Jenny would be struck by how much she was changing, how much she already had been transformed.

As she had waved good-bye to her parents outside her dormitory the previous September, the trees still leafy and green, she had watched carefully as they climbed into their car, square-looking, a dark blue color, her father's eyes slightly misty, her mother's gaze stoic. And she had fleetingly recalled their leaving her behind the morning of her first day of kindergarten and how from the classroom window she had watched their car drive away. She had experienced a sinking within, her first sense of loss. Many Septembers later, once her father's car had vanished from sight, her heart beat fiercely, not because she had any regrets about leaving home, but because she was overcome with excitement about what was before her.

Her roommate, Arlene, salty-tongued and edgy, was petite and slim, her dark hair short-cropped, her bangs were long and full, falling past her wispy eyebrows.

Over the first few weeks they had attempted to enjoy each other's company, to hopefully discover between themselves an enduring affinity. But no matter how diligently they tried, there was no connection to be found. It was not long before they mutually understood that although they would be able to tolerate living together, they would never be intimate friends. As an only child Jenny had always prided herself on her flexibility—it was the only way she'd known to get along with others. Her flexibility, she believed, benefited both of them. Arlene, the second child of five, had confided to her during those early weeks that she had learned from a young age that the more flexible she was, the more she would be taken advantage of. Whereas Jenny had learned flexibility for the purpose of acceptance, her roommate had learned to be inflexible in order to survive. Jenny believed they had understood this about each other and for that reason they had been able to last out the year together. Arlene's major was biology—she had every intention of going to medical school—and while Jenny's major was comparative literature, she had no desire like others in her field of study to eventually pursue a career in international law.

Arlene had grown up—and her family still lived—in a town only a two-hour drive from the college. She had a steady boyfriend from high school named Barry. He was attending college on a part-time basis so he could work, and he lived at home in order to save money. Whenever Arlene spoke of him, her sarcasm evaporated. As much as she could adore anyone, she adored him. Jenny soon gathered that Arlene envied what she called Barry's iconoclastic nature. One night when she was drunk, she had told Jenny that what she loved most about Barry was his fearlessness—hadn't she realized yet that most things frightened her? Jenny was studying at her desk and Arlene stood close to her; with her small hand she pushed aside her bangs and looked deeply into Jenny's eyes, unnerving her. She took quick breaths.

Jenny didn't answer her directly, but told her she looked tired, that she was drunk and needed to sleep. After a few moments the tension between them dissipated; Arlene shrugged and then went to bed.

Barry would come to visit every few weekends. He was of average height, broad-shouldered, and although friendly he was not talkative. Whenever he came, Jenny would have to find another place to stay for two nights. Because the timing of Barry's visits was relatively predictable, she was able to plan in advance. But one of those weekends, a weekend when he had called Arlene in the middle of the afternoon to say he would be coming that night instead of the next Friday, Jenny did not have a place to stay. It was the second weekend in November, early evening, and Barry would be coming within the hour. Arlene anxiously paced back and forth across the room because Jenny had not yet found a place to stay. Jenny knew it was because of Barry—he was the only person she knew of who could make Arlene act in this way. She was unraveling because he was coming—any look of sarcasm or defensiveness had been wiped from her expression. Throughout the school year, it had been surprising and disconcerting to witness her change in this way.

It took Jenny a while to glean that although Arlene was an independent person intellectually and in her professional aspirations, she dreaded the thought of losing her relationship with Barry. Jenny had found this quite baffling but knew well enough not to mention it to Arlene. Perhaps she would have if she had been a better friend, or if they had been closer.

Soon she began to pack a small overnight case with her belongings, trying to imagine who she would stay with that weekend, while Arlene stood before her in her half-slip and bra, her arms crossed, her eyes darting, her voice tense as she made suggestions: "Caroline? Debra? Camille?" Then there was a blunt knock and Arlene scurried to find her skirt and sweater. Once she had put them on Jenny carefully opened the door, expecting to be met with Barry's impatient yet warm gaze. But instead it was the dorm proctor, who said that someone had come to see Jenny and was waiting in the foyer. She thought it might be Todd, a student from another college she had met at a mixer the previous weekend. He had said he would try and stop by on a Friday or Saturday evening. She was pleased. She had enjoyed talking with him. Already she was imagining spending the evening with Todd, perhaps going out for a pizza, then seeing a movie. Later she'd knock on the door of a friend's room, one of the women Arlene had suggested.

She turned away from the proctor and glanced at Arlene, who nodded, her eyebrows knitting together in her attempt to show concern for Jenny's situation. Jenny put on her coat and then picked up the small case from her bed and soon followed the proctor through the hallway and then down the one flight of stairs to the entrance way. As she turned the corner to walk toward the foyer, she froze. Leaning lightly against the reception desk, his arms folded, was Eric, the worldly Eric. He was dressed in a dark gray suit, the jacket long and fitted, a square-shaped gold clip on his moss green tie. He looked too old and foreign to be there. When he turned and caught her gaze, he lifted his eyebrows, quietly surprised. Her heart sank. How strongly she disliked him. Over the past summer she had not allowed herself to form an honest opinion of him—it had been her way of distancing herself from Eric.

He pointed to the small overnight case in her hand; she clutched it more firmly. "I have caught you at an inconvenient time—you are going home or away with a friend?" His light dismay was appealing—momentarily lessening her dislike of him.

Without flinching and with a forced confidence she explained to him about Barry's unexpected visit and told him she was planning to ask her friend in the next dorm if she could stay with her. She motioned with her free hand in the direction of the building. But when she gazed back at him he was smiling calmly, his blue-gray eyes set with an odd look of contentment. At the same time there was something about his stance, how his shoulders tensed, that made her believe he was holding himself back, that he was guarded with her. She read it as hesitation, and it relaxed her. He pressed his fingers over her hand that was pointing in the direction of her friend's dorm. Firmly lowering it, he said, "Let's have an early dinner, you can ask her later. I have a car. I've been in town on business for a week and thought I'd come by to see you before going back. I should have called to warn you . . ."

She interrupted him, asking roughly, "Did Mother ask you to check up on me, Eric?"

He looked surprised, then turned his head away and said,

"I haven't spoken to your mother since I took you to dinner last August." She felt herself blush; she was not naturally caustic.

They drove into the city for dinner. It was a surprisingly warm night for mid-November. She unbuttoned her coat. From the car window she looked out at the stars. Eric was quiet and she wondered if he had something on his mind, maybe something to do with his work. She wasn't certain exactly what he did. The few times they'd been to dinner together over the summer, he'd been reluctant to talk about it. Business was what he had said, his voice sounding both determined and uneasy. She didn't know what type of business it was and he hadn't allowed her to ask about it. She was unsure if it had been out of humility on his part or embarrassment. But her mother had implied that whatever it was, it was quite a profitable business. He traveled a great deal around the country and the world. Because Jenny had been convinced ever since she met Eric that he would not be part of her future, she had not needed to know. Countless times she had told her mother that he was too old for her.

Since meeting him on the beach the previous summer, she had often wondered whether or not she had encountered him in the past. If his parents had been close friends of her parents, why had she not known of them? Or had she met his parents in their Hartford living room when she was a child? If so, had Eric been with them? She did not know. Over the summer she had attempted to bring up the subject with her mother, but Johanna dismissed her questions. "How am I to know whether or not you have seen Eric or his parents before? We know of them from Trieste. I don't speak with them often." And her mother's indifference, which Jenny believed was feigned, had made her uneasy.

Now as she studied Eric, one of his hands firmly on the steering wheel and the other relaxed on his leg, Jenny searched for any signs of familiarity. There was something recognizable about his clean-shaven face, his high cheekbones, his chin, how it subtly jutted forward, in more of an attractive than an unattractive way—as if he were graciously and perpetually trying to make one point or another. And then his crown of curly hair, incongruous with the rest of his appearance, which was cautious and neat, as were his mannerisms. "What is on your mind, Jenny? Have you had a long day?" he asked, his voice warm and cajoling, a tone he had not adopted when she had been out with him before. Over the summer he had not inferred any sort of intimacy between them and although he was not directly doing so now, in his words there was an unmistakable suggestion of it.

When he looked over, waiting for her answer, she smiled and said no more. He turned his head away and said, "You like to be mysterious, don't you, Jenny?" She heard a gentle sarcasm in his tone.

Although he'd been mostly quiet in the car, she was more surprised he was not talkative at dinner. The previous two times they had been out together as well as the day she had met him on the beach he'd been gregarious. He'd spoken mostly about how it had been for him to come to America when he was twelve years old, adjusting to the American school system, often being teased because he was European, how he believed his friends—the few that he'd made—hadn't quite trusted him, but had given him the benefit of the doubt. "You see, I was so different, Jenny," he'd said again and again. He had gone to a private high school in the city. But he had never alluded to what had happened to him after he had turned eighteen, his college and professional years. And she had not been compelled enough to ask. But this night he was different, more quiet, not asking much about her, nor speaking of himself. His eyes were steady as he perused the menu. He pointed out a certain item, pressing his finger beneath it. She noticed how well-manicured his nails were and felt both disarmed and annoyed by his obvious attention to himself. After they had placed their orders their gazes starkly met—it was as if they were at that moment exposed to each other—their hurts, their hates, their passions. But once she lowered her eyes and he, his, it was as if it had never been. He spoke first, asking if she had decided yet on a major. His English was clear, impeccable. She told him for a brief time she had considered philosophy but now was more or less settling on comparative literature. He smiled, and said, "Dante—is it because of Dante, or is it Stendhal?" his eyes glistening. She told him she had not yet read either, and that although she had read Madame Bovary, she had been drawn to the field not because of that novel alone but mostly because she had been compelled by the idea of comparative literature, the range of it. He smiled and said, "Ah, Flaubert—you have much to look forward to, Jenny." Briefly he closed his eyes as if trying to recall something and when he opened them, he pointedly asked, "Do you view Emma as a victim or a victimizer?"

She was surprised by his direct question, and her heart beat more quickly. "I do not think of her as one or the other—she is a romantic, but when her sense of romance takes an erotic turn, I suppose you can say she loses herself."

"Does that disturb you?" he asked, his eyes narrowing with interest.

With his wrists firmly resting on the rim of the table, his body leaning toward her, she sensed something feral about him. "Why should it disturb me?" she asked. "I am an adult."

At first he grinned, but when he answered his tone was serious. "And so you are, Jenny."

When she asked him where he had gone to college and what he had majored in, he diverted her attention to a woman sitting across the room who was wearing a large hat, which seemed out of place. She was facing away from them. Eric nonchalantly said he'd spent the afternoon negotiating with her and then said nothing more. Jenny did not know if he was speaking the truth, understanding it wasn't only because of his manner that she doubted what he had said, but because of her upbringing where furtiveness, secrecy, and deflection were not only taken for granted but expected. When their gazes met again, she knew they intuitively understood that about each other. She felt an inner disgust. She did not want to carry within a fear of honesty, a fear she had resented in her parents. Studying Eric, his steadfast but inscrutable eyes, the finely etched lines on his face, she wondered if he were more a citizen of Trieste. As if reading her thoughts, he asked, "You are happy to be have been born here, Jenny?"

"This is my country," she said, her voice raised. He nodded and smiled quickly. The waiter came with wine, and then food. As they began to eat, Eric asked what Trieste meant to her, if anything.

Closing her eyes, she recalled the city of her parents' births. "Gray skies, calm waters, exuberant people," she said. "That is a superficial view, but any depth I feel for Trieste has to do with my relatives there, not the city itself." He nodded, then solemnly asked if she was aware of her parents' past life in Trieste.

Hedgingly she spoke, avoiding his gaze. "I know my parents' existence in Trieste during the war is a very painful subject for them. They don't discuss it. After living with them for eighteen years, it is as if I understand their experience—it is like osmosis, I guess you could say. I know they were terrified as most were during the war. It was a traumatic experience for them. That is enough to know, I suppose. I never inquired about the day-to-day details. I never needed to. I didn't want to hurt them. If I asked too many questions, I knew I would. And there was no guarantee they would respond. Of course I've been to Trieste many times, but no one discusses the past there either. People are concerned about their current lives, the future, what is happening in their city in present time." She paused.

Eric reached across the table and grasped her hand. Their gazes locked, his pained, and for the first time she understood the depth of his sadness. He didn't say anything. Willingly she accepted his touch. He soon signaled for the waiter to bring the check. She remained silent as well.

Jenny left the restaurant, not knowing where they would be going. She understood he would not be driving her back to the college. She understood he intended to tell her about her parents' past. Deep within, she comprehended how much she needed to know.

They drove for a long while. She peered out the car window at the passing dark November night. The air was chilly now. No longer was she able to make out any stars. Eventually Eric stopped the car. She didn't know where they were; leafless trees surrounded them. She looked over at him and spoke for the first time since dinner. Despite the blackness of the night she could clearly see his blue-gray eyes. "Tell me, Eric," she said, hearing the fervency in her voice. "Tell me." Her tone frightened her; her words seemed to be coming from another person, reverberating through her, like a deep and endless echo. It was as if she were lost in a dark forest, injured, crying out for help.

He looked away, then started the car. As he drove, she readied herself for what she was about to hear.

Within thirty minutes they were in his hotel room. After she took off her coat, he handed her a glass of brandy. Then he sat on a sofa across from her. With her free hand she gripped the arm of the chair; he explained in a dispassionate voice the details of how his parents, his family, at great risk to themselves, had protected hers during the war. And even now as she sat in the train station she could not recall his exact words. His tone was what she remembered, mostly even, descriptive, at times bitter, and between his words she had heard a begrudging acceptance. In his voice she heard truth, fear, and an unrelenting hopelessness. Though she had been in a fog as she sat there gripping the arm of the chair, she understood that Eric's father and mother, because of their standing in Trieste society, had been able to shield her parents. Her father had joined an anti-fascist group and had been active in it. He'd been interrogated twice by the authorities, Eric had said, one finger lightly stroking his chin, before his parents, close and longtime friends of her mother, had interceded to help the newly married couple.

Across from her, she now saw the elderly couple rise. She heard the train coming. When she embarked, she chose a seat near the window, leaned her head against the glass, and began to feel a sense of nostalgia about her life one year before, and about going home for the next three weeks. Although she had visited her parents twice over the school year, her time with them had been short, interrupted by visits from Eric. She had not seen them since the semester break in January. Three weeks seemed a long time now. She thought of their small home, their backyard, their busy street, Jonas's house next door. Her mother had told her he had returned that month—that he wanted to be an artist. She thought of the previous summer, his studio in the basement, his muted painting of the seagull, and the various other ones. But he seemed young now, innocent, and she had become too old. The weight of the past bore down on her, and willingly she had succumbed to its pressure. For she had learned that she could not deny what had occurred.

She and Eric were not intimate until months later. The delay had been because his visits to the college had been sporadic. His business took up much of his time, and when they were together he spoke often and for long periods over the phone. She would go to his hotel room and fall asleep on the bed while he spoke to a colleague about one deal or another. She never paid much attention to what exactly he said, only to the relaxed insistence in his tone.

When he came to pick her up one Friday night in mid-February, she immediately realized their relationship would take another turn, would deepen. He seemed more solemn than usual. Instead of eating at a well-known and busy Philadelphia restaurant, they dined at the hotel. When they went up to his room, he did not pick up the telephone, but turned to her and said he had no calls to make that night, that unless she was opposed, they would make love completely. It had been that simple.

From that night forward, she would await his visits with a searing sense of anticipation and deep somberness. During the intervening time, she would throw herself into her schoolwork. She became more distant from Arlene, and she rarely called her mother. She wanted to hide her odd passion for Eric from them, from anyone she knew. For it was odd. She was drawn to him for reasons she did not fully comprehend—but she understood there was a darkness in her need for him, a fervency, as there had been when she had begged for him to tell her about the past. A fervency she had become aware of only at that moment. And in their intimacy it was as if she was forever reliving that moment when she had pleaded with him to tell her about her parents' past. It was a feeling that had stayed with her, that had become more intense in her most intimate moments with Eric. He no longer seemed too old for her—they were the same. She had always been grown up in this way but had been unaware of it until then. Eric, on the other hand, had been stunted by the war. As he was a child during those years, he could only go so far. If he delved too deeply into his emotions, it would cause him too much pain; he would not be able to survive. She had come to comprehend this about him those past months, and so they had clung to each other all the more.

They had decided to marry a year from the following September. After another summer of classes, her coursework would be nearly complete. She insisted Eric go alone to see her parents, to inform them of their pending engagement. For she did not want to witness her mother's glee or her father's relief. In front of Eric they would be more subdued.

With one last thrust the train pulled into South Station. Her father would be waiting for her in the car, while her mother would be home preparing dinner. Before disembarking she took a final look out the window and was met with her own reflection. How serious she appeared, uneasy, comprehending that it was because she fully believed Eric had not told her the complete story—she deduced there was more. Yet in marrying him she would be fulfilling her obligation to her parents, a realization that afforded her both an added confidence and melancholy.

Five

Sketching

When Jenny had said, "not tonight, Jonas," he had been dispirited. He had other errands to do, he had answered loosely, and said hopefully they'd run into each other again before she returned to the college. Jonas noticed a brief expression of sadness crossing her face, a warm breeze moving her fine dangling earrings. She parted her lips as if about to speak, but she didn't. He understood that she accepted his words in that disciplined way of hers and strode on.

After taking three or four steps, she turned round, as if aware he'd been watching her. When she caught his stare, he saw she had taken off her glasses. She moved closer. In the sunlight her eyes appeared more gray than brown. "Jonas," she said, her gaze penetrating his, "I knew you had left San Francisco. I am happy and pleased for you. I believe you have potential." Her voice was warm and her eyes sincere, he thought. But before he had a chance to respond she was walking at a swift pace toward her home, her form partially in shade from the passing cars.

There had been a guardedness in her voice, tempering her earnestness, a subtle warning not to pursue her. He was deflated—he found her young. Despite this, he had been hoping they would share a strong friendship. Once she disappeared from sight, he smiled ironically and thought, friendship, wasn't the joke on him?

When he got home, he went directly to the basement to work on a charcoal drawing of one of the waitresses in the coffee shop he visited every morning. From the tag on her uniform, he knew her name was Violet. He'd rise early, and would often go there with his sketch pad. One morning he had gone earlier than usual; his mother had not come home the previous night. Cora had told him, her eyes sincere and apprehensive, that she and Belinda were planning on going to a very late movie and she would be staying with her that evening. Nodding his head, his lips closed, he had understood his mother was disclosing that she'd be spending the night with Harold. When he had walked into the coffee shop that morning, no other customers were there; the coffee smelled freshly brewed, more so than usual.

He sat at the counter and soon Violet sallied over with a mug of coffee in hand. She placed it on the counter before him and began to speak as if they were old friends, revealing details about her life, her two marriages, her one child—a son, who lived mostly with his father. Her expression thoughtful, she would from time to time look away from him. She spoke in a factual way; she wasn't inclined to feel sorry for herself. He liked that about her. In a surprisingly soft voice, pointing to the sketch pad he had placed on the counter, she asked if he was an artist. He nodded and shrugged at the same time. She seemed to accept and digest his response. Then, as if it were an afterthought, she added that she was thirty-six. He was pleased she had told him her age; he would not have guessed it—at certain moments she appeared quite young, yet she looked significantly older than her age when the light was dim.

At his desk now, his accidental meeting with Jenny no longer foremost in his mind, he switched on the lamp and began to sketch the faint lines he had noticed that morning surrounding Violet's mouth, the smallness and roundness of her eyes, the pearl-shaped irises. But he was having difficulty recalling the exact contours of her face, whether or not her cheekbones were defined or rounded, the relative distance between her lips and her chin, the width of her mouth. His desire to work that afternoon had begun to wane.

After dinner he mentioned to his mother that he had run into Jenny that afternoon. Lounging on the sofa, drinking coffee, they had been discussing the coming summer, his tentative plans—working on setting up his first exhibit by early fall—as well as her more definite ones: two weeks off in early August to visit an old friend who had moved to Texas. His mother, no longer in her work clothes, wore a pair of cotton slacks and a short-sleeved tan-colored top. In the dusky light, he studied her profile, the upward tilt of her nose, the shadows beneath her eyes.

In twenty minutes or so he would go down to his studio and work more on his sketch of Violet. Once he went downstairs Cora would either turn on the news or open the Zane Grey novel he had observed her reading the previous few days.

He had been home for two weeks and he still had not met Harold. His mother approved of his knowing about Harold, but she simply and sincerely did not want them to meet—it was his understanding that, with sober deliberation, she had chosen to keep those two parts of her life separate. From time to time he would ponder her decision and eventually would conclude that she was preventing him from meeting Harold in order to honor the memory of his father.

When he now spoke of Jenny, Cora in her quick and exacting way placed her cup in its saucer that lay on the coffee table. Then, turning to him, her eyes startled, she said, "Jonas, I have explained to you about Jenny." His mother, appearing to have lost her natural confidence, sighed uneasily—there was a part of her that took Johanna Smila too seriously, he gleaned. He had never witnessed this uncertainty in her before, her unwavering belief in another person. She continued in a pointed and confiding voice, "There is somewhat of a mystery surrounding Johanna's family during the war and the part Eric's family may have played in helping them. Johanna rarely speaks directly. Between the lines I have gathered there are exceptionally close and binding ties between Eric's family and Jenny's. I would not become preoccupied with Jenny. I would not be surprised if she were to marry Eric relatively soon. Johanna has not said anything conclusively, but she has alluded to the possibility." His mother looked quite serious, so much so that Jonas was filled with unease. Then she spoke again, her voice determined, though wavering some, her hands now clasped: "The past of others can hurt the unknowing," she said. "I don't want to see you hurt, Jonas."

Annoyed with her attempt to interfere in his personal life, he firmly put his arm around her narrow shoulders, less sturdy than he expected, and said, "Don't worry, Cora, Jenny's too young for me, and Eric is too old for her." It was the first time he'd addressed his mother in this way. Initially he felt her stiffen, but soon she relaxed and met his gaze, her eyes attentive, and he felt her confidence rising. He continued, "If Eric is what Jenny wants and needs, it is a relationship I can easily accept. Friendship is all I have ever hoped for from Jenny. Today she said she would be returning to the college soon for the remainder of the summer, and so I imagine a friendship between us will not materialize." When his mother smiled warmly in response, he knew he had sounded firm and convincing. He kissed his mother on each side of her face. And with renewed energy, he hastened down the basement stairs to his studio. His memory sharper now, he worked diligently on his sketch of Violet.

He rose early the next morning. When he drew apart the beige and gray curtains his mother had sewn and peered out the window, he was met with a misty day, the clouds low and heavy.

The sunrise would not be visible. He quietly left the house, carefully shutting the front door. As he began his daily walk to the coffee shop, he stopped and paused in front of Jenny's home. He assumed her father would not be leaving for work for another hour and a half. All the lights were off, and there was a somberness about the Smilas' small ranch house. It was a dark brown color, and a few of the brick steps along the front path were broken, grass sprouting between the cracks. Although his home was about the same size as theirs, it seemed larger. He believed it appeared so not only because it was a pale yellow color but because of his mother. Despite Cora's small size and generally exacting nature, there was something extraordinarily large about her presence. There was a staidness about Jenny's home that saddened him. He stood there unable to move, just staring; he was overcome by an emotion he'd not experienced before—a mixed feeling of both hopelessness and hopefulness. He caught a movement in the drapes in a front window, a narrow parting. As their homes were similar in design—he had been inside Jenny's living room a few times the previous summer—he guessed it was her father checking the weather from his bedroom window. But he soon realized it was Jenny. It struck him as odd that her parents had given her the master bedroom. Only part of her face was revealed, and her long bare neck. With each hand she held on to the drapes, now bringing them closer together, shading his view of her, then suddenly she swiftly drew them farther apart. Her hair was pulled back. She was looking off into the distance as if in a trance. Her expression was both luminous and slightly degraded. Before she looked down, he began to walk quickly. He was shaken; he had been privy to another side of her, one he had not desired to know, a darker and more private side. Had the figurative mask he believed she wore, a second skin, so to speak, been at last removed and tossed aside?

He had been disoriented by Jenny's sudden appearance at her window, and so, when he stepped inside the coffee shop, he did not, as usual, seek out Violet. After a minute or two, in his search for an empty seat, he happened to glance in her direction and noticed that, despite the gray clouds, Violet appeared quite cheery, looking much younger, smiling broadly. She stood behind the cash register, promptly ringing up the check for a customer.

Jonas found a vacant stool at the counter. As he rested the sketch pad on his lap, Violet approached to take his order. He made no attempt to strike up a conversation, nor did he subtly study her face in order to sketch her more accurately when he returned to his studio. Each morning he refrained from drawing her while he was at the coffee shop—he didn't want her to know he was interested in her in that way. The previous week she had noticed him sketching others who had come into the shop. She had come over and had asked to see his work, smiling slowly as she studied with a ruminative gaze what he'd been drawing.

With a few gulps he now drank his coffee, then smiled curtly at Violet, motioning to her that he was ready to pay. She appeared offended by his brusqueness; her small eyes, which he likened to two periwinkle shells half buried in a tan-colored sand, narrowed as if she were hurt. Instead of coming over to him, she struck up a conversation with the customer she was serving. Eventually she came over and slapped down the check next to his empty cup. Her expression was pensive and he sensed she was deciding whether or not to converse with him.

"Where is your art pad today, Jonas?" she asked with a tinge of sarcasm, her earlier happy state having folded in his presence. She stood on her toes and peeked over the counter, pointing to it resting on his lap. "Aren't you sketching today?" she asked, her cheeks reddening. He lowered his head, ignoring her question. "You look a little pale today, Jonas," she said flatly.

As he opened the door to leave the shop, out of the corner of his eye, he saw Violet frown. He wondered if she had surmised that he had been sketching her privately. Jonas had not asked permission to do so. He'd gathered that she would not have approved—his assumption was she would have thought it a furtive activity of his.

When he returned home, his mother had already left for work. Within moments he was climbing down the basement stairs.

The studio was more untidy than usual—he did not allow his mother to clean his work area. Yet often he would become involved in sketching or painting and forget about tidying up. Although the window was narrow, a thin layer of light wended its way into the room. The sky was no longer gray and the sun was coming from behind the clouds, the morning light picking up particles of dust.

At his desk, he switched on the lamp; the unfinished sketch of Violet lay before him. He thought it only vaguely resembled her. Instead of working more on the drawing, he put it aside. With exactitude he loosened a blank sheet from his art pad and, without a second thought, he attempted to draw Jenny. Not the Jenny he recalled from the previous summer, but the mysterious woman he discerned that morning, peering out her window, the darkness inherent in her gaze. He imagined how she would have appeared if he had been in the room with her, facing her in direct light, the drapes no longer covering the sides of her face. Pressing the piece of charcoal too firmly onto the paper, he tore into it. Reflexively he crumpled the sheet, tossed it into the basket, and began drawing on another sheet. He sketched her eyes, the natural downward cast at the corners, then the upward tilt of her eyelids, the arch of her rounded chin, the vertical line above her lips, her high and flat cheekbones. But suddenly he stopped and stared at his work. For it wasn't remotely Jenny's likeness; instead he'd drawn a sketch of Belinda!

He held the drawing close to the light and froze. After a few minutes, his heart began to pump furiously. He could not comprehend what he'd done. What trick had his mind played on him?

Whenever he painted with a brush or worked with a piece of charcoal, he had been guided by both his hand and eye. He considered himself to be a visceral artist, one grounded in reality, more than a cerebral one. And as he knew he was not insightful in a psychological sense, he thought as he examined the sketch of Belinda he might as well have been looking at a page written in ancient script.

His mind wandered to his aunt—he had not seen her in over a year, not since she had visited him in San Francisco with his mother. At the time she'd been, and he believed still was, involved in a relationship with an ex-priest. She had seemed preoccupied during her visit, often on the phone, wrapping herself in the long springy cord. After each call, she'd tuck a five-dollar bill in Jonas's shirt pocket. He recalled her mercurial personality, how she had been the one to tell him how his parents had met, but most poignantly, the memorable conversation he had had with her in his boyhood about his father, her fine dark hair sprawled across her back, how she had tightly clutched *A Tale of Two Cities* as she spoke of David, the lone tear rolling down her cheek. Yet Jonas was aware his memories of his aunt were circumscribed; it was as if he were viewing her through a telescopic lens. He'd been a child then; he didn't know her as an adult.

With a sense of resolution, he put aside the drawing of his aunt and turned to his sketch of Violet. Although he had not paid close attention to her that morning, surprisingly, the general cast of her features was now fresh in his mind. Thoughts of the change in Jenny and his inadvertent sketch of Belinda slipped from his consciousness; he became absorbed in the drawing. For he was envisioning the contours of Violet's face more and more clearly. Soon he was immersed in his work.

~

He did not speak to Jenny again during her three-week visit that May. And other than that early morning at the window, he'd noticed her only one other time. It was at the movie theater, about a week after he had seen her at the drugstore. It took him a while to realize it was Jenny. It was a cool night, and she wore a dark green sweater. She sat five rows in front of him, next to Eric, Jonas assumed. He had not seen Eric before, but because of Jenny's detailed description of him the previous summer, he was easily recognizable.

Jonas was alone. He had considered asking Violet that morning—she had become friendlier over the last few days—but he was skittish about becoming involved in a serious relationship. On some mornings Violet would ask to see his sketches and then comment on them and make suggestions after she guessed which customer he was drawing. She once asked if he needed to ask permission to draw a person. He told her he didn't know what the ethics of an artist was, but it was only a sketch, his impression of the person, so it didn't really matter. She seemed to ruminate over what he had said but had not responded.

He studied Eric, who wore a jacket with a collared shirt and no tie. He recalled Jenny's haunting expression as she had stood peering out the window that morning a week before. Her body leaned in Eric's direction while he sat straight, looking up at the screen. From time to time she'd raise her hand to the back of his neck and stroke it, but Eric did not take her hand nor did he put his arm around her.

After a while Eric rose from his seat and walked up the

aisle. Jonas saw Jenny turn to watch, her eyes solely on Eric. Because of the dim lighting, Jonas could not decipher the expression in her eyes. It was more of her posture, her doting on Eric, that disturbed him. For she had always come across to him as quite independent. His past interactions with her briefly crossed his mind. He thought of how she'd examine his paintings, not really caring if she was overly critical. Or how she had avoided him whenever she was with her friends, though she had invited him to come along. It had taken him a while to realize she had invited him out of politeness, that she really did not want him around when she was with her friends. She had preferred to be alone with him. Jonas thought that with him she invariably had the upper hand. But that night she was not the Jenny he had known the previous summer. He wondered if there was more to their relationship, a pending marriage, as his mother had implied. Although Jenny appeared cool and contained, she was quite caring and he believed she would be protective toward anyone she considered to be a friend or a lover. Because of this it was difficult to determine what she desired, which direction in life she would choose. Then, uneasily, he thought of her at the window that morning, her haunting presence.

When Eric returned to his seat, Jonas noticed a stealthy yet upbeat agility in his walk that was so inharmonious he found it jarring. Jenny didn't look in Eric's direction; she now seemed to be completely absorbed by the movie. But once Eric sat next to her she turned to him. There was something about the movement of her head, her profile in silhouette, that caused Jonas to sense a pleading quality in it. He was disquieted, and he diverted himself by focusing on the movie, a movie whose title he would never recall.

What he would remember was that it was a movie about an older woman in her late forties and a younger man who was approximately thirty years old. It might have been a French movie, which from time to time would come to their small city. But he was not certain whether or not he had had to read subtitles that night. All he'd recall was that the couple meet at a party and she at first speaks to him in a somewhat maternalistic way, chides him for spilling his coffee as she watches over him at the dessert table. Then she shows him how to pour it properly, holding the pot higher, not close to the cup. Neither of them speak; it is all explained through movement and shaking of the head or nods. The younger man shrugs it off; he isn't chagrined by her instruction—he is a poet. With filled coffee cup in hand, he leaves her and walks confidently across the room to speak with a young woman who obviously admires him. Jonas would not remember more about the plot, but he'd recall that a short time later the late-forties woman and the thirty-year-old poet were in bed together.

From his point of view, the movie paralleled his perception of the relationship between Eric and Jenny. During the film, his eyes would often stray from the screen to the two of them. But the more the movie progressed, the more Jenny and Eric seemed immersed in it.

When the film was over, Jonas lowered his head as Jenny and Eric made their way up the aisle toward the exit. When he thought they had passed his row, he cautiously raised his eyes. They had come to a standstill; the couple in front of them was immersed in conversation with another couple and they were blocking Jenny and Eric from moving forward. Jonas lowered his head again, yet his gaze drifted left and he was met with the sight of their hands, how urgently Jenny pressed Eric's, which were behind his back, both of hers clutching his. He had no need to worry that she might notice him; she was fixated on Eric. Her eyelids were lowered, heavy—as if she were drugged.

Eric, Jonas thought, appeared indifferent to Jenny's adoration of him. He accepted it, Jonas concluded, as he would have expected a delicious dinner at a well-known restaurant or a nearly flawless gem at a prestigious jewelry store.

By the time Jonas left the movie theater and was walking toward home, the two of them were no longer in his thoughts. As a couple, they were not an uplifting sight. They were a heavy sort, he decided—he did not perceive the seesawing from banality to excitement he noticed in the relationships and marriages of his friends.

Despite how uneasy he had felt observing Jenny and Eric, when Jonas returned home that evening he felt a strong sense of renewal. He knew that all he wanted now was to paint, to draw. Painting and drawing soothed him, distracted him from the dissonance in humanity. His natural irony and tendency to be skeptical could no longer shade him from darker realities; he turned more and more to art.

He found his mother sitting quietly, staring at the blank screen of the television set. In her lap was a book. Jonas went to her and put his arm around her, wondering if she and Harold had had an argument. He fleetingly recalled how as a young boy he'd touch her hair whenever he had come upon her sleeping. He had an urge to do so now, out of habit, nostalgia. But she seemed solemn. "Jonas," she said softly, smiling warmly. He knew at that moment she was not sad and that things were probably fine with Harold, that maybe she had been savoring her general sense of contentment. Jonas told her he was hoping not to be living with her too much longer, maybe a year at the most. He needed to be independent. He was twenty-eight.

She looked steadily at him, pursed her lips, and then said, "I understand, Jonas."

That night he dreamed of Jenny; the man she was with was not Eric, but the man he had seen in the coffee shop, who he'd thought might be Harold.

About a year later, during one of his trips to New York, Jonas thought he spotted Jenny and Eric. Jenny had not planned to come home that summer, his mother had told him, as she would be getting married in early September. Eric and Jenny, he believed, were in front of a clothing store on Madison Avenue, but he wasn't certain it was them. He was coming up the street—he had just been at the Metropolitan nearby. The woman who he thought might be Jenny was pointing to something in the window and the man she was with was looking in the opposite direction. Then they disappeared inside the store. By the time Jonas got there and went inside, they were nowhere to be found. He rushed out and looked up the street, but they were not in sight. He could not fathom how they could have gone in and then come out without his seeing Jenny and Eric; his eyes had been glued on the store ever since he had first noticed them. Then he wondered if it had been his imagination, after all.

His mother received an invitation to Jenny's wedding. It would take place in Milan so that both Jenny's relatives and Eric's family could come from Trieste. Eric had wanted a honeymoon on the Riviera, according to what Johanna had told his mother, a sort of an apologetic explanation for having it so far away.

Jonas had gathered that the Smilas no longer had many friends in the United States and that most, like Eric's parents, had returned to Trieste. They had come to America to escape memories of the war and, to an extent, to be reborn—but it had been difficult to achieve a sense of renewal, and so they had returned. Because of Jenny, he knew, the Smilas had stayed.

His mother was indecisive. Harold—whom Jonas still had not met—was, according to his mother, not interested in attending. Cora, who had not been to Italy before, was becoming more and more intrigued about the possibility of seeing the country of her ancestors. She looked at Jonas as if considering whether or not to ask him. That is when he suggested Belinda. "Belinda no longer likes to travel," she said, surprised that he had mentioned her as a possibility. He recalled his sketch of his aunt the previous year, and felt discomforted.

Eventually his mother convinced Harold to attend. Following the wedding they would spend a few weeks traveling around the country. Harold had agreed to go as long as they made a side trip to Liverpool, where his grandparents had been born. Jonas was occupied with an upcoming exhibit of his work at the gallery he had worked in two summers before.

When his mother returned from the trip she spoke about their travels, but not of the wedding. A few months later she introduced Jonas to Harold; she left them alone while she went out Christmas shopping. Harold and he had a superficial chat, but after shaking hands before they parted, they both knew they had no interest in knowing more of each other. Harold left before Cora had returned from her shopping excursion.

During the time Jonas lived with his mother, she never brought Harold to their home to spend the night. He didn't at all resemble the man Jonas had seen in the coffee shop. And after meeting Harold, he rarely saw him—only if he was coming to pick up his mother or driving her home—yet whenever his name was mentioned Jonas would envision not the actual Harold, but the man in the coffee shop he had imagined to be him.

Jonas lived in his mother's home for a few months short of

two years, and left in early 1975. He had just turned thirty years old. He'd had a few exhibitions of his paintings at galleries downtown, but his art was not supporting him. Through the contacts he had made during what had become his monthly trips to New York, he had been offered a job as a portrait artist at an upscale art gallery.

Although he would be painting people of means, at least he would be painting, not selling, and he'd continue his own independent work as well.

He regretted that he had not had a chance to see Harold and his mother interact. All he knew of them as a couple was that vague conversation he had overheard the night he had spent in the basement three years before. He had often thought that if he had observed his mother and Harold together for a certain amount of time, he would have understood something about his parents' marriage or how she might have appeared with his father. His mother could not have possibly known how much he had wanted her to marry Harold or at least live with him. And in terms of Jenny's marriage to Eric—Jonas was bewildered. When he left for New York, he had no sense of what the true meaning or purpose of marriage was. No longer retaining the idealized vision of his parents' relationship he had as a boy, he instead carried with him the dry and stilted definition of marriage he'd read again and again, as a young adolescent, late at night, in his mother's old Webster.

SIX

SUMMER AND FALL

Summer heat, intense and persistent, filled her with a sense of longing. In her dormitory room, at her desk, book in hand, she peered closely at the text, the whirring fan close to her emitting soft, warm air. The words on the page did not appear clear and crisp, nor did the characters seem as strong and vibrant as the subjects she had analyzed and written about during the school year; instead they were hazy, as if she were viewing them from a distance, across a murky pond, the sun in her eyes. They were blurred and undefinable. It was becoming more and more challenging to keep her coursework foremost in her mind. The papers she wrote were rambling and unfocused. Her emotions superseded her intellect.

The summer of 1973, she took four courses—two in the first summer session, occurring mostly during the month of June, and two in the second, which began after the fourth of July and ran through the second of August. She would study late at night when at times it was cooler—though many evenings the heat was unbearable. Then she would get up from her desk, go to the open window, and stare out at the still grounds of the campus. Usually no one was in sight. One night Jenny spotted a woman who worked with her in the office, her supervisor. She was strolling across the campus, holding hands with a man Jenny recognized as a security guard in the main building. He was much younger than she was. Jenny could not clearly see their faces until they walked beneath the lights of her dormitory—how loosely they moved, how ecstatic their expressions.

There were moments when she'd ask herself why she had bothered to take classes over the summer. What was the rush? She'd be married in September of the following year; she planned to take that semester off, then return in the spring to complete her coursework. Yes, what was the rush? Others had questioned her plans; those who worked with her in the admissions office were surprised she had set up such a rigorous schedule. What was the purpose?

A few weeks later, Eric surprised her, showing up unexpectedly in her office to take her to lunch. She had not seen him in nearly a month. Over the summer she had arranged her work schedule around her classes. Now that her summer studies were complete, she worked in the office full time.

It was an early August day, and although the temperature was over ninety degrees, Eric wore a gray linen suit that accentuated his blue-gray eyes. When he stepped into the office their gazes met and she said, "I missed you." The words escaped her lips like a soft sigh. No one else was working at the noon hour, but she knew she would have said it regardless. He had wanted her to finish her coursework—he had no intention of distracting her, he'd said the last time she saw him. Then he had disappeared until this day. His expression was impassive as she spoke, but that was his way and she was never quite certain what he was feeling beneath the surface—only when they were in bed together. It was the only time his feelings would be aroused, when she experienced his anguish. It was as if she held power over him when he cried. And she would hold him close, ask what was causing him such pain; she would run her finger across his forehead then down his nose to his mildly pointy chin until his eyes were dry.

Over lunch he told her about his travel plans for the next year, where he would be going until their wedding in early September. It was only thirteen months away, he said, matter-of-factly; he was never one to be emphatic.

"Are you happy, Jenny?" he asked suddenly, his gaze both hopeful and distant. She heard a touch of irony in his tone. They sat outdoors, and the sunlight caught the gold of his cuff links and she again noted his manicured nails. She looked at him steadily, thinking how she had not considered happiness, but obligation, since meeting him. She felt agitated. The waiter came to pour more water into their glasses and Eric was diverted. When they were alone again, she turned the question to him. "How could I not be happy, Jenny?" he responded so simply that, raising the water glass to her lips, she felt her pulse quickening.

Although he had told her where he would be traveling over the next eleven months, he had not told her why he would be going to Madrid or Tel Aviv or London. He did not tell her about his business, and it did not occur to her to ask. She was certain her mother and father knew. If it was something untoward, they would not have encouraged her to be with him, they would not be so overjoyed by their engagement. She trusted him, she trusted them. There was no point in not doing so. During the school year, she relished her coursework, her plans for a career—outside her passion for Eric, it was her sole interest.

Eric was more intrigued by her classes than she was his business. She now told him about the two courses that ended the previous day. One was a comparison of Svevo's *Zeno's Conscience* and Joyce's *Ulysses*. He smiled. It pleased him whenever she spoke of literature, especially European. He asked her what she would like do after she graduated. They had agreed not to have children for ten years. He was not ready and neither was she. She told him she might teach. What else was there to do with a degree in comparative literature? "Compare, I suppose," he said, jokingly.

"Compare what?" she asked, smiling. He leaned across the table and whispered a sexual comment, which she shrugged off; it had dampened the carefree mood between them, she thought.

Eric would be in town for the next ten days. He would be meeting with clients in Philadelphia, and then a week holiday on Maui together would follow. He wanted her to be refreshed before she began her second year of college. She was apprehensive; they had not spent this much time together before. While he was in town, she would go to his hotel every night and he would drive her to work the next morning.

She preferred Eric's luxurious hotel to her dormitory room; in the lobby there were huge sparkling chandeliers and thick handmade rugs, mostly a deep red color. When Eric wasn't looking, she'd slip off her sandal and touch the carpet with her bare foot; she'd experience a thrill within, the arch of her foot pressing into the sensual texture of the carpeting, and she'd reflect on where she had come from, how young she was, how much of life there was before her.

She sensed it would be different with Eric now. Not having been in his company for a month, she noticed a certain edginess in him that hadn't been apparent to her before. And over lunch when he had made the sexual comment, she had been surprised; she hadn't believed he was inclined to such talk in her presence. But now as they rode the elevator to the room she chalked it up to her own lack of experience, her naïveté. She did not love him less, but only more—she appreciated the many sides to him. Whereas at first she thought his remark had dampened the communication between them, by the time they were walking down the hallway toward his room, she believed it would make their intimate moments more complex. She was both somber and elated.

Once inside the room, he locked the door, then turned to her and beckoned her to come to him. Their gazes met; gingerly she approached. He pressed her close, so close she could barely catch her breath. Suddenly he released her. When she looked up at him, there was an expression crossing his face she had not been aware of before. She was accustomed to his sadness, his mournfulness when they had made love in the past. Now she witnessed a strictness, how he lifted his chin. Yet she trusted him.

"What is it, Eric?" she asked, meeting his gaze, noticing strands of brown in his irises. She was not able to read or interpret his intention. Her eyes rested on the shadows beneath his eyes. She knew he had been working late and was under much pressure, as businessmen are during certain months. He had mentioned to her before that late summer was a stressful time for him. She had been surprised that he had arranged the trip to Maui, but then had assumed it was because of his work.

"Nothing in particular, Jenny. I know you are quite independent and would not have any qualms about walking away from me, breaking our engagement."

Her heart pounded; she again met his gaze. "Do you want to break our engagement, Eric? I am confused. Do you not love me, do you want us not to be together?" Her imaginings of their future life together began to scatter in her mind like autumn leaves falling prematurely from a tree.

He embraced her again, with more caution now; her face rested against his chest. She was not able to see his expression. "Let's take a walk," she heard him say. His voice sounded somewhat distant, as if coming from a television or radio in the next room.

She stepped away from him, her hands still on his arms. "If you need to speak, Eric, I'd prefer you do so in this room." She was forcing herself to say those words; within she was uncertain. It was a new experience for her.

He smiled and said, "Jenny, you always surprise me. Sometimes you appear confident and composed and at other times young and naïve."

Shaken, she went and sat on the edge of the bed and tightly closed her eyes, not from sadness but as a way of gathering herself, readying herself for a deeper strength she knew she would need to reveal. She was keenly aware of the difference in their ages and how because of it he held much knowledge and experience of the world over her. Worldly Eric, she thought with deep irony. It struck her that honesty, her newly developed frankness, was what she possessed, was what would help her counter his experience.

When she looked up, his back was to her. He stood near the window; he had pushed aside the drapes and was looking out. She wondered how much she would be able to comprehend what he had experienced during the war.

He turned to her and said, "We are different, Jenny, maybe too different." Their gazes met; his was determined. She forced herself to speak.

"What is wrong, Eric? What has happened since we were last together? I will not stay with you if you believe we are so different." She pulled off her engagement ring and placed it on the table next to the bed. "I will go, Eric. You are free now. We are no longer engaged." She read amazement in his eyes. This was not what he had expected from her. Or was his expression of amazement his way of hiding how startled he felt? Startled by his own words? Did he think he had so much control over her? Tears began to gather in his eyes.

"Don't leave, Jenny."

"What happened this past month, Eric, that makes you this way—so committed at one moment, so distant at the next?"

No longer melancholic, he appeared strained, unsure. She continued, "Or was it much before that? What are you not telling me, Eric?" His name coming from her lips sounded sharp and constricted.

He went to the door and she believed he would leave her now. She was getting too close. He stood at the door. She knew he was not certain. She understood him only through her parents, their life—that was the root of her comprehension. Closing her eyes, she took a deep breath—it was one of indecision. She was not sure whether or not their engagement should continue. It was a moment of uncertainty for both of them. Who was more unsure? Who was more reliable? Which one of them was less destructive? Directness had been a struggle for her for most of her life. She had been taught to be evasive.

His hand gripped the doorknob. Her heart pounded.

Fleetingly, she imagined her life with him and then without his presence. Which was more promising? The many trips to Europe, his love, having his children? Or her complete independence, her freedom? Then she thought of her parents and was convinced she would never be free—for her, freedom was an illusion. She honored their experience during the war. Would she ever be able to shake herself from its bonds?

Eric turned to her. He had taken his hand off the doorknob. She could not read the expression in his eyes that were now clear, not one trace of unshed tears. "Take the ring," she said, pointing to the table next to the bed. He came to her and lowered her hand.

"I want us to be married."

"No doubts?" she asked.

"None whatsoever," he said. But though his voice was firm and assured, his eyes were distant. Yet it was his low and confident voice that reached her. Its sound caressed her like a warm high wave engulfing her. She threw her arms around his waist and he kissed her with a disquieting fortitude.

"A lovers' argument," she said, gazing up at him, hearing how hollow her voice sounded. He ran his hands down her back; there was an impatience in his touch.

He nodded, his eyes slightly less distant. In this moment he was with her, she believed.

It was a little after midnight. Rustling sounds filled the room; in the darkness they made their way to the bed. They had just come in from a very late dinner, five courses, much wine. Eric's intention had been to celebrate their being together again after a month separation. He had not anticipated their argument, their near breakup. Since they'd been together they had not argued, until that day. Eric had not had as much wine as Jenny had. He was careful never to drink too much; he was always on alert, it seemed. He was always in control, and she understood this about him, as she was not so dissimilar. Tonight though, from the tension of the near breakup of their engagement, from her uncertainty, she had allowed herself to open up more, to not be aware of how many glasses of wine she'd drunk.

On the drive back to the hotel, her words slightly slurred, she had teased him, chided him about his pointy chin, like an orchestra conductor's. He was smiling in the dark, a relaxed smile, highlighted as they passed beneath a street light and then lights from an oncoming car. "Jenny, Jenny," was all he had said. Despite his mostly impassive expression, she had heard unbounded relief in his voice. It had been wonderful to tease him. She believed they were closer now. Their disagreement, their near separation had been worth it, she thought.

In the dark she slipped out of her clothes and tumbled into bed. Silence. Soon she realized Eric was no longer with her; he was not in the room. She lay in bed waiting. Forty minutes later the door cracked open. He did not switch on the light. She could see him in silhouette, undressing. Then she felt his weight next to her in the bed. Within moments he had turned his back to her. She stared up at the ceiling, a blank white sheet, as the night passed into morning.

~

It was early September, the first week of her sophomore year of college. Her life at school was different than it had been the previous year, mostly because she did not have a roommate. Arlene had transferred to a state school closer to her home, and Jenny had not found out until the week before. She had been disappointed Arlene was no longer at the college. She would miss their eclectic conversations. Arlene had enhanced her life in that she had been her only experience with a sibling of sorts. Jenny had called her a few times, but after exchanging initial pleasantries Arlene was always in a rush. She did not want to talk more. Jenny assumed this was her way of coping with their separation, and she understood there would be a day when they would no longer communicate.

Others did not approach her as much as they had the previous year. A classmate might ask her what the homework assignment was for the next day, or when the next paper would be due. Women suspiciously eyed the engagement ring on her finger and it was noted that she had her own dorm room. She was considered mature. She was no longer truly part of the college environment. She was like a shadow of a student whose essence was elsewhere.

Her thoughts were mixed about her new status. At times she felt more sophisticated and knowledgeable than other students. In class, she spoke out, neither too much nor too little, but with confidence, and only to make a particular point. She was now an experienced woman who had known love and passion, who had her career before her with a successful fiancé at her side. She was no longer thought of as naïve Jenny.

She often asked herself if she missed those early months the previous year when school was first beginning, before Eric had walked into her life. Yet as much as she tried, she could not bring those days to mind, or recall the early excitement. Perhaps she had locked away the experience because it simply was not relevant to her life any longer. She was not dismayed or even reminiscent. She thought first of her present reality, and then she'd remind herself that her parents would no longer exist if Eric's family had not intervened, and how in their doing so, they had allowed her to be.

Her path in life was very clear. Did she love Eric out of a sense of filial duty? Whenever she asked herself this question, she understood it was unknowable. Her situation was complex and involved—any attempt to answer such a question would sound insincere and perhaps even false. Someday she hoped she would have the maturity to comprehend why she loved Eric, why she was committing herself to him. Although he was older, she believed she was the more grounded one. She hesitated to ask him about his days as a child in Trieste during the war. She did not know how much he remembered. He had dreams of horror. She'd hear him call out in his sleep. His cries would awaken her and she'd sit up in bed and watch over him; she'd wait until his sleep was again sound. In his conscious life, his life unburdened from his dreams, she believed he had no awareness of his childhood. He had shut those days out of his life as she had drawn a shade over her carefree days when she had believed so profoundly in her independence. His method of shutting down the past was unconscious, while hers was accomplished in full awareness.

She had attempted to research Trieste, what had happened during the war, the anti-fascist group her father had been part of, but she had not been able to unearth much; it still was an enigma to her, and so not quite real. All she knew was that Italy had declared war on Nazi Germany, October 1943. Her imagination roughly filled in the rest. She had come to understand that Eric, other than that night he had first spoken of it, mirrored her parents in that it was a subject he did not want to approach, let alone discuss. She understood why he had been compelled to reveal the truth; he had needed her to be cognizant of her parents' past and their connection to him and his family. Yet he had not said more. Their linkage had become nonverbal—it had been evident in his lovemaking, which ran the gamut from high emotion to detachment and distance. On her part it was evidenced in her devotion to Eric, or at times her dispassionate objectification of him. There were days when she would wonder if it was possible that she hated him. But she would remind herself she had never hated anyone.

It was the end of the first week of September, 1974, and they had been married for seven days. They would spend another week on the French Riviera, heading to the Italian side the following Saturday. It was wonderful to lie on the beach. Although the air was only slightly cooler at this time of year, the sun was strong, beating down relentlessly over their half-naked bodies. She had never before felt such a surge of physical strength and well-being as in those days by the sea.

Two nights before, Eric had disappeared for a few hours, but was back in their room by eleven. That night his lovemaking had been hasty, less inclusive, and she had felt like a bystander. The next morning she was uneasy and doubts started to creep into her mind about their marriage. But the previous night after they had spent the entire day together, he had been as caring and as romantic as his nature would allow, fully revealing his melancholy when they made love. It was at these times when she most understood Eric. When he disappeared for a few hours, which he had for two nights of their week-old marriage, she had been uneasy. She had no idea where he was. When he returned, she'd ask him where he'd been. He'd avoid answering her directly. He had his contacts in Europe, he'd say. And she would tell herself he was seeing his business associates, as he had indicated he might before their wedding. But she never fully believed him. She was beginning to understand there was a part of Eric she would never know. That was where their age difference asserted itself. While she was a young child, he had begun to establish these contacts. It was his world without her. Although she knew she must allow him to live it, given who she was she did not believe it would be possible for her to easily do so. Was that the sacrifice expected when there was an age difference such as theirs? Was it a sacrifice she would not be able to make?

For when she had asked him where he was, his response had always been the same: "Business—I can't stop working because we are enjoying a very long honeymoon. I am not that wealthy, Jenny." There had been neither scorn nor pleading in his voice; his tone had been low and factual.

That night she lay alone in bed. Her back was badly sunburned. It was difficult to fall asleep. The windows were open and there was a caressing breeze. When Eric was not with her, she liked to listen to the rush of the waves.

Above the sound of the ocean, she now heard people talking on the terrace, the clattering sound of waiters clearing dishes and silverware from the tables on the patio just below. It was a small, intimate restaurant—the ocean a stone's throw away—with round tables and white linen tablecloths, a candle and a vase with one flower adorning the center of each one, waiters in white jackets scurrying about.

It was one o'clock in the morning. She experienced a sense of contentment, the scenery, the night, the light conversations below. It was idyllic. Then she thought of her marriage and her feeling of wholeness dissipated. For a moment she wished Eric would only be the Eric she preferred and that they would live this life forever, that they would not go home. She closed her eyes wishing. But then she thought of home, of school, which she would again attend in January, and she knew they must return. They would be living in Philadelphia then. That was what belonged to her, her schoolwork; it represented her life, her future as an independent person, as independent as she could possibly be.

She heard voices from below again, louder now, a conversation. There were many people talking. Three or four men, two or more women, she thought. They were from various places, she gathered, as they had different accents, though they were all speaking English. From time to time one lapsed into French, and then another person would respond in French but soon they were all speaking English again. They were too far away—she could not determine their exact words or what they were speaking of.

Slowly it dawned on her that one of the voices was Eric's. His tone was different. He was laughing and he sounded as young as the others. She was accustomed to his subdued and at times stern voice, ever confident. She had always thought this was because of his age. Yet now she heard how young he was. She imagined him sitting out on the patio, wearing blue linen pants and a white cotton shirt with the sleeves rolled up—how he was dressed when she had parted from him in the early evening, just before he had slid into the car he was renting, telling her he had to meet with an old client and wasn't certain when he'd be back.

Now she heard his laughter, his light tone, and for a fleeting moment she was hopeful. Then she heard chairs scraping against concrete.

Ten minutes later Eric walked into the room. She heard him place the key on the table next to the bed. She pretended she was sleeping, though her heart beat wildly. He sat next to her. "Wake up, Jenny," he said, urgently. She smelled alcohol on his breath. Her eyes opened. He leaned over and switched on the light. As he got up, she felt his weight leave the bed. Standing now, he slowly undressed, his leg grazing her bare arm.

In Lucerne the dark mystique of Halloween hissed throughout the city. The weather was quite cool. During the day, the sky was mostly gray. Their hotel room looked out over the turbulent river that snaked through the city; its covered bridges appeared more white against the dusky sky.

The next day they would begin their trip back to the United States. Those few days in this old city marked the end of their two-month honeymoon. It had been one of highs and lows, and she was not certain if their marriage would be a successful one. She had learned that Eric was erratic, to say the least: kind and emotional at one moment, stern and demanding at the next. Fortunately she had been able to ignore his spurious wants, diverting him whenever possible, never succumbing to him when he was so inclined. At such times their relationship devolved into a seemingly endless game of dodgeball.

It was now close to five o'clock. They walked through the streets, not holding hands as they would have during the early days of their trip. Each gazed off in another direction—she was searching for she knew not what; Eric's stare was with purpose. He stopped in front of a department store and, without turning toward her, said he needed to go inside. They would be attending a Halloween party at their hotel that night, and she knew he was looking for a hat that would go with his costume. She sat outside on a bench across from the entrance; she preferred the cool evening air more than the hassle of shopping in a large store. Her mind drifted to the uncertainties of the past two months and again she wondered if their marriage would last. She rationalized that it was too early to know; they had many years before them to discover more about each other. On the other hand, their marriage was fraught with complications—in particular, Eric's inability to talk in any depth about his past or his work. Although she had not insisted on knowing much—she had put her trust in her parents' judgement—she had lately begun to ask direct questions about what he did, especially since he'd been disappearing for hours. When he'd return, he'd expect her to react as if he'd been away for only twenty minutes or so.

He would appear surprised by her questions; he felt he didn't need to answer in any depth, because he would provide for her. He told her she only needed to know specifics if his business for some unknown reason took a turn for the worse. She was relieved they would not have children for a while. Given the difference in their ages, having a child now would be difficult; they had much ground to catch up on before they would be ready for that step.

They were an hour late to the Halloween party. She was dressed as a shepherdess and Eric was a pirate—not a very compatible pair. She was wrapped in a white sheet, one shoulder exposed, her hair in a loose ponytail that reached down to the center of her back. She held a staff in one hand. Eric had a black patch over his eye and he wore a short red jacket and black pants. He had not been able to find an appropriate hat at the department store.

When she glanced across the room, her pulse quickened; she had spotted a familiar form, a woman, standing next to the buffet table. Without thinking she began to approach her, her heart pounding. The woman wore a black mask and was dressed like a feline. Pausing for a moment, Jenny turned back to look for Eric. She did not see him. She was not certain where he had gone.

Her curiosity was boundless. She felt slightly dizzy as she walked toward this familiar form; the lights in the large room seemed to blend together and shimmer. Now she was next to her. The woman turned to her; she was holding a glass of wine in one hand, a canapé in the other. Jenny did not say anything, only peering into the familiar eyes. The woman put down her glass, and with one swift motion, she removed her mask. "Arlene! Why are you here?" Jenny cried out, her heart in her throat. Before Arlene answered, Jenny looked quickly about the room, but she did not see Eric. It was as if he had been consumed by the crowd. Her hand on her forehead, she felt how moist it was. She looked again at Arlene. She was smiling now. She had always liked the element of surprise, Jenny thought, recalling how Arlene would disappear on certain nights and would not tell her the next day where she'd been. She'd leave unexpectedly and return in the same mysterious way. Jenny had never known whether or not to report to the dormitory proctor that Arlene was missing.

"Semester abroad," she said now, her lips moving in an exaggerated way, perhaps because there was a density about the room; although no one was talking loudly, there was a sense that if you spoke, you would not be heard.

"In Lucerne?" she asked skeptically.

"Zurich," Arlene answered again with her lips.

Jenny's eyes filled with tears. She turned away to search again for Eric. All she saw were the tops of heads, some with odd-shaped hats that she imagined suited their costumes, and then cigarette smoke trailing just below the ceiling. It seemed she had lost Eric. When she looked back at Arlene, she noticed that her face was flushed. Arlene picked up her wine glass and as she sipped from it, she looked askance at Jenny. She noticed an engagement ring on Arlene's finger. "So you are engaged," Jenny said, nervously. "Barry?"

She shook her head. "I met someone in Zurich, a banker."

"That was fast," Jenny said in a noncommittal way, her heart thumping.

"I suppose you could say we fell in love." As Arlene spoke, her eyes were nearly vacant. It was as if she was a different person with a different spirit in the form of Arlene.

"Is he here?"

"Yes, he is a friend of Eric's. I think they have gone off somewhere."

"A friend of Eric's? How did you meet him?" Jenny felt herself shaking within, thinking how odd it was for Arlene to be in Lucerne, to be engaged to a friend of Eric's—more strange than anything she had witnessed or experienced with Eric.

Arlene looked at her in that old way of hers. And for a moment Jenny felt a sense of familiarity—it was as if they were back in their college dorm room. "Life is full of coincidences," Arlene said, gulping down the remainder of her drink.

Jenny looked away and spotted Eric across the room, deep in conversation with a man she assumed was Arlene's fiancé. He was evidently older than Eric. And Jenny thought of the young and vibrant Barry and how heartbroken he must have been when Arlene had announced she was engaged to someone else. Those early days with Eric during her first year of college flashed across her mind, and then she looked again at Arlene. Arlene had always seemed a backdrop to their relationship. She had only seen Eric briefly that first year of college, on three or four occasions, and had not appeared to be impressed in the least with him. Jenny had thought she was always comparing him in her mind to Barry, and she had assumed Eric was the one who had come up short. Arlene had let Jenny know in subtle ways that she believed Eric was too old for her—especially when she emphasized how wonderful it was to be involved with someone her own age. And here Arlene was now with a much older man, older than Eric.

A sudden surge of strength bolstered Jenny; she was not as naïve as she had been when she had lived with Arlene. No longer did she hazily, dreamily think there was more to Eric's story; she knew there was, in a way she had not fathomed.

Seven

Winter

On a bitterly cold Saturday morning, late December, 1980, Jonas learned of Eric Stram's death. For an hour he had been sitting near the door in a coffee shop on Seventh Avenue, assailed by a draft of cold air each time someone came in or left. His table faced an ice-framed window; he peered out at the bleak scene, the malaise of winter encroaching upon the city. The sky was colorless, and pale, vacant expressions clouded the faces of the pedestrians.

He forced himself to consider his future. The new year was a few days away, and in a month, he'd turn thirty-six. There was something of significance about that age; it was a marker of where one was, what one had achieved. Should he continue on as he had for the last while or should he turn his career and life in another direction?

More than five years earlier, he had come to New York and he still was uneasy there, though he grudgingly acknowledged he'd never felt attuned to any setting—not in the small college environment in western Massachusetts where he had spent the first four years of adulthood, nor in the years he had lived in San Francisco as a middling art salesman. And in terms of his home close to Boston, even as a young boy he'd viewed it as a place-in-waiting.

The man at the next table who had not removed his knit cap the entire time he'd been there suddenly got up and left; the newspaper he'd been reading was sprawled across the Formica-topped table. Reflexively Jonas's gaze wandered over and he noted at the top of a page Eric Stram's name in bold dark letters. As it was early he was still sleepy and so at first the name didn't register. He looked away and then spotted a woman crossing the street who he thought seemed familiar, perhaps someone he had painted, but realized within seconds that he'd not seen her before. And then his gaze wandered back to the newspaper and up to the name of Eric Stram, and at that moment it dawned on him that Eric Stram was Jenny's Eric. Jonas got up and snatched up the newspaper; clutching it with both hands, he stood and read the article with a mingling of intensity and dispassion.

What he determined from his first read through was that Eric's death had been an accident, but there was no description nor any details about the accident. "Successful businessman," Jonas read; but there was no clarification of what business he was in. Jenny was mentioned only at the very end along with his parents, who were living in Trieste, Italy, as his survivors. No other siblings were mentioned but Jonas vaguely recalled having heard from either his mother or Jenny that Eric had had an older brother who had died at fourteen at the beginning of the Second World War. He also noted that Eric had passed away six weeks before. He wondered why his mother had not contacted him, but remembered she was in Florida visiting Harold, who owned a condo near Palm Beach. He was retired now and lived there full time.

Jonas knew where Jenny lived. After she and Eric had moved to New York, she had come into the gallery where Jonas worked on several occasions—though now he had not seen her in over a year. She had enjoyed talking with him, he thought, because he was her connection to her life away from New York. A few times they had gone out for a glass of wine or coffee. During those times she had told him that Eric was out of town on business. But she had come to him only sporadically; months would pass between her visits. Jonas had not been able to determine whether she was happy or miserable with Eric. Their conversations only lasted a certain amount of time and were general. She'd ask him if he were painting landscapes in addition to his portraits. She had told him that she had mentioned him to Eric, and her husband had suggested that Jonas paint her. And he had recalled uneasily how he had been incapable of sketching her several years before, and how instead he had drawn his aunt Belinda. His inability to sketch Jenny had always stayed in his mind like an embarrassing reoccurring dream.

His head now throbbed; he was at a loss. Images of Jenny, a succession of them, rapidly crossed his mind, as if he were watching a film in fast forward—Jenny as a fourteen-year-old girl, bouncing the tennis ball with determination and force against a brown patch of earth on a warm dry day in May; Jenny walking toward him, holding her finger in a page of *Women in Love*, as he stood at the backyard gate separating their homes; Jenny asking him to kiss her before he returned to San Francisco; Jenny refusing to see a movie with him the following spring. His most intense memory was of Jenny walking out of the movie theater clutching Eric's hands, her gaze revealing a dark passion. But most painful of all was the image he had retained of Jenny at her bedroom window, grasping the drapes with each hand, her expression wavering between hope and degradation.

He hastened out of the coffee shop and soon found himself outside the building where Jenny lived. A cold gust of wind brushed against his face and he put on the woolen cap he'd been holding; his hands were red, his gloves were not in his pockets.

When Jenny had told him where she and Eric lived, he had not been certain if she had wanted him to visit. She had not asked him to call first and had said to stop by at any time. Once he had asked if she would like him to come when Eric wasn't there. He had been surprised by his boldness. He'd had a few drinks and his speech was more loose than normal, but he had managed to turn it into a joke. Even still, he was surprised he had been that careless with her. He had not wanted to lose her friendship, as sparing as it was. But she had looked back at him, her gray-brown eyes steady beneath her fine brows, and had said, "It doesn't matter whether Eric is home or away on business."

In response he had barely smiled, less affected then by the alcohol, his sense of irony prevailing, preventing him from comprehending the inference in her words. Instead he had felt at more of a distance from her.

As he looked up at the building, trying to assess which apartment might be hers, he recalled the first time Jenny had come into the gallery. He had not recognized her initially. He'd been working there for a little over a year and was told as he stood in the back studio, painting a portrait of one of his latest clients, that someone was there to see him, a Mrs. Stram. He had not made the connection between Eric's last name and Jenny and was puzzled. He had looked apologetically at his client, and then turned to the person, a young man who worked at the reception desk, and said he would see Mrs. Stram in ten minutes. He had assumed it was a woman who had wanted her portrait painted in order to surprise her husband.

After his client had left, he sat for a moment to compose himself. He had never been comfortable on a first meeting with a potential client. He had felt awkward and unconfident, not certain whether he would be able to please her or him. Expectations were high—clients anticipated a dignified portrait; they wanted to be viewed in an optimistic and strong light. And Jonas had not felt this would be possible with every client. Some people's natures were too dark, and as he himself was not particularly insightful, he was only able to intuit a person's dark side while painting. He could never refute what he felt; he could not make it better. It was surprising he had not been fired. But he had come to realize that not every client witnessed the darkness he had perceived; they had been pleased by the effect. They had interpreted what he had thought to be darkness as strength and determination and he had been able to heave a sigh of relief on many occasions throughout that first year. But still he would be apprehensive whenever he first met a client. For he knew there would be a person at one point who would comprehend the truth in his portrait and would be angered by it.

When Jenny had come into his studio, her cheeks had been flushed, her gray-brown eyes flashing. It was a breezy early spring day. To him she was out of context and it wasn't until she said, "Oh, Jonas," and reached out and clasped both of his hands that he knew for certain it was Jenny. It wasn't that she had physically aged—she was nearly twenty-two and had been married for about eighteen months. It was her expression he had not recognized—although she looked her age, her eyes and posture were that of a much older person.

As she held on to his hands, he kissed her on each cheek. "Sit down, Jenny. I did not know you were in New York."

"I've, I mean, *we* have been living here for the last four months. We were in Philadelphia for the first year and then Eric thought for the sake of his business it would be best if he were centered in New York, and we were coming here more and more often. So we decided it would be best if we moved." He thought she sounded breathless and he vaguely wondered if it was from anxiety about seeing him. She soon told him she liked walking about the city and took a long walk nearly every day. Despite himself, his natural skepticism, he could not help but smile as she spoke. He was pleased to see an old friend and to know she was living close by. They exchanged addresses and realized they lived about ten blocks from each other. He was still lonely in New York—it was before he had made a few friends and so he was delighted someone from his hometown was in close proximity to him. At the time he had been traveling home often on weekends to visit his old friends. For the most part those trips had been disappointing.

As he debated whether or not to ask how she had found out that he was living in New York and where he was working, she told him. Crossing her legs and unbuttoning her jacket, she said she had kept up to date about his whereabouts through his mother. She would call Cora every now and again and ask about him. Once she was married, her mother had not approved of her asking about Jonas. With a light smile she told Jonas she had taken it upon herself to call his mother. "I've always felt comfortable with Cora," she said to him as freely as most twenty-two-year-old women would have, but he saw in her eyes a darkness and seriousness that was not in accord with her age.

What had she seen? What had she experienced? Those questions crossed Jonas's mind and, as gratified as he felt at seeing an old friend, he had been uneasy with her as well. He knew she was older than he was in certain ways; she knew things he did not and had experienced them as well. But that first time together he knew not to ask her any probing questions. He had sensed she hoped to drop in to the gallery to see him on occasion. And now as he stood before her building he realized that both had turned out to be true. His conjecture at the time had been practical. She was new to the city and as he himself had been there for only a little over a year, it was still a new enough experience for him to understand how pleasing it was to visit an old friend. And after fourteen months in the city, he had still felt almost as new to it as she had. He had studied her as she looked about his small workplace. Her eyes were steady, her gaze hopeful and ascertaining.

She turned to him and asked, "Do you still paint seascapes? I remember your painting of the seagull hovering above the waves." She uncrossed her legs and bent forward, clasping her hands together. Her posture did not appear natural. But at that point he wondered what was genuine about her. They hadn't had any prolonged contact since she was eighteen, and now that she was nearly twenty-two, he realized how scant his knowledge of her had been. And what did she know of him—what he had experienced over the last three years? The rejections and slight successes? Yet, studying her, he saw that she believed she knew him quite well. It was the confidence in her tone, the way she assessed him as if knowing what he would say next, nearly completing his sentences.

Had nearly five years passed since she had first stepped into his gallery? he now asked himself as he rang the doorbell to her apartment. He saw that Eric's name was still on the tag next to the apartment number.

It had been an early September evening the next time she had come to the gallery. She had walked in a more sprightly way, seeming more her age than when he first saw her. Her eyes were pensive and sad, but her tone was light. "I was just walking by and thought I'd stop in. Eric's out of town for two weeks. Maybe we can have a drink together. Are you almost through for the day?"

Her sudden appearance had caught him off guard. He had not seen her in six months, and it had slipped his mind that she and Eric were living in New York. In that six-month period he had begun a relationship with a woman who often came into the gallery. He felt himself smiling at Jenny with skepticism. Would she only come to see him when Eric was out of town to pass the time, to help with her loneliness in this new city? "I am going out at eight, but we could have a quick drink now," he said.

"So you have a date, Jonas," she had said with a steady smile. He nodded.

"I don't want to interfere," she had responded evenly.

"You aren't. You are an old friend," he had answered with a touch of irony. And now as he looked up at her building he recalled how dismayed he had been when they had parted that evening. He had regretted his slight sarcasm, his distance from her. That had been a little over four years ago. She next appeared the following year, and then a few more times after that.

But on those subsequent visits she had been more restrained with him, less familiar.

Jonas now looked up at the building. He didn't think Jenny was in her apartment—maybe she was with her parents or with Eric's mother and father in Trieste; he felt a tug of disappointment. He walked briskly down the front steps and took a right turn, his head down, his hands dug deep inside his pockets. Approaching the corner of the street, he looked up; Jenny was coming toward him.

Eight

Lost

She did not recognize him at first. He walked quickly, his head lowered, the coldness seeming to enclose him; just before he raised his eyes she grasped that it was Jonas. Blood rushed to her face. Her bare hands thrust inside her coat pockets were now suddenly paralyzed by the frosty air. No longer was grief inoculating her from the frigid weather; she was stung by it.

Later, when Jenny would recall that moment, she would try to summon up what it was about Jonas that had convinced her of his identity. She had been in a fog the month following Eric's death; there were times when she would be unaware not only of the date and time, but of the day of the week, the year, and sometimes the city in which she lived. No one could comfort her. She had had no desire to seek or to be comforted. Had it been Jonas's loose walk in contrast to the way he held his shoulders, high and tight, or had it been how he moved his lowered head, as if mulling over a problem he found irritating? What was it that had caused her to step out of her haze and acknowledge him? Or maybe it was because it had been a shockingly cold day and, despite her state, she had been yearning and searching for the warmth of recognition from a familiar face. But what she would most remember was how upon seeing her he had at first stared at her as if she were a mirage, nearly walking past her. There had been an uncharacteristic dreamy quality in his gaze, his face quite pale, as if viewing an apparition of sorts, followed by a fleeting and sharp look of skepticism. Yet soon his expression revealed a submissive regard for her.

After a brief and painful embrace, her cold fingers pressing his jacket, Jenny inclined her head in the direction of her apartment building and said, "Please come in—it is too cold," her words clipped by the frosty air. He nodded and followed her.

She gathered he had heard of Eric's death and that was why he had come—yet she sensed his uncertainty. She wasn't surprised he had not visited her over the years she had lived in New York. When she had invited him to stop by and see her at any time, she assumed he wouldn't have done so because she was married, intuiting that he was careful in that way. At first she had genuinely wanted Eric to meet Jonas, but the timing had never been right. One day when she and Eric were a few blocks from the studio, she had nearly suggested they go in, but had refrained from doing so. Had she been fearful of Eric's reaction—would he have been critical of Jonas? Would he have put on a supercilious air? She would not have been able to bear any of that. And so Jonas had never painted her portrait—Eric had been interested in him doing so but it wasn't something he had thought a great deal about; he had relied on her to remind him.

Those thoughts ran through her mind as she ushered Jonas inside her apartment. She had felt a simple relief in coming upon a familiar face; it had lessened her sorrow, and his presence was a reminder of her life as it had been before she had known Eric. She thought of Jonas's quick and petite mother, Cora, and how her own mother, Johanna, would often confide in her, the puzzlement she had felt as an adolescent at how different their mothers were and how she had secretly yearned for her mother to possess Cora's frankness. Jenny longed to be back in that world, a world she now perceived as innocent.

Jonas sat across from her in a white-cushioned, high-back chair, Eric's favorite; he leaned forward, his hands clasped between his knees. He studied her for a long moment, his gaze serious, mournful, then he looked about the room. She could see he was somewhat impressed by the objects and the artwork. She noticed his eyes lingering over a copy of a Degas done by a promising young artist who painted replicas of the masters to earn a living. It wasn't unusual for her to have moments of clarity like this, but then she would soon be submerged by her own sorrow and guilt. She felt guilty that she was alive and Eric wasn't, she supposed, and understood her guilt was for reasons she was aware of and had yet to digest.

His eyes again on her, he said, his voice careful, slightly edgy, "I don't know what to say, Jenny. It has been a year since I've seen you, and now this." He motioned with his hand and he might have been speaking of the contents of the room as well as Eric's death. But he followed it immediately with words of condolence, not knowing how she must feel, telling her how deeply sorry he was. She followed his expression as he spoke—the arch of his brows, the sharpness of his nose, which always seemed to correlate with his inbred skepticism, the paleness of his skin as if he were still in shock from seeing her. How thin he was, she thought, bringing herself back to reality again—he was like a refreshment. He was refreshing because he was familiar, and she was no longer familiar to herself. She had to look to the outside, to her parents, to her friends, and now to Jonas—they validated her, who she was, who she had been, but not what she had become. They saw the old Jenny, albeit a sad Jenny, one who still to varying degrees elicited their trust.

She stood up and told Jonas it wasn't necessary to express his sadness for her. Inwardly she was frustrated by his attempts at sympathy. She asked him if he'd like something hot to drink; she knew her voice was calm and perhaps too low. He looked up at her and in his eyes was an acknowledgement of what she said, how she felt. He nodded, and she went to the kitchen to make tea.

When she came back into the room, carrying the tray with the pot and cups, she saw that Jonas was not in the chair but was peering at a bronze sculpture of a lynx that stood on top of a side table; his hands on his hips, he gazed down at the work with an expression of both interest and doubt. Was he doubting the quality of the work or her ownership of it? Aware of her presence, he turned toward her and smiled loosely; his tone was neutral. "It's a nice piece," he said. But she didn't believe he really thought it was.

"Eric found it somewhere," she said, hearing the blandness in her voice. "It was before I knew him," she continued, carefully placing the tray on the coffee table. "I don't know the story behind it. I never asked."

He nodded, accepting the cup she gave to him. She purposely did not look at him; her eyes were glued to the cup and his assured hand grasping it. It struck her that though they had known each other for years, they were in a sense strangers. He had no true awareness of what her life had been like with Eric. She had not confided in him those times over the past four or five years she had visited him at the gallery, and he had not revealed to her very much about his own life. She had not told him about her strained relationship with her husband; she had admitted very little even to herself and only once had she berated Eric. She felt pierced by this thought and bit her lip as if in doing so it would help her subdue the pain. It had been one of the last nights of their honeymoon—the night of the Halloween party in Lucerne when she had come upon Arlene. Arlene, her college roommate who had disappeared soon after their short conversation. She had told Jenny she was going to the women's room to refresh her lipstick, but she had not returned. When Arlene had left her, Jenny had looked around but she could no longer see Eric or Arlene's fiancé. She had waited near the table for Arlene to return for nearly a half hour. About forty-five minutes later Eric had come up to her. By that time she was sitting alone in a corner, her thoughts on Arlene, recalling the year they had lived together, whether there had been any signs. . . . Eric was somewhat drunk, unusual for him, and hadn't realized her anger. "I am going to our room now," she had said to him, her voice hostile. He had nodded and said he would join her soon. He did not come until two hours later. She had been pacing for nearly the entire time. Angrily, she watched as he closed the door, his face shaded by the muted light. "You are a liar, Eric," she cried out, raising her clenched fist.

He studied her for a moment and said evenly, "I do not know what you mean, Jenny. I have been with an old friend, a banker from Zurich, who happened to be here. I wanted to spend some time with him, to catch up."

"And this friend of yours," she retorted, "do you know who he is engaged to? My roommate from college. It is bizarre, Eric."

He smiled slowly and said, "What is so bizarre about it? Jenny, your imagination gets carried away. He met her while she was doing a semester abroad. He told me. It is a coincidence."

"I don't believe you," she cried out, louder this time. Then she sharply pounded her fist on the bureau. But he was silent. He had not refuted anything she had said, had not attempted to explain or deny. In his way he had stunted her anger. At that moment it struck her what her marriage would become—it would be up to her whether or not to accept it. For the remainder of their marriage there had been no more outbursts or confrontations on her part or his.

Jonas asked her now if she'd be staying in New York and she barely nodded, reflecting on how within herself and throughout her marriage, she had been harboring a deep resentment toward Eric, one that she had been neither willing nor capable of shaking, yet she had not been able to leave him either, despite knowing their marriage was doomed.

She heard herself say, "I will stay in New York at least until spring, and haven't yet decided what I will do afterward." But even as she spoke those words she could not relate to them—they sounded as if they were another person's plan, another person's words, and she was only experiencing the reverberation of them.

She hoped Jonas would grow restless from her inability to carry on a sustained conversation; she wanted him to leave her alone with her sadness. It was not because the source of her sorrow was what Jonas likely had understood it to be, but because it was the opposite; therefore his presence only confused her.

He rose again, holding the cup in his hand. She wondered if he intended to stay longer. He seemed in no rush to leave; he gave her the sense that he wanted to linger, the way he walked about the room with ease, now standing before a high glass table, picking up one of the wooden sculptures Eric had collected, most of them purchased before she had known him. He'd had a predilection for small wooden sculptures of naked subjects, many of them with expressions she found mystifying, not knowing if she were witnessing asseverations of fervor or horror.

Jonas turned to her. Drawn in by his deep interest and intent, discarding for a moment her pain, she rose and went to him. She realized how much of his growth as an artist she had missed. It was as if he were her child and she had been a parent preoccupied with her own life, her profession, and was suddenly aware now that her offspring was twenty-one, and she had missed the course of his development. Given her state, she regretted as much as she possibly could the superficial and infrequent conversations they had had over the past five years.

She picked up one of the sculptures and handed it to Jonas. It was one of the few of Eric's selections she liked. He had purchased it a year after they had married. They had been staying in the California desert—it was a wooden figure of a Native American woman—and at the time it had brought to her mind the photographs of Edward Curtis. The figure's eyes were nearly closed, lips not quite smiling, finely sculpted beads covering her breasts. Jonas took it in his free hand gingerly, almost lovingly, she thought, his eyes intently gazing at it, his face gleaming. His natural skeptical expression was now erased and in its place was his passion, his need to comprehend how the work had come to be. Quietly she told him where they had found it, and that it was one of the few pieces Eric had purchased since she had known him and that she had encouraged him to do so. After a few minutes, Jonas looked at her, met her gaze, and said, "It is an exquisite work."

"You don't sculpt, do you?" she asked softly, looking away, across the room, toward the window, gazing out at the bleakness of the day, as if confronting the depths of her loneliness. Even with Jonas, someone she had known for some time, she felt it, and because of his presence she was acknowledging it. But nevertheless, it pained her beyond anything she had experienced, even more than those difficult times with Eric, when he had left her in the dark about himself and his activities and she had felt as if she were in an enclosed room with no light, feeling her way to the door. Whenever she thought of those days she'd shiver, her sense of isolation increasing.

"Are you okay, Jenny?" Jonas asked, putting down the figure next to where he had placed his cup. She thought he sounded uneasy, as if he had been hesitant about asking, had not wanted to get too close.

She smiled wearily at him, tepidly noting his anxious look, her eyelids feeling heavy now; it was an effort to fully lift them and directly gaze at Jonas. "I am better than you may think," she answered; she felt a certain freedom in expressing herself in this way, and mildly grateful to him for having given her the opportunity to do so.

"Yes, Jenny, I cannot imagine." She thought his voice sounded somber and restrained. He took her hand, guided her to the sofa as if she were wearing ice skates on solid ground and he flat-heeled shoes. "Maybe you'd like to rest now," he said, his eyes solicitous. And she smiled—that look seemed unlike him, she fleetingly thought. He sat next to her, still holding her hand.

He spoke cautiously, "If you need to talk about what happened to Eric, his accident, or of what your life has been like these past eight years, then I am more than willing to listen. I am your friend. I want to know. But if you do not want to speak or are not ready to do so, then I will not pry." When he loosened his grip, she placed her hand on her lap, and saw he was now looking toward the door. He wanted to leave her. Her pulse quickened; she now did not want him to go. Yet at the same time she knew she was not ready to reveal anything to him—it would take a while to do that. Maybe Jonas would be the one she could confide in—he was someone she had known for years and at the same time she did not know him very deeply; he would provide her with a sense of anonymity that might free her to ultimately speak. But deep within, she knew this would not be the place as Eric's imprint, his presence, so to speak, was evident throughout the apartment—from the small wooden figures to certain pieces of furniture he had insisted on buying. Even the colors displayed in the room had been primarily Eric's choices. It had been his money, she had thought at the time, and she had had other things on her mind—should she apply to graduate school or look for a job—but most incessantly she'd pondered her deeply disturbing marriage. In comparison, furniture (cherry wood as opposed to birch), red or white Oriental carpeting, decorations (embroidered versus silk drapes), the large postmodern paintings, devoid of the artistic nuance of a Rothko or a Pollock, that Eric had been drawn to, that she had found cold and satirical—it had all seemed essentially mundane to her then. And so she had left it entirely up to Eric to choose and he had enjoyed doing so. But now here she was—all those things she had not really cared about were facing her, were now her companions of sorts. The only exception was the one wooden figure—the only object she had felt any affinity to because it had reminded her of a Curtis photograph. Jonas seemed to stand out in stark contrast to these remnants of Eric. She understood that Jonas derived comfort from his skepticism. Yet she also discerned that he possessed the gleaming and intent look—unselfconscious on his part—of one who paints to discern. She had forgotten or not realized how long and pale his face was, especially now that he no longer wore a mustache.

When she saw him checking the time on his watch, she stood up, felt color rise in her face, and asked, "Do you need to go, Jonas?" The strain and warmth in her voice seemed to swirl around her, engulfing her like an unexpected fog. She looked at him directly and experienced no sense that she was pleading with him as she would have done with Eric. She caught her reflection in the large and ornate mirror on the wall by the foyer and thought that despite her height she looked small and wavering—overwhelmed—in the midst of Eric's objects; the ceiling had never seemed so high, the paintings, each one a large blob of color, never so oppressive, the Oriental carpeting never so intractable. And when she glanced into the mirror again, all she saw was Jonas's reflection and how his shoulders tilted as he turned toward her.

She knew he was uncomfortable, that he found this apartment ostentatious; she could almost read his thoughts. He had only been inspired by a few of the wooden figures; he had appreciated the raw artistry of them, but not of any other object in his sight—the statue of the lynx had been only a curiosity. Everything else in the room created an emptiness within him, she believed—a sense of nothingness—and he needed to extract himself from it. She imagined what Jonas's apartment must be like—small, with clean lines and much light, marginally untidy, a few of his paintings on the wall, perhaps a print of an artist, one whose technique he was presently studying, hanging in his bedroom so that he could gaze at it when he awoke.

His fingers pressed the woolen cap now in his hands. "I will come by again, tomorrow," he said. His voice was sincere, his look mildly apprehensive.

"I need to see you, Jonas." The words cut through her as if originating from an unknown source.

He seemed to freeze, but then said almost breezily, his somberness lifting for that moment, "Until tomorrow."

As they moved toward the door, she asked, "Why don't we meet somewhere else, a place where we will be free to talk?"

He answered, as if it were an afterthought, "Tomorrow is Sunday. I plan to go into the gallery in the morning. Why don't we meet there at one or so?"

When she closed the door behind him, she felt an immense sense of relief. She was a little less sad, a little less guilty—though she knew she never would be free of remorse; it would be there no matter how she rationalized or what she believed. And she did not know how long it would be before she again would be overcome with sorrow. Yet the next time, she thought, when the melancholy overtook her, maybe she would be more hopeful, maybe she'd be able to lift herself out of it or at least attempt to imagine herself doing so.

From her bedroom came the sound of the phone ringing. She knew it was her mother; she called every day at this time, hoping to convince Jenny to go with them to Trieste in April. Her parents would be traveling earlier this year, in the spring, not during the summer. Jenny believed they would retire in Trieste as Eric's parents had. Like Eric's parents they had never adjusted to America. But the United States was home to her—she did not wish to go with her parents in April. And she did not want to see Eric's parents. They didn't completely trust her—she knew that. They believed their son died because she had not loved him enough—she had not been careful. Six weeks before, she had been in Trieste for his funeral. His parents had insisted it take place abroad and she had not had the will to fight them. Selfishly, perhaps, she thought, she had not been opposed to having it there—for when she returned home, it would be as if she were starting her life anew in America.

When she answered the phone, she thought her mother sounded more circumspect than usual—she knew her mother well, and could sense her mood instantaneously. But Johanna did not mention Trieste. Jenny assumed she was preoccupied with a more pressing matter. She nearly asked her what it was but she did not want to know; she didn't want the hopeful feeling she had derived from Jonas's visit diminished in any way. Before Johanna had a chance to ask, Jenny told her she had decided to go to the Caribbean in the spring. Her mother sounded weary in her response, wishing her a good time, hoping she would be traveling with a friend so she wouldn't be too lonely—after all, she was accustomed to Eric's presence. She couldn't imagine how it must be for Jenny. Yet Jenny felt there was something more—she was not convinced of her mother's sadness as she had been on other occasions; at those times she had felt her mother was honestly empathic with her situation in more ways than she would have imagined. Jenny often wondered if her mother had been aware that her marriage to Eric had been quite painful, but had not allowed herself to acknowledge it. This time her mother sounded less heartfelt, not because she wanted to be but because something else was diverting her. Whatever it was, if it was of importance, she would eventually reveal it to her.

When Jenny hung up the phone she realized this was the first time she had admitted to herself that she would not be going with her parents to Trieste in April, that she would take a trip on her own—she would not ask a friend—she needed to be alone in warm and caressing weather. How cold it was now.

When she went to bed that night, before she fell asleep, she thought of the flight home from Zurich after their honeymoon. She and Eric had not had much to say to each other. It seemed as if the years lay before them—it was a stark and barren landscape she had envisioned and she guessed Eric had felt the same, but perhaps in his mind he had peppered it with moments of color and excitement, his sort of excitement. There must have been something of significance about the flight home or she would not be recalling it now, she vaguely thought as she drifted off to sleep. But when she awoke in the middle of the night, startled by the sound of a truck passing by outside her apartment, it occurred to her what it was. As they had sat in the plane, drinking coffee after their meal, he had leaned toward Jenny and had picked up her hand. She had noted as always his manicured nails and she had felt a shiver run through her—she had found his hands even more distasteful than she had in the past. But this time Eric had noticed. "Do you despise me that much, Jenny?" he had asked in his level and dispassionate way.

When she looked up at him, she had felt tears coming to her eyes. She had not wanted to hate him, but she knew then that she did, that she had ever since she had first encountered him on the beach. She chided herself within for not having followed her instincts. She had fallen in love with him four months later because of her parents, their life during the war—in his subtle way Eric had evoked in her feelings of guilt and sadness. Sitting up in bed, she realized why this memory was so firm in her mind—for though she had believed she was in love with him, even in their most intimate moments, she really had despised him—her passion for him had been one of hate.

She got up from the bed and went to the window. Crossing the dark sky she saw faint light; dawn was beginning to break. She thought of Jonas's visit, concluding that he had been repelled by the apartment—had found it cold and uninspiring. Eric's taste in art and music had not been sophisticated; he preferred light music over jazz—he didn't like too much intricacy. But this was because of where he had come from—his life had been filled with complexity; it was why his taste had been more on the superficial side—that had soothed him more. He would not be pressed to think or feel too deeply. He had married her because of her youth and inexperience; she lacked profundity and any true connection to what her parents or he had experienced. The more she had realized this, the more and more anger she had felt toward him. Eventually she had become indifferent, involved in the life she was beginning to patch together for herself, less concerned about Eric's whereabouts, his activities—and so the accident had occurred and, yes, she had been responsible.

Nine

Restless

When he awoke the next morning, his mind was filled with a myriad of thoughts—both practical and speculative. As he walked the ten blocks from his apartment to the gallery, a light, wet snow began to fall, clinging to his jacket and eyelashes.

He was becoming more and more disgruntled at the gallery. Painting portraits at first had been good training, but now it had become routine. He had begun to liken himself to an author of formulaic fiction, harnessed to a particular brand of writing, unable to develop an independent style.

It was becoming increasingly impossible, he comprehended, to define himself as a painter. Perhaps it was because he was too exacting with his portraits, he concentrated too much on detail and accuracy. While painting the image of one of his clients, he would think of Sargent to incite himself. But his brush did not possess Sargent's psychological acuity. Although he painted with exactitude and his clients generally were pleased, Jonas would be disappointed with the lack of nuance in a portrait. His initial charcoal shadings were penetrating, poignant, and rife with potential, but he had discovered that when he attempted to transform one of those sketches into a portrait painting, something was lost.

He desperately wanted to discover his true form, but he had expended so much energy on the portraits of his clients, he had not been able to accomplish this these past five or so years. And so, as in San Francisco and then at the studio in his mother's home, he had come to a dead end.

From time to time he would think longingly of those days in his mother's basement when he was experimenting with his own style. But eventually it had been more imperative for him to support himself; the money he had saved while working in San Francisco had begun to run out and at thirty years old he had not wanted to depend on his mother's generosity.

Now that he'd be turning thirty-six at the end of January, he was at a crossroads yet again. It had been more simple the other times—it had been effortless to quit his job in San Francisco and become a waiter while working during the day on his paintings. Then, after he had returned to his mother's home and realized he needed to support himself, the goal had been to look for a job as an artist, one that would not be solely for commercial purposes, one where he would be able to foster his craft. Now his goal was more amorphous—he wanted to develop his own style and it seemed that the route he should take to do so was not as clear and explainable as it had been in the other two instances. He supposed he could work less at the gallery, take on fewer clients, but he had always put so much effort into his work that even though he might not take on as many clients, he might easily put more energy into each portrait instead of less. No, he thought, he needed to make a clean break. It was then—because of his mounting restlessness—it struck him that Jenny might be stopping by to see him in the afternoon.

To escape the cold, he went inside a shop. Standing in line, he noticed a couple in front of him who were intently conversing—he could not determine if they were commiserating or angry with each other. It struck him how fury and empathy could be closely aligned. And soon he was ruminating over Jenny's marriage to Eric; it bewildered him. He had no sense of what it must have been like for her—Eric had been so much older than Jenny. When he was in her apartment the previous day, he had tried to imagine Eric there. He recalled how Eric had walked in that casual but insistent way as he had come down the aisle in the movie theater that night, how he had walked as if his chin were his compass. And Jonas had imagined him crossing the living room in his apartment in the same way. He had seemed old and distant to Jonas, and Jenny in turn had appeared beholden to him, adoring of Eric. And then Jonas had tried to conjure Jenny and Eric conversing, how they might have interacted—would she have been assertive with Eric as she had always been with him, or would she have taken on a pleading demeanor similar to how she had appeared with Eric at the movie theater? But despite these attempts, Jonas had been at a loss—he could not fathom anything, could not hold on to any image of the two of them together. All he concluded was that marriage significantly had changed her.

As he left the shop with coffee in hand, his thoughts wandered again to what he should do next in his life, how to break away from the gallery, how to support himself and develop his own style at the same time. It was a dilemma, one that he found both hopeless and invigorating. If Jenny was feeling less mournful in a few months and if she was still in New York, he would discuss it with her. He hoped she would be able to experience happiness again. He believed she had always possessed a sense of contentment, something that had invariably eluded him. He had relished watching her sustain her optimism in the face of having to cope with strict parents. They had perceived American life so differently than she had as an eighteen-year-old. Then he remembered seeing her at the window that early morning after he had left San Francisco for good, that commingling in her expression of degradation and hope.

He walked into the gallery and went to the back where his studio was. It was early and no one had yet come in. The gallery wasn't open to the public until the afternoon, and so he was hoping he'd have a quiet morning, touching up the two paintings he was currently working on—one was of an elderly man, who reminded him of an older version of his mother's boyfriend, Harold, the narrow forehead, the round green eyes and the way he smiled, his lips thin, in a sly yet appealing way. There were times when thoughts of Harold would come to mind more often than imaginings of his father. Whenever Jonas realized this, he'd become annoyed with himself, and then impulsively he'd rummage about for the photo of his father he liked best, the one of him with friends in front of the hardware store. He could not clearly see his father's expression, but because of how shadows and light encircled him, it was the photo in which Jonas most comprehended who David Hoffman was—perhaps confident by his assured stance, content by his relaxed posture, questioning by the tilt of his head. But Jonas would never know for certain.

The other portrait he was working on was of a young woman, who appeared to lack a sense of curiosity; she appeared disinterested when sitting for him, her thoughts elsewhere, not seeming to care how she would be depicted.

Before he began to work, he thought of Jenny the previous day, how she had been at her best when she had shown him the wooden figure of the Native American woman—it was then, despite her sorrow, that her hopeful nature had been evident in her appreciation of the work. He recalled how she had handled the piece graciously but firmly, her expression studied and resolute. But moments later she had appeared as hazy as she had been since he had come upon her on the street not far from her home.

After reading the article about Eric's death, he had gone promptly—almost without thinking—to her apartment, and yet when he had spotted her walking down the street toward him he had been startled by her presence—he realized that even when he had made his way to her home he had not expected her to be there. He had gone because he had thought it was what he should do. But he had not expected her to be home. Should she not have been with her parents or in Trieste with Eric's, or traveling with a friend? Why be alone at such a time? But she had chosen to stay and in doing so she was augmenting her grief instead of trying to cope with it; she was allowing it to consume her instead of simply facing it straight on. But then again, what did he know about the grief she was experiencing? The only form of grief he had known was for a person he had never met—his father, his parents' marriage, for something that had never existed for him. And at that thought he felt a deep pain. Perhaps his grief was worse than most because it was ongoing and unexplainable; most would not understand why he still clung to it. He would even chide himself from time to time for feeling that way, yet it would return and he'd become caught up in his sorrow for what had not been, before becoming dismayed with himself for sliding back into that sort of thinking. Then he'd sink into his work.

Jenny did not appear until nearly two in the afternoon. Jonas had lost all sense of time and had stayed longer in the studio than he had intended, working on the hands of the young woman, soft and plump in contrast to her thin and agile form.

She knocked twice before he registered there was someone at the door. For a moment he was caught off guard, as if he had been awakened from a deep sleep. He carefully put down his brush and then hurried toward the door, opening it. She stood there looking both hesitant and pleased, he thought, pleased that she had made the effort to come, to get out of that oppressive apartment. Her gaze did not meet his, but instead wandered about his studio. She went over to the painting of the young woman and stared at it for a long while. "She doesn't seem very happy, does she, Jonas?" she said, not turning away from the painting but studying it all the more, leaning in closer to the canvas. She was wearing blue jeans and a quilted jacket that fell to the middle of her legs, a scarf around her neck that was a deep violet color. He had not before seen her dressed in such a casual way: even the previous day she had worn loose but graceful pants with a silk blouse, the top button undone, a fine gold chain round her neck. But her demeanor, as it had in the past, had not reflected the calmness and serenity of her clothes; instead, there had been much angst in her expression—a lack of focus in her brown-gray eyes, her lids hooded, her cheeks more hollow, her lips appearing flattened instead of full.

Today she was more composed, he noticed, but in her composure there was an anguish that she seemed to be pushing against—her attempts to sound almost too definite in her comment about the painting, in a sense showing him she was fine or would be so shortly.

Now she turned toward him and smiled. "I like your studio, Jonas; it's inviting, and then there is your work," and she motioned with her hand to the two paintings. Again her words sounded forced, not because she was insincere, he thought, closely watching her, but because she was attempting to override her sadness.

"I am glad you have come, Jenny," he said. Her expression suddenly fell as if she were tired, her eyes weary. He supposed she had not slept well.

"It wasn't easy to come to the gallery," she said simply, honestly, her voice soft; she had lost her bravado, he thought.

"Let's leave then," he said, suddenly feeling confined by the studio, the paintings he wasn't really pleased with. It was as if his flaws were on full display. Not only did he not want them to be revealed to her, he didn't want to have to look at them straight on at this moment. He needed a break, and though he was tentative about being with Jenny, her sense of loss and how she was struggling to fight against it, he believed in a more neutral setting they each would be invigorated, perhaps in a trivial way even return to the rapport they had shared years before. But later when he would look back on that day, he would realize how naïve and self-centered he had been; his first thoughts had been on his career, and Jenny and her experience with Eric had only been secondary. He had understood the tragedy of a man passing before his fiftieth birthday, but on the other hand he had believed that after a certain period of mourning Jenny would be ultimately free to live her life. He had been unaware of all the subtleties and complications. His thinking had been superficial at best and may have indirectly caused her more strain than he had intended it to.

They spent most of that Sunday together, stopping in at cafés, visiting different galleries, and then the Metropolitan. They ended up having an early dinner in the restaurant at the museum. Her presence offered him a freedom from his worries and he thought his might help deflect her sadness.

They would meet every ten days or so in the same way, saying very little to each other; he hid any concern he had about his future from her. She obviously had no financial worries and he had many—he wasn't certain he wanted to accept any help from her as he knew she would be more than willing to give; money was not a high priority for her, let alone foremost in her mind. She would be the same Jenny, he understood, with or without the financial freedom she now possessed. And at times he longed to be in her position—how he would be able to paint without worry—but he would shake that thought from his mind. He felt greedy thinking in that way. For he was torn between his allegiance to her as an old friend and his need to go forward with his work.

It wasn't until three months later—the end of March—that she spoke of Eric's accident. It was a surprisingly warm day; the trees were still bare but the earth smelled of early spring. A balmy caressing breeze uplifted them as they walked through Central Park. They had not seen each other in three weeks—it had been the longest separation since he had gone to see her the previous December. Two days before she had returned early from Saint Lucia; the experience had reminded her too much of Eric—she should have chosen to go to a place where she had not been with him, as her intention had been to free herself for a week or two from her mourning. It was how she had explained her early return to Jonas.

Each time they had met over the previous three months, he had encouraged her not to be sad. And on that day he had been more adamant about it than usual, his words more forceful. While she was away, he had decided he must make a change himself, and so his intensity with her had to do with his need to spur himself on as well. The reality was that he and Jenny—for different reasons, of course—were each stuck, and he guessed she was aware of it as much as he was.

After strolling through Central Park, they walked down Fifth Avenue, crowded with tourists. Then, suddenly, the sun disappeared behind the clouds and the air became much cooler. He realized they would need to go inside soon. A painting he had recently begun came to mind. He wanted to show it to her; he was curious to hear what she thought of it. After walking another few blocks, he suggested they take a taxi to his apartment; he explained about the painting. She had not been to his apartment before and told him she'd like to see it as well as the painting. She had appeared less sad at first that day, and had seemed more receptive to his words of encouragement than she had in the past. But the more they walked the more she seemed, he thought, to sink back into her mournful self. He thought a trip to his apartment might help her forget, might distract her.

Inside the taxi, she sat next to him, her fists almost clenched, her hands looking cold, and twenty minutes later as he unlocked the door to his apartment she seemed hesitant about going inside. But then she took a deep breath as if to steel herself before following him across the threshold. He noted how she looked about his apartment. Her gaze slid over to the photo of his father and mother on their wedding day; he had framed it and placed it on top of a small table in the corner beneath the window. She walked over to it and picked it up. "It's Cora," she said quietly, gazing down at it. Whenever he heard his mother's name, he'd feel a tug; it was as if he were for that moment no longer the Jonas he had become. He studied Jenny but could not make out her expression—it was almost vacant—yet the way she had sharply lowered her head to study it, how her fingers tightly grasped the frame revealed her intensity. Still her eyes were neither sad nor expectant but eerily dispassionate. She said nothing else, made no reference to his father. It was as if he were only a shadow. Then, as she placed the photo gingerly back on the table, she looked up at him and asked, "What is it you want me to see, Jonas?" Her words, precise and sharp, stung him. He didn't answer her directly. He moved toward the small alcove next to the kitchen where he worked and she followed him. He pointed to the painting he had begun a few months earlier.

"It's not nearly finished—it's just an idea," he said slowly, looking over the painting, forgetting for a moment her tone.

"You have set the figures at a distance; they are not definable, not fully formed and may never be. My guess is it will be up to the viewer to determine who they are. I think I will like it, Jonas."

There was something in her words—supercilious, intellectualized—and he felt suddenly angry. He turned to her and asked, his tone slightly sharper with her than usual, "What happened to Eric, Jenny?"

At first she was restrained. Maybe she'd been waiting for him to ask, he thought, maybe he was the one who'd needed to be ready to hear, maybe it was why she'd cut short her vacation in the Caribbean: she had needed to talk and he was the one she'd wanted to talk to.

Then a look of alarm crossed her face. She was still for a moment, and then as she began to speak, tears slid down her face, her brown-gray eyes darting. "I believe I am responsible for Eric's death."

His heart beat quickly. He didn't touch or attempt to comfort her. "How are you responsible, Jenny?" he asked, his voice stark and honest, almost echoing.

She turned away and soon was sprawled out on his sofa; she had removed her shoes, her head on one arm rest, her feet on the other, her arm dangling, her thumb pressing a tissue into her palm, her fingertips touching the floor. He lay on the rug across from her, his legs out to the side, his head propped up with one hand, and listened as she told him about her marriage to Eric, about how she believed he had had an affair with her roommate from college, and had assumed there were other women as well. He would be warm at one moment and cold at the next. She paused for a while, then said she had fallen in love with him because he'd given her a sense about her parents' life in Trieste during the war—she'd viewed Eric and his family as her mother and father's saviors and so hers as well. She'd felt bonded to Eric because of it, and mature, but soon after they were married it had dawned on her that she had been naïve. She raised her head and looked over at Jonas. "I was filled with illusions, Jonas. I believed I was mature—I was completely fooled, but only I am responsible for that."

His heart pounded as she spoke but he was determined not to reveal to her his anxiety; his expression remained neutral and he did not attempt to interrupt her words. He longed to ask her again about Eric's accident but refrained from doing so.

She talked more about the difficulties in their marriage, how she would stay up at night, wondering how she could extract herself from the situation without hurting her parents or herself, or causing Eric's parents to distrust her and her mother and father—they had aided her parents at a very tragic time; they had, without a doubt, saved them, after all. Eric had had an older brother who had died during the war. Then ruefully she said that Eric had never truly revealed to her what his childhood had been like, and ultimately his reticence had caused her to dislike him even more. After Eric's death, she had promised herself, she said, again looking over at Jonas, that she would discover what had happened to him during the war, but she honestly had no desire to know. She had understood even before she married him that he was a scarred person; she had been drawn to him because of it. It wasn't that she thought she could change him, but that he would be bonded to her because she appreciated his pain, his flaws.

"I began to hate him, Jonas—hate—an emotion I thought was beyond me. But now that I look back on it, I realize it was my illusions about him, about us, that I hated even more."

As she spoke, he was inwardly distraught. Why hadn't she just walked away from the marriage?

Then she added that she and Eric had not been intimate for two or three years. Eric's work was taking up much of his time and he had become concerned about losing clients. The previous fall he had caught an unusual and severe strain of the flu but had insisted on going on a yacht with a client and his friends. "The waters in the Keys were rough, and they had been drinking—though Eric had always been careful about drinking too much, especially when he was with a client. In most situations he had been guarded about drinking because he could become hazy after only one drink; his tolerance had been low. He'd been taking a lot of medicine too. He leaned over the side of the boat, the waves were high and overpowering—he should have been with the others below, not out on the deck. He was swept overboard; it was dark and they could not locate him."

"How is the accident your fault, Jenny?" Jonas asked, his voice meek and awestricken.

"Don't you see I could have prevented it? I could have insisted he not go. I knew how sick he was, but I did not interfere. I drove him to the airport. I let it happen. I knew he was worried about this particular client, and that he was not well enough to go. He was foggy from the medicine. But I did not stop him. I wanted him not to come home."

Jonas did not respond; he watched as she closed her eyes, her face pale. Talking had exhausted her. Within minutes she was asleep. Jonas took a pillow from his bedroom and gingerly placed it beneath her head. His heart heavy, he covered her sleeping form with an extra blanket he found in his closet, then he went to the alcove to work more on the painting.

TEN

A NEW YEAR

Her gaze rested drowsily on a tall enamel lamp in the far corner of the room, the muted light emanating from it and the ensuing shadows striking the wall. She heard a clock ticking softly. A few minutes passed before she became aware of the pillow Jonas had placed beneath her head. She pulled the blanket closer, then propped herself up on her elbows; slowly turning her head to the side, she hazily noticed there were no blinds or drapes on the two adjacent windows. It was dark outside. Her first clear thought was that she might be alone. Where was Jonas? Had he disappeared because he had been so disturbed by what she had told him? Was he walking the streets of New York moodily pondering her words? She imagined his loose walk, his head down, his expression edgy, his shoulders high and tense, as he made his way down a crowded street, not far from where she now lay, and she felt a tightening in her throat.

She listened but could not hear the traffic outside. The windows were closed, yet there was not even the diminished sound of horns honking or cars passing below. She found the silence and stillness in Jonas's apartment overwhelming, more so than in her own home the last few months.

But then she sharply remembered, her heart racing, her thoughts turning to the previous November and the horrific quiet of that evening. In the late afternoon, she had received news of Eric's drowning and learned that his remains had been recovered in the early morning hours.

Not hearing her own steps, she had paced about her domelike living room for what had seemed like hours, not calling his parents or hers. She believed if she withheld the information long enough, it would no longer be true. As she paced, crossing the black-and-while tiles in the foyer, then over the plush Oriental carpeting to the large flat red painting on the far wall and back again, she rationalized that she had not wanted Eric dead; instead she had only wanted him not to come home to her again. At that thought, she sobbed uncontrollably but kept walking, her arms spread out as if welcoming her sorrow.

Eventually, she picked up the phone to place a call to Trieste. Her mother-in-law answered in her sharp and stoic voice, hewn from her days during the war. It was three o'clock in the morning in western Europe. At once she understood what Jenny was attempting to say. Jenny refrained from mentioning, and would never reveal, that Eric had been ill, that he'd been taking medicine that might have caused confusion. She had spoken only of the accident, attempting to comfort his mother in the best way she knew, her hand shaking as she held the receiver to her ear. That had been nearly five months before, but it seemed to her as if it had taken place years and years ago or that it had been a dream, or rather, a nightmare—one from which she had not fully awakened.

Once she had informed Eric's parents, she knew it would not be necessary to call her own. Agitated, she waited by the phone. Finally, it rang. Yes, they had received the news from Eric's parents, and were phoning to let Jenny know they would soon be with her, they would go to the airport, take the shuttle to New York, and would be ringing her doorbell within two to three hours. If they missed the last shuttle, they would drive to New York. She only listened and then put down the phone. Ten minutes later her doorbell rang; it was Annette, a friend who lived on another floor, her hair unbrushed, her eyes sleepy but mournful. Johanna had called and asked that she stay with Jenny until they arrived.

The weeks following were a blur for Jenny and even to that day the haze had not entirely dissipated—the difference was she was now accustomed to living in this state, and was able to haltingly recall what she had done on a prior day, whom she had spoken with, and, albeit cautiously, had made plans for her trip to the Caribbean. She also had arranged to meet with a friend or Jonas every so many days. But she still could not remember much about those two weeks after Eric's passing. What stood out in her mind, perhaps because it had been most striking for her, was the priest in Trieste who had given the eulogy. Although she knew very little Italian—her parents had spoken this language as well as German on occasions when they had needed to converse privately in Jenny's presence, wanting to prevent her from knowing what they were saying to each other, and she had known Eric to speak only in English—she understood the context of the priest's words, especially when from time to time he'd emphatically pronounce the word *destino.* Her mother, to her right, would shift in her seat whenever he spoke it. But she could not remember much else about that time. Afterward at Eric's parents' home, people she did not know offered their condolences to her in either Italian or German—her mother introducing them to her, her father sitting in a corner, a napkin covering his knees, a glass of wine in his hand, his eyes wide open, his expression alarmed, as she imagined he must have appeared when he first heard the news. Or maybe he had been thinking of the past in Trieste, the war; perhaps seeing certain people he hadn't seen since the war had stirred his memory.

Eric's parents were stunned, yet strong and gracious; his mother, Alma, in her late seventies, was tall and stately with dark hair and blue eyes, the same color as Eric's. Whenever she looked over at Jenny, Jenny would shudder. She thought Alma had not completely trusted her when she had been introduced as Eric's fiancée. She had been disappointed in Jenny's youth.

The plane ride home was also vague, and she barely remembered staying with her parents until early December, or what she did, where she went. Had old friends from high school stopped by to see her?

On the fifth of the month, her parents had driven her back to New York, then stayed with her for a few days, saying before they left that they would come again at Christmas. But a few weeks later, they both had come down with colds, and so they had not come for the holiday. Jenny did not travel to Boston to see them until the first day of the new year.

During her two-week stay in January, she refrained from telling them that Jonas had come to see her at the end of December and that she would continue to see him. They were still not fully well, and she was uncertain how they would respond to her reconnecting with him.

Whenever she'd walk out of their house, she'd look over at Jonas's old home; the lights would be off and there would be no car in the driveway. When Jenny returned to New York in the middle of the month, Jonas would tell her his mother had been in Florida with Harold.

On afternoons when her parents were resting and the temperature had risen to the mid-thirties, she would walk around her old neighborhood. One day she went to the playground of the school she had attended, remembering how she had not known anyone when she had come from Hartford at the age of fourteen and how alone she had felt, sitting in the car as her mother drove her to school. She went to the very spot where she had stood that day in early spring, her first one there, feeling the warmth of the sun shining down on her, superseding the chill in the air, and how the other students one by one began to approach her. She smiled when she thought of how she had made friends quickly. She had been in the eighth grade and the other students had taken to her almost from the start. It was as if she were a celebrity. In their young minds, Connecticut was the exotic equivalent of New York City or Los Angeles. They'd sensed she was different, but it was a difference that had drawn them to her. By the time she was in high school she was one of them; she was no longer a welcome and mysterious stranger, but a member of their community. She'd kept her parents at a distance from her friends. Most of those students had had no idea about World War II, other than knowing of an uncle who may have gone to battle overseas, or one of their fathers, perhaps, but it was not talked about or discussed. It was always viewed from a distance as if whoever spoke of it was looking through a telescope to see and then speak of the constellations, without any knowledge of the difference between the Big Dipper and Orion. They all had been born in the mid-fifties like herself, when the war was no longer a reality, just a distant occurrence that if not mentioned would be soon forgotten. And even Jonas, whose father had died before being sent off to Europe, did not understand the agony of the war—for it wasn't the war that had caused his father's death, but an illness. She had always been different in that way from her school friends; she had always carried with her an extra burden that no one else seemed to bear. She had experienced the reality of war in her parents' anguished expressions; they were more restive than other parents, more protective, more grounded in a dark reality and so less hopeful, and they spoke with noticeable accents. At one point she began to deny what she was experiencing, convincing herself she was like her friends from school, an American, and only marginally affected by a war that had occurred so many miles away, across what seemed to them an illimitable Atlantic Ocean. But she could only fool herself for so long—as she visited Europe with her parents for a month every other summer, she knew the distance was much shorter than her friends realized or she wanted to acknowledge.

She now heard the apartment door open and she sat up erectly. Another light was switched on and she sharply turned her head. Jonas was coming through the door, carrying two bags filled with groceries, one in each arm.

"I thought I'd make dinner," he said, meeting her gaze, and her first thought was that he seemed unmoved. He appeared no different; he looked at her in the same way, his eyes both objective and sensitive. He had not changed toward her. She was at a loss for words; she was overcome by his acceptance.

"You don't despise me?" she asked, staring at him. He turned away and her eyes followed him as he went toward the kitchen. She heard him placing the bags on the counter. Then within seconds he was standing before her.

"Why should I despise you?" he asked. "Because, understandably, you wanted Eric not to come home?"

Staring up at him, she nodded slowly. Then she stood up,

the blanket sliding to the floor, and said, "Jonas, don't be too easy on me."

"Eric's death was an accident. He could just as easily have fallen into the water if he were in perfect health. Unless, if there was foul play involved—someone had pushed him overboard."

She began to shake and then felt the pressure of his hands clasping hers. "People feel responsible when they are close to one who has passed—that's just the way it is; they always find a way because they want to be a part of it as they were part of the person's life," he said.

She felt herself smiling and her trembling begin to subside. His hand felt warm on hers and she felt grateful to him—extremely so. He kissed the top of her head.

"Thank you, Jonas," she said, wrapping her arms around him.

Jonas's plainspoken words had moved Eric further from her emotions; in the following days he began to seem more and more at a distance from her, more of a phenomenon of some sort, no longer a person to whom she had been married, but more like a portrait of a well-known historical figure she had seen again and again, a painting that reflected his or her role in history, for good or evil, or both, one whom she could not touch, whose existence she could only imagine. And so her memories of Eric became both circumscribed and unreal. She would recall his appearance on the beach that hot July day, the bright sun illuminating his curly blond-brown hair, the sound of waves crashing against the shore, and how he had said her name that first time, his pronunciation almost lyrical, seemingly guileless. And then how he had shown up in the foyer of her college dorm—how well dressed and sophisticated he had appeared against the backdrop of the college campus—the easy way in which he had unfolded his crossed arms as she approached him, revealing his tie clip, pure gold. But whenever she'd think of their honeymoon, how often he would disappear, and the receding tenderness then near indifference in his lovemaking, her impression of him became harsh—so much so that she needed to stop herself from remembering.

Once she moved on to this next phase in her life, she became more aware of those around her. She recognized that her parents were older now, not very old, but her father, she supposed, would be retiring in the next five years or so. Her mother's memory was no longer as sharp as it had been in the past; her father moved with less vigor and was working at the shoe store four days a week instead of five. And in the eyes of her few female friends, she witnessed not only their support of her, for what she had experienced, but how their support of her fatigued them as well. Then there was Jonas—it was now clear to her he was struggling financially and he needed to make a change in his career. She wanted to help him, but she did not know how to offer assistance; she did not know how much his innate pride would come into play. More than anyone else and mostly by his presence alone, he had helped her comprehend the previous eight years.

On a Sunday in mid-June, she and Jonas were walking from the art gallery to a café a few blocks away, one they often frequented. The sun was bright and the air warm and close. Throngs of pedestrians surrounded them. As they approached the café, there were fewer people about. Jenny, feeling relaxed and enlivened, remembered Jonas's latest work. She asked him about the painting he'd been working on, the one she had seen in his apartment a few months before. He hadn't mentioned it since the day he'd brought her to his apartment and shown her the beginnings of this work. He turned to her and said, "I've finished it." His voice was clipped and she wondered if he had been offended she had not asked about it sooner.

In truth, she had not thought about it until that moment. After her revelation to Jonas that day in late March, her efforts had been concentrated on freeing herself from the specter of Eric. She had begun by redecorating her apartment, then spending a long weekend alone in Chicago, a place where she and Eric and not been together. Only of late had she begun to view her parents and friends with her former sense of empathy. She now stopped walking and said simply, "I'd like to see it today." She thought he was deliberating as he did not answer her immediately. Instead he looked away, in the direction of a group of tourists equipped with cameras and shopping bags, coming out of a restaurant across the street, studying them as if expecting to see someone he knew.

Then within moments, he hailed a taxi and they were on their way to his apartment. They didn't speak during the ride. He neglected to explain why he had called out for a cab; they could easily have walked. Had he wanted to get her there before she changed her mind? Or was he impatient to see what her response would be? She looked at him, but he was staring directly forward, as if he were driving the taxi.

He did not look over at her until the driver stopped the car in front of the apartment building. He smiled uncertainly as she got out of the cab. When they walked into his apartment, he motioned for her to sit down and said he would bring the painting to her, but then he hesitated and asked if she would like a glass of wine first.

"Let me see the painting," she said, as she sat back on the sofa, remembering how in that very same spot just a few months before, she had revealed all to him, and she felt uneasy. It had been a turning point in her life but she wasn't convinced she would not be sad again. A sense of freedom had buoyed her after that day. Vaguely, she understood she might be repressing more grief and uncertainty. But she had opted for happiness; she had not wanted to be sad for so long. She was at an important age—it would soon be necessary for her to make decisions about her future with a clear mind.

He carried the painting into the room, then knelt before her, the canvas leaning against his chest, his hands cupping the edges. She noticed how lean and hungry his fingers seemed. Then she focused on the painting and was immediately struck because she found it different from his other works. It was both more personal and less personal, closer in perspective and more distant. She leaned closer to it and saw the two figures in the background, leaning against a wooden railing—it seemed from the past at first, from another time, but then she saw it was very much of the present. She could not determine whether or not the figures were male or female, one of each, or both the same. It was not an intimate interaction, but one of warmth and fluidity. At the front of the painting were thick patches of grass and bushes, a lime green color, and the figures were dressed in pants or maybe not—it was difficult to tell. Their forms were partially turned away from the viewer, partly covered by the foliage—all Jenny could see clearly were their profiles, one with a flat look and the other a more prominent one, a Roman nose. It was provocative—not in a seductive way, but more in a thoughtful one. They trusted but did not trust each other. They were both calm and anxious, assured and not confident. It really was a study in contrasts, but it was happening all at once.

She looked up at Jonas and asked, "What were your thoughts when you painted this?"

"Thoughts?" he asked, smiling. "I don't necessarily have thoughts; I see images, have impressions—one leads to the next."

"But your portraits," Jenny began, assuredly.

"Yes, my portraits are filled with thoughts—that is the problem. I think of what each customer wants, how each one wants to be depicted—it is if I am holding my brush wearing handcuffs, painting each circumscribed stroke a subject desires, choosing colors he or she hopes to be portrayed in. Except for the young woman I painted recently—she didn't care, but I felt I was led by her mother, who wanted me to paint her, I think, so she could discover who her daughter was."

"But these figures are not definable at all—I am not even certain of the sex of either of them. Is one a man and one a woman? Are they both men, both women?" Jenny could not take her eyes from the painting. All she wanted was answers—she wanted to know more about Jonas. Who was he? Maybe she was not unlike the young woman's mother, she thought, needing to find out through a painting the reality of a person.

She felt him studying her, and she now looked up from the work to meet his gaze. "It isn't important what sex they are, or who I think they are—it is for the viewer to decide," he said earnestly, his voice devoid of his usual skepticism.

She felt disoriented as he spoke—she had always longed for order. Through this painting he was refuting her sense of structure. It was his view of things, she understood; she had not realized how foreign it was from hers—she had firmly believed, taken for granted, that their perspectives on life were similar.

"So is this the new style you are trying to develop, Jonas?" she asked, gauging his expression, anticipating that at any moment he would return to his old self.

"I don't know, Jenny—I am just playing around with things. But what do you think—does it or does it not work?"

"Does it work?" she asked with intelligent caution. "I don't know—all I can say is, yes, it does work for me." She heard the sincerity in her voice yet while she spoke he looked at her bemusedly.

She watched as he easily stood up and carried the painting back to the alcove; she then heard him placing it on the easel. When he came back to her, he said nonchalantly, as if his thoughts were on other things, "Let's go." She was deeply disappointed; she did not want to go. He appeared intent on leaving. She wondered if he was meeting someone. He was in a hurry—as impatient as he had been to get there, he was as equally restless to leave.

She stood up and began to follow him to the door. Within seconds she stopped; meeting his surprised look, she said, "I don't want to go, Jonas—I want to stay. I believe we have something to accomplish together. I am not certain what it is. I don't want to leave until we know."

Later, when she'd recall that day, what would first occur to her would be the bewildered expression on his face at that moment—it was as if she had unmasked him in some way, had pushed aside the skeptical façade he had worn as protection for so long. And then she'd wonder what had prompted her to speak so directly to him; she had not intended to say a word.

He remained silent; her heart beat erratically. Then he said, "I am not sure what you mean, Jenny, what you are trying to say." He scratched his head, sat down on the sofa.

She guessed he was trying to determine in what way she wanted him. He appeared to be at a loss, and despite her anguish she smiled because she realized she was at as much of a loss as he was. Then he stood up, and as if on cue they both began to pace. There was not much space in his living room, and they soon ran into each other. She could never remember who laughed first, or maybe she cried because she had not wanted to run so quickly from her widowhood. She had not mourned enough, yet she could not prevent whatever was to occur next from happening. She was compelled to not leave Jonas, and was convinced he should not leave her either. She would look back on that day and wonder what had taken hold of her—had it been pure instinct? Had she wanted to release herself from her mourning? Was it because she wanted to help Jonas as she knew she could, support him in his endeavor? But she never would wonder if it was because she had fallen in love with him. After Eric, she had promised herself she would not do so again.

On that mid-June day they decided they would form a partnership, that, yes, they would marry and perhaps would have children, and Jonas would continue to follow his dream of becoming an artist. They passionately liked and, yes, loved each other. They sat up all night talking excitedly about their future together, how they should have realized it years ago, that she should have left Eric once she had connected with Jonas in New York, maybe he would still be alive today if she had, maybe if she had left him, he would have returned to Trieste and carried out his business from there. Jonas interjected and said that was the past and it was best not to relive it; neither she nor Eric should be faulted for their decisions.

When their lips met, she held Jonas by his arms, assertively, firmly. He moved closer to her, his fingers running through her hair.

His strength, she knew, was rooted in his dedication to his work, while hers lay in her ability to reach out to life—hers, and to the lives of those surrounding her. She knew she had embraced her parents' anguish too fully, perhaps, and Eric's as well. Now it was Jonas. But she believed he would provide reciprocity—he had not experienced the darkness her parents and Eric had, and so she was hoping for a fulfillment she had not before known.

After the first few hours of their fervor had passed, Jonas suddenly was quiet. He sprang up in the dark and said he wasn't certain about marriage—he had never really witnessed one in his life—he'd never seen his parents together, and his mother had kept her relationship with Harold at a distance from him. He'd not really lived with another woman before—he had attempted to but had always held on to his own apartment. He really was a novice at all this. She could only see the outline of his form. She got up and went to him. Finding his face, she stroked it and said, "I understand, Jonas but all those things don't really matter. You could say I am as much as a novice as you are. My parents were scarred by the war—I don't think their marriage is a very healthy one—and because of his experiences as a child and the age difference between us my marriage to Eric was even more unhealthy. Don't worry, Jonas. We will prevail."

The more she spoke, the more she understood how much he questioned her words.

Over the summer that followed, in his free time, Jonas would wander the city streets, trying to convince himself of the purpose of marriage. Other than what she had told him the one time she had spoken of her and Eric's strained relationship and her late husband's accident, Jenny had not revealed more about them as a couple. In his darkest moments Jonas wondered if there was something she was shading from him about her marriage to Eric. Had she donned her mask yet again? He had not the audacity to ask her to lift it.

Recently he'd come across the sketch he had begun of Jenny that had turned out to be Belinda, his aunt. It struck him he'd done the drawing as if he'd been imagining Jenny in a stark light, not through shadow—that had been a mistake, an obvious one, one a novice would make. Surprisingly it had taken him years to realize.

During his walks he'd observe couples, older ones, younger ones, some appearing content, others seeming ill at ease. In doing so he was not attempting as he had in the past to glean what his parents' marriage had been like but instead to conjure what his and Jenny's would become. After each outing he would return to his studio and submerge himself more and more in his work.

~

They were married the following January, the first day of the year. In respect to Eric's passing it was a quiet ceremony. It took place in the afternoon. The reception was held at a restaurant in their hometown, across the road from the ocean, close to where Jenny and Jonas had walked that late August night, prior to his return to San Francisco and before she had left for college.

Later when Jenny would recall their wedding day, she'd think of her father, her often inscrutable father, standing in the lobby of the restaurant, looking out the window at the turbulent sea, then checking his watch, the hostess approaching, asking if he was waiting for someone. And how her mother, while others were up and conversing, had sat alone at the table, her soft, round hands resting on her lap.

There had been something about the expression on Johanna's face that Jenny had not understood, her mother's eyes darting with a hint of suspicion, her lips closed in a half-smile, revealing a piercing sort of love. At that moment Jenny had been possessed with a strong desire to know the truth; she moved toward her mother. But as she began to approach, she felt the warmth of Jonas's fingers running across her shoulder. He whispered into her ear that he wanted to introduce her to an old friend of his, and the intensity of her longing to know more of Johanna dissolved.

They had decided to join their names, and from that day forward, with an ironic expression and a firmer stroke than before, he signed his paintings Jonas Smila-Hoffman. And she, who had not thought the name Smila on its own, or Stram, in any way, had suited her, was pleased with Jenny Smila-Hoffman; it better reflected who she was, shade and light.

Interlude

Tilting Toward the Light

It was a snowy winter and because of it Jonas and Jenny Smila-Hoffman, over the first months of their marriage, remained mostly inside their apartment. There was a prevailing sense of stasis in the air and whenever they'd venture out, a woolen scarf flung round each of their necks, gloved hands burrowed in the pockets of their heavy coats, their mouths restricted by the cold air, Jonas would point upward and comment on how the buildings appeared frozen against the backdrop of the gray sky. White flakes would fall, or, if not, soon would be swirling toward them as they'd make their way to a café or movie theater. Sometimes the snow would be light or in other instances heavy, and invariably mounds of it would be clustered against the curbs of the sidewalks; in one form, or shade—grayish or white—or another, it was present.

Each morning, awakening before Jenny, Jonas would wrap himself in a blanket; bare-footed, the woolen material trailing behind him, brushing the cold floor, he'd shuffle over to the lone bedroom window and look out at the piles of snow and icy ground and shiver. Then he'd turn his head to the side to check the clock on the bureau; inadvertently he'd catch his reflection in the mirror. His image, the uneven slope of his nose, the angularity of his visage, and the intensity of his stare would strike him as unfamiliar. He appeared more serious than he'd realized; it had to do with his qualms about his work—he felt confined by his job at the gallery and then there was his unease with aspects of their marriage, which, he believed, Jenny shared. Erasing these thoughts from his mind, he'd put on sweatshirt, pants, and socks, and with sketch book in hand go into the kitchen; his padded feet on the rungs of the chair, his head lowered, he'd begin to draw the teapot on the counter or the shelves above the stove before breakfast and then his eventual walk to the gallery.

Jenny would open her eyes to the sound of Jonas softly, exactingly rubbing a piece of charcoal against paper; she'd find it lulling, comforting at first, but then she'd feel at a distance from him. She'd get out of bed, put on her robe and slippers in a sleepy albeit perfunctory way, and go into the kitchen to join him.

Four mornings a week she attended a journalism class at a nearby university, its extension division. She cautiously was attempting to shape a career—one course at a time—but she believed it was necessary to do so at this point in her life. She was in no rush for anything. For there were instances when she'd become mesmerized by unexpected and hazy images of her first marriage. Whenever they came to mind, it was as if insensibly she had shaken a water-filled paperweight, a tiny village encased inside it, and though she'd strain to view it, the falling white flakes she unwittingly had released prevented her from clearly seeing the miniature houses, fences, and tiny figures. She'd become frustrated, then angry. She was not ready and might never be to fully comprehend memories of her first husband. She was fearful of what she would discover about Eric, about herself, and maybe even about Jonas.

Her marriage to Eric had passed at a frenetic pace, so much so that it had never been quite real to her. And now in its aftermath she was attempting to adjust to her current life, her unabated passion for Jonas.

In class she would appear focused, her eyes gauging her professor, her chin down, her posture composed. Only fleetingly would she become distracted by the falling snow or icy rain striking the classroom windows, or the unusual style of boots the woman had on in the seat next to hers.

Whenever her professor, a bland-looking man with pale eyelashes, appearing older than his age, set his gaze on Jenny, she'd be steadily taking notes. One day he called out her name and immediately she experienced a sinking sensation. He asked her to clarify to the class what he had just said. She answered slowly, carefully, and soon he understood she really hadn't been listening to him. For dawning across his face, she had witnessed his realization of her inattention, a shimmer of annoyance then understanding. Wasn't she the one who had lost her first husband in a yachting accident and at such a young age, too—she believed she could read his thoughts.

On that day, the third one of spring, Jenny and Jonas had been married for nearly twelve weeks. Their life had taken on a predictability that reflected at times calm, but at others an intrinsic edginess. When he awoke that morning, Jonas did not wrap himself in a blanket before he crossed the room but instead stood, his feet bare, before the window. Over breakfast he said he'd felt a mild chill—it wasn't yet as warm as he liked. But he could see spring in the sky, still pale, though a warmer blue and the more encompassing light from the planet's tilt toward the sun was uplifting.

As Jenny listened, her pulse quickened. Soon, she sensed, he would suggest a honeymoon; he'd been mentioning it every now and again. But she had no desire to go on a honeymoon this year. She wasn't quite ready. There was something final about the idea of a honeymoon, and that it would be her second one was disturbing. Second honeymoons were for those who were more established in their relationships. And there was something disorienting about experiencing another honeymoon—it evoked troubling memories of her first. Apprehensive, she waited for him to continue.

"Would you like to travel this summer, take a honeymoon? We've not had one, unless you'd call a visit to your parents and my mother every so often a vacation." He now tossed aside his sketch book in the way he did whenever he was not pleased with his work.

Hearing the implicit irony behind his sarcasm, she didn't answer, only shrugged. "Not this year; we've much to do, much to settle."

"Do you find it unsettling to be married to me?" he asked, half joking, half serious, scratching the side of his face; it was as if he were daring her to say yes to prove to her and himself that he was not meant for marriage.

"Jonas," she said, reaching for his hand, her face reddening, "I don't like the idea of a honeymoon now—it would be my second one; you are my second husband but I'd like to think of you as my first."

"But I literally will never be your first husband. You may have met me first."

"I knew of you first," she said and smiled.

"Isn't that what is most important?" he pointedly asked.

Removing her hand from his, she didn't respond. If only Jonas understood—she had attempted to explain it to him—how confused she was about Eric, his life. Now that her mourning had lifted, she realized that she felt a great deal of pity for her first husband. And though initially she had been infatuated with him, she now deeply believed that she had never really loved him; he had been secretive and detached from her, and she had become more and more aware of it the longer they had been together. During their marriage, her attitude toward Eric had ranged from compliance to uncertainty to distaste to indifference and finally anger. Following his death, there was at first an all-encompassing guilt that eventually was replaced with pity. And Jonas was a reprieve for her, his frank kindness, her passion for him, a reprieve from the overwhelming pity she felt for Eric.

Jonas left the apartment before she did; he said he would be meeting with a new client who wanted to commission him through the gallery to paint a portrait of her husband for their anniversary. And though Jenny did not have class that day, she had scheduled a meeting —her next assignment was to conduct an interview. She had chosen to interview a fortune teller—she thought it would be intriguing, as she'd never been inclined to go to a clairvoyant for her own sake.

From the front window, she watched Jonas make his way down the street. He appeared freer without her, she thought, feeling discomforted. In his snug jacket, his hands in its pockets, his firm shoulders and narrow waist seemed devoid of any encumbrances as he stepped past the shrinking grayish piles of snow.

She knew that Jonas had decided to continue working at the gallery for a variety of reason, but mostly because he did not want to be without a salary and have to rely fully on her. Jenny wasn't certain how long Eric's money would last. Over the last few years of their marriage, his finances had not been as plentiful or secure as they had been when they first met. Toward the end of his life, Eric had made risky investments—not completely out of character—that had not panned out; his losses had been significant, but salvageable to an extent.

She understood that Jonas was not established in the art world nearly to the degree he had hoped. She was relieved he was staying on at the gallery for a bit longer, not specifically for financial reasons—she thought if they were careful (they had opted to live in Jonas's less expensive apartment) they could get by for a while—but because it put their life together on hold.

She turned away from the window and went into to the bedroom to shower and dress. Since it was spring, she wanted to wear something more colorful, even though she knew it was too early in the season to be completely free of any winter clothing. She thought of how in the not-too-distant past she would often wear beige, and now she preferred a variety of colors.

In the bureau drawer she found a pale yellow cotton sweater that would keep her warm enough. After she finished dressing, she took a quick look in the mirror then put on her coat. She wasn't looking forward to the interview, as she had not been enjoying the class; it concentrated on the technical aspects of interviewing. The mechanics of an interview—that was to be her focus today, not necessarily the content. The professor had advised against choosing a subject that would be compelling, but she had done the opposite. Wasn't there something exotic about interviewing a fortune teller? Her assumption had always been that a clairvoyant would come to conclusions about you based on what you gave away without realizing you were doing so. Jenny had made it clear to the fortune teller that it was an interview only; she wanted to know about her work, and was not interested in having her personal fortune told.

She slowly walked down the street not far from the garment district, looking for the shop where the fortune teller had explained that she rented a small room on the first floor at the front of the building. Jenny had phoned three clairvoyants but had settled on this one because she sounded the most disinterested in doing the interview. Her indifference was what had appealed to Jenny. She had concluded that if the woman was apathetic, perhaps she would inadvertently reveal more just to get the interview over with.

She checked the number; it was the right address. The door made a groaning sound as she opened it. Immediately she saw that the seat behind the desk was empty. It struck her that she might have been presumptuous, that the psychic might be even more disinterested than she had revealed and would not show up. Jenny sat down in the chair across from the desk, checking her watch; she decided she would wait fifteen minutes. Then she looked about the room, and her gaze fixed on a series of photos on the side wall. There were three of the same woman and perhaps her partner or husband, and then one of a little girl. She wasn't certain if it was the woman as a young girl or perhaps it was her daughter, but her subdued presence in the other pictures seemed different than that of the little girl, whose personality appeared explosive; she had her hands on her hips if she were about to skirt away from the view of the camera and then pounce on whomever it was who was taking her picture. And it occurred to Jenny that a child's behavior was not necessarily indicative of how she would appear as an adult, sometimes it was the exact opposite.

Jenny crossed her legs, clutched her hands together, and leaned forward in the soft plastic chair. She felt a slight draft coming from the closed window behind her. She checked her watch again—only five minutes had passed and she felt incredibly restless. Maybe she should not wait the entire fifteen minutes, but then she remembered that in a week she would need to pass in a report on the interview. She abruptly stood up, crossed her arms, lowered her head, and peeked out the window. Then she began to pace before sitting down again. But within moments the door creaked open and the woman who was in the photographs walked in. She was surprisingly petite—she appeared of average height in the pictures—and wore no make-up. She had wispy, light brown hair, and her eyes were nearly identical in color.

She wore brown wool pants, a beige sweater beneath an unbuttoned raincoat, and a shoulder strap bag that crossed her chest. Jenny was taken aback—she had convinced herself that the fortune teller would not show up.

Observing her after adjusting to her presence, Jenny concluded that the woman's understated appearance might disarm her clients, cause them to forget that she was a clairvoyant, and then they in turn would reveal more than they were aware they were admitting. She stared directly at the psychic while these thoughts ran through her mind, then dropped her gaze. When

Jenny lifted her eyes she thought she caught the end of a slight grin crossing the woman's expression.

"You want to interview me and do not want your fortune told," the clairvoyant said, her voice soft and detached, then she lightly clapped her hands together. "Naturally I will charge you for my time as if you had made an appointment to have your fortune told." With the same softness and detachment the clairvoyant now spoke in a sing-song voice.

"I will pay you," Jenny said hastily, exactingly, and felt her cheeks warming, "but one does not usually pay someone who has agreed to be interviewed. People in the arts or in business usually feel it is helpful, it helps promote them."

When the fortune teller looked down, a shaft of morning light crossed the top of her head. Jenny noticed how fine the clairvoyant's hair was and she suddenly felt cautious; the woman might be more fragile than she had first thought. She had not envisioned a fortune teller in this way. The woman now met her gaze and responded slowly, her voice still low but more precise now, "You are a student, the interview will not be published in a magazine or newspaper, will it?"

"No, it won't," Jenny said readily. She was pleased to get this part over with. She had many questions to ask this woman. She did not mind paying—she only was charging the price she would a client. Jenny opened her pocketbook, drew out her wallet, and then placed the money in front of the fortune teller. She hoped by laying out the money the financial discussion would come to an end. In accepting the fortune teller's conditions, she believed she was asserting herself.

Half smiling, the fortune teller sat back in her seat. Jenny understood that the woman felt she had conquered her on a certain level. But that was fine, let her have her illusions—aren't illusions what clairvoyants depend upon? "You can begin," she said, checking her watch. And Jenny realized that the clairvoyant was not fragile but instead forceful.

Though her voice remained soft and indifferent, Jenny noticed that the fortune teller's gaze had slightly sharpened. She had composed a long list of questions on a writing pad in her pocketbook and now thought it best not to take it out. In some way she found the fortune teller inhibiting. Jenny asked how long she had been a psychic and what had made her choose this type of work.

"Is that it?" the fortune teller asked. Her tone was not mocking but it could have been; it was, in fact, soft and direct. She was about ten years older than Jenny, and though Jenny was accustomed to being in the company of older people, she had not been undercut by anyone, older or younger than her, in this way before. The fortune teller's voice now was gentle and she again spoke in that indifferent sing-song way of hers. She said she had been telling fortunes for fifteen years—from a young age she'd been able to assess people intuitively and then rationally predict their futures. She did not need cards or any other props—it was natural for her to do so. Then without a change in expression or tone of voice, the clairvoyant, her elbows on the desk, leaned forward and asked, "Why have you chosen to interview me, a fortune teller? I do not believe you would go to one. You appear to be settled in your views, your perspective, and incurious about your future. That is why people come to me; they need to know what will happen. They do not want their futures to evolve; they want it handed to them on a silver platter. I imagine you desire to fill your own platter."

As the fortune teller spoke, Jenny noticed that she wasn't looking at her but around the room, her eyes fixing on the photograph of the young girl with her hands on her hips. It seemed as if she were already bored with the discussion, with Jenny's presence.

Jenny noticed a worn deck of cards on the desk, but the clairvoyant didn't touch them or even look at them. When she soon caught Jenny's gaze on the cards, she simply said, "A red herring."

"Do you mean like a crystal ball, or the supposed reading of a person's palm?" Jenny directly asked.

"I said I do not use props; I observe a person's demeanor, posture—I hear what is unspoken." Then she sighed, a big deep sigh that rattled Jenny, but the fortune teller's expression still did not change, still dispassionate and close to indifferent.

Jenny wanted to leave, distance herself from this clairvoyant who suddenly struck her as odd. Jenny put on her jacket, and said, "Thank you," then stood up.

"Have I said enough? Will you be able to write your article?" the fortune teller asked in a factual way. Jenny understood that she wanted to be fair, that she intended to keep her end of the bargain.

Jenny shrugged and said, "Yes, I'll be fine," but she was terribly disappointed. The interview was a failure—she had not taken any notes as the fortune teller in a sense had taken the reins from her, preventing her from asking any real questions.

As Jenny walked toward the door, she tried to think of someone else she could interview before the week was up. But within seconds she heard the fortune teller call out her name; her mind had been going at a fast and panicked pace that she had nearly forgotten about the clairvoyant's presence.

Jenny turned to face her and though the clairvoyant no longer held her interest she felt her mouth quivering.

The clairvoyant rose from her seat and extended her hand; Jenny went over to the desk and shook it hastily. Before the fortune teller unloosened her grip, she said, "I see no ring; you are unmarried." Jenny glanced down at her left hand as she withdrew her right one from the fortune teller's grasp.

"I left it at home—I did not want to be late for the interview."

The fortune teller shrugged, her expression impassive, her voice soft, " Good-bye, " she said, and smiled evenly, slightly nodding her head.

Once she closed the door and stepped outside, Jenny took a deep breath. It is warmer, she thought. And then immediately she felt freed from the oppressive presence of the clairvoyant. Walking in the direction of her apartment, she acknowledged that the fortune teller had shaken her. Then she forced herself to remove this experience from her mind and decided that instead of finding another person to interview, she would piece together this interaction as best she could, concentrate on the practical aspects of the meeting—describe the room where the fortune teller saw her clients, the photographs on the wall, the deck of cards on the desk and how the clairvoyant had referred to them as a red herring.

As she increased her pace, various thoughts rapidly crossed her mind, and soon Jenny was again reflecting on the interview. It was becoming more and more clear that the fortune teller's intention had been to subtly point out to her that she, Jenny, didn't truly know herself, that there was much more that needed to be unraveled. Half incensed and somewhat ponderous, she stopped for a coffee at a neighborhood café, where she drew out her pad and began writing notes on the interview.

When Jenny arrived at their apartment, Jonas had not yet returned and she guessed he wouldn't be there for another few hours. He was meeting with a new client and usually that took longer. She approached the window in the front room; looking out, she pressed her hands against the sill and watched the pedestrians pass below. Seemingly elevated that it was spring—she could tell by the lightness in their steps—their expressions became grim once a strong wind blew, rattling her windowpane.

Most of them now dropped their heads to steel themselves, waiting for the gust to subside.

She then went into the kitchen and made herself a cup of tea. She concluded that, yes, she had found the fortune teller unnerving, but she was determined to shake the image of the clairvoyant from her mind, her dispassionate look, her wispy appearance, her voice, at times melodic and at other times indifferent.

By the time Jonas arrived, she was less perturbed by her experience with the fortune teller. Before dinner they brought chairs to the front window, enjoyed a glass of wine while observing the sunset.

"The difference in the light now from just a week ago is remarkable," Jonas said, smiling. He drew his chair closer to Jenny's and she soon felt his arm around her shoulders. He asked about her interview with the fortune teller.

"We didn't connect well at all—she was disinterested, smug, and unnerving."

"Unnerving? Did she try to tell your fortune?"

"Not in so many words—she said I wasn't a person who would ask to have her fortune told—she viewed me as personally clueless, I believe. She didn't say very much about her work other than that she observes and listens, and doesn't use props, but somehow I'll manage to write a report."

"You are practical, Jenny—realistic. You don't sound very bothered by her. Wish I were more like you." Then he told her about his encounter with the new client, how he had been compelled by her earnestness, her desire for him to paint her husband's portrait. "I believe they have been married for fifteen years. But I wonder if there is more behind her insistence, her wish to have her husband's portrait painted. Guilt? Or is she looking for reciprocity—she doesn't believe he loves her as completely as she loves him?" His expression puzzled, he shook his head. "But the challenge for me is to paint an accurate likeness when I will not be observing him in person. She wants it to be a surprise."

"Will she bring you many photographs? " Jenny asked, supposing that Jonas would need to make do with pictures as she would have to make do with the scant information she had elicited from her interview with the fortune teller.

"I have not painted anyone only through photographs. I do not feel great about it. But she wants his portrait painted and she explicitly said that she wants it to be a surprise. I asked if there was a coffee shop he went to or if there is any other way I could get a glimpse of him. She said she would think about it and was obviously hesitant. She didn't think about it very long, though, because just before she left she said that she had decided that she wants the painting done only through photographs."

"Well, I guess you will have to go along with what she wants," Jenny said musingly. "It is her husband, and she is the one asking for the portrait to be painted in such a way. Maybe she want it to be illusory, less real. Maybe the reality of him is taxing for her. I do not know what I am saying, Jonas, I am just searching for any possible reason she would choose to have his portrait painted in an indirect way. If she wants it to be a surprise that is fine, but she should let you see him in person." Jenny paused, then asked, "Is her husband with her now?" It struck her that he could be away or that maybe they had agreed to a separation for one reason or another.

Jonas shrugged. "I do not ask questions. I just paint and see what characteristics evolve about the subject as I work. I do not like to assume or put in what is not visible. I'll try and do the best I can with the photographs."

"I believe you would want to see him in person," she responded, glancing out the window; the setting sun was now hidden behind a building, its orange rays reflecting harshly, warmly against the side of the tall glass structure a short distance away.

"Yes, that is what I would choose to do. But maybe I am intrigued by what she is asking of me. It may be difficult, or it may be easy. I am not certain. I think as long as I do not use only one photograph—as any one picture would also be a reflection of the person who took it—I should be okay. If there are enough photographs taken by different people then I possibly could piece together an image of him, my own translation, you could say."

But as he continued to speak, weighing the pros and cons of painting a subject with only photographs, she knew he was a purist and would not agree to the portrait unless he could in one way or another observe the woman's husband in person. If the man were not alive, that would be a different matter. If he refused to accept the woman as a client, she knew Jonas might lose his job at the gallery. She clearly understood that he needed to work on his own art now. Just as she knew that she'd be able to piece together the inconclusive and jarring interview she had had with the fortune teller and write a report. She was not a purist like Jonas; her temperament inclined her not to expect perfection—she would always make do.

That night as they were about to get into bed, Jonas went over to Jenny, lifted her hand, turned it over and studied her palm; with a slight grin crossing his lips, his dark eyes intent, he said, "Let me tell you your fortune."

Jenny placed her finger over his mouth and said, "No, Jonas, I will tell you yours." She grasped his wrist; staring into his palm, she said exactingly, "Your honeymoon will be delayed because in the next few months you will leave your job at the gallery to work entirely on your own paintings."

Spontaneously, he reached out and hugged her tightly. Jenny, tilting back slightly from the pressure of Jonas's body against hers, caught in the light emanating from the bedside lamp, a momentary though pronounced look of stark determination in her husband's eyes—a reflection of her own unflinching gaze.

August

Those early years are hazy and unfocused in memory, pale brushstrokes of a newly begun painting. Through the lens of time I recall a silk-like scarf draped over the arm of an unfinished chair, a necklace with a stone, the shape and color of which I strain to envision, resting on the bony chest of a woman whose face is a blank, an inkling of a stain on the rug near the door. Images lacking the distinctness of firm color, pressed against my dim recollection of the first apartment I lived in with my parents—I was too young to perceive more, to fill in forms and hues.

Of the Saturday soirees in August, the month my mother and father entertained, I only am aware of what I was later told. Reminiscing, their expressions ponderous, they would say how hot and close it was—over fifty people crowding together, conversing, while from the record player, opera—most often *Aida* and the voice of Caruso—resounded throughout the room. My father then would cross his narrow, firm legs and clear his throat, and my mother, her ankles touching, her shoulders erect, would raise her eyes as if to inspect the ceiling; in a pensive and respectful way they'd speak, in near unison, of Giorgio, a former colleague of my father's, engineers during the pre-war days of Europe. They described him as small-framed and thin, his hair and mustache thick and full, overpowering in contrast to his lithe physique. Whenever the heat became oppressive, Giorgio rolled up his sleeves, unbuttoned his shirt, and thrust open a window; sitting on the ledge, gripping the sill with his small hands, he leaned forward to catch a breeze, his legs dangling against the side of the four-story building. Some would laugh with excessive delight, their faces flushed from wine or alcohol, while the sober ones expressed their unease.

One night, Giorgio, his head bowed, asked to sleep on their sofa, explaining that his wife was away, visiting family in Venice. When my parents awakened the next morning, there was no trace of him; vanished, my mother added with emphasis. They would never see him again. It was assumed though not verified that he had joined his wife in Italy. Not concluding their story of Giorgio, my parents would say no more. They'd sit back in their roomy chairs and look into the distance, as if gazing across the rough, blue Atlantic, then in to the world of their pasts.

Their guests, immigrants mostly from Trieste, like themselves, had left Europe following the war. Later, in the next apartment where there were no parties, friends and acquaintances from past days occasionally would visit on a Sunday afternoon, some of them smoking heavily, a few with pronounced shadows beneath their eyes. Their smiles revealed a range of emotions, from unflinching wariness to pure contentedness. Over time I gleaned that they had been shaken from the misplaced loyalties in their country of origin; they had come to America to forget, to start anew, to regain their composure.

I left Hartford a month short of my fourteenth birthday. In the back seat of the car, shoes off, knees raised, my hand grazing the vinyl material of the cushion, my parents silent in the front. From the radio I heard the news, the reader's words at times sounding staticky, more often soft and distant. It was March 1968, and like my visual memories, my auditory ones are vague as well, a faint word here and there, often repeated, not seeming to connect to the next one—"Warsaw"; "King"; "North Vietnamese." Words I heard from time to time during those years, words that elicited a distant confusion as if I were living beneath low gray clouds that might never disperse.

My mother wore brown that day, and the zipper of her dress was not fully up; the back of her neck was full, freckled and protruding. I cannot recollect how she appeared when she turned to ask if I was hungry or thirsty, or what my father's expression was either—all I remember are his steely and darting eyes, peering into the rearview mirror. I sensed they were ambivalent about the move to the outskirts of Boston.

What was most clear was that I was leaving behind a particular place in my Hartford bedroom. I inhabited it and so it had become an extension of me, of where I chose to hide. It was next to the window, from where, sitting on the hardwood floor, I would stretch my neck and view the activity on the street below, a radiator beneath the sill. I'd sit and often read, believing it was my territory where I could view, imagine, and learn about the planet. I'd feel empowered. I kept close a book with a map of the world, and oftentimes, spreading out two fingers, I would place one on Europe and the other on North America, straddling both continents, the blue Atlantic in between. I belonged in both places, but not by choice. In this small space I would experience a sense of order, an inner contentment that evaporated once I stood up and mustered the determination needed to walk away.

One

The Postcard

Summer, 1984. A wet June evening, the rain strong and heavy, falls in spurts, flooding the windshield, blinding our view; my second husband and I, driving north, pass the sign to Hartford. Up ahead there's been an accident; Jonas presses the brake. In profile, his face appears longer, more angular; the hollows in his cheeks not tempered by the round turn of his chin. Lights flash and a policeman in bright rain garb, directing traffic, signals for us to move forward. On the side of the road, close to the ambulance, a woman sits on the curb, her legs extended, her face pale, her features undefinable. I see no more; we have passed the scene.

The glistening road and frenetic movement of the wipers draw me to an image, a memory of a man wearing charcoal-colored pants. His step was long and brusque, the fabric clung to his legs; my head parallel to his kneecap, my bare feet nestled into a warm rug. A woman whose face was unrecognizable sat in a chair against the wall, her legs spread, a red stain on her lap. Neither frightened nor angry, I watched the man walk swiftly past her; I was deeply aware that this moment, in one form or another, would always be with me.

Though the rain is now a soundless drizzle, the traffic on the highway remains heavy; we make several stops along the way. The drive from our apartment in New York to my mother and father's home outside of Boston takes longer than usual.

Past midnight, we pull into the driveway. Quietly, we let ourselves in with the key I've kept for the past twelve years. We tiptoe past my parents' bedroom, go down the short hallway, and into the room that once was mine.

Unable to sleep, I replay the unearthed memory in my mind. Jonas shifts his lean and wiry body; his back to me, I run one finger down then up and across his skin as I would as a child on the beach after the tide receded, drawing lines in the moist, firm sand. While the adults were embroiled in conversation, anticipating the long drive back to Hartford, I would lower my head, my heart beating fiercely, and touch my face to the wet sand. Then I'd run to the sea to wash it off; the muddy weight of it pressing my cheeks and forehead.

The next day is bright and clear, the midday sun glinting over the surface of the automobile; we drive toward the ocean and a mild breeze caresses us. My parents are in the back seat, their expressions stoic in different ways.

We dine at a restaurant across from the shore, with an encompassing view of the Atlantic, the windows open, light streams in; we linger over our lunch. As a party of four passes our table, a shadow crosses my father's high forehead. He wears a tan-colored shirt, his complexion appearing less gray. Fully engaged in our cursory discussion of politics, his responses are exacting, practical, yet his eyes reflect disquietude, more so than usual. My mother is dressed in a yellow-gold dress, a large onyx ring tight on her second finger. She is animated today, buoyed by the glare of the sun.

I lean forward and announce that in August we plan to take a belated honeymoon, that we are looking for a place near water; Jonas hopes to sketch, I say, then take a sip of coffee.

"Are you considering Trieste, Jenny? Jonas?" my mother suggests, sounding more ambivalent than encouraging; her hand outstretched, her palm upward, she taps the stone of her ring against the table. Bemusedly she eyes my father, her lips part, the lower one quavering; he signals for the waitress, and orders a second martini.

Later we visit Jonas's mother, Cora; she opens her front door, appears preoccupied as she greets us. Though once seated, her legs crossed, her pants cut just above her ankles, she intently studies Jonas, then me. Gradually her gaze becomes less and less penetrating, her eyes drift away, now focusing on the wall behind us; perhaps a photograph of Jonas as a young boy has caught her attention. Petite, her movements concise, her presence is never burdensome—as if her purpose in life is not to oppress. Her half smile is sweet and ironic, like Jonas's; it reveals they are mother and son. Her erect form is softened by the late afternoon light.

Lowering her eyes, she speaks of a possible vacation; she's thinking of driving north, into Canada, maybe Montreal. Montreal, a city that reflects who she is—small, intricate, active, never overbearing. Alternately, she taps each forefinger on her lap, debating, it seems, opposing viewpoints in her mind. Is she considering traveling with Harold, her partner of many years, whom she rarely mentions, and with whom Jonas is minimally acquainted? Despite her restiveness, she is, invariably, steady. For Cora's natural warmth, quietly expansive, supersedes her innate sense of order and moments of preoccupation; a woman whose husband unexpectedly passed away prior to his deployment to a world war and birth of their only child.

Before dinner, my mother, her cheeks flushed from the warmth of the stove, serves each of us an aperitif. With glass in hand I go into the bedroom to look for a book I left behind the last time we visited, a biography of Caravaggio. After perusing the volumes on the shelf without success, I place my drink on top of the desk.

Half listening to the muted conversation between Jonas and my parents coming from the living room, I open the bottom drawer and notice Roth's *Goodbye, Columbus*. With bemusement—for now it would not capture my interest—I pick it up. Holding it, I dismissively flip through the novella. But soon, lodged between two pages of the book, I discover a postcard. With no recollection of having received it, I hold the card up to the fading light; on the front is a picture of a large and uninspiring hotel overlooking a glistening Mediterranean Sea. The edges of the card are still firm and the face of it as glossy as it must have been the day it was sent, though the angle of the picture and the quality of the paper suggest it is not from the present. When I turn the card to the other side, my heart thumps erratically. For the slanted signature is that of my late, first husband, Eric Stram; the date on the card is August 1, 1972. His letters are close, difficult to read. At the time I did not know him well. He did not mention that he hoped to visit me soon; it was a superficial greeting from an acquaintance.

For over a decade the novella and card have lain untouched in the bottom drawer of the desk in this bedroom where I spent the last four years of my youth. Over my eighteenth summer, I read *Goodbye, Columbus* three times, and Lawrence's *Women in Love* once. I was drawn to both because each work introduced me to a concept that for the most part was foreign—one of unabashed freedom.

The voices of my mother, father, and husband sound more distant now, as if coming not from the present but from years ago, and it is not the polite but reserved exchange they share with Jonas; instead it is as if they are with Eric, and I imagine their speech as intense and rapid, how it was whenever they conversed with my first husband. I put the book back into the drawer, and with postcard in hand I stare out the window at the growing twilight through which the passing cars appear to move in slow motion. Abruptly realizing I should join my parents and Jonas, I tuck the postcard in the back pocket of my blue jeans, pick up my glass, and walk out of the room, closing the door behind me.

August light, golden yet muted, falls through the open bedroom window, circling the edges of the beveled mirror frame. I lean across the bureau, my weight on my wrists, gauge my reflection in the glass; with purpose, I say, "I was Jenny Smila until I became Jenny Stram; now I am Jenny Smila-Hoffman—yet I am not a name." From time to time in the same spot I will speak this sentence. The words are a prayer of sorts, a mantra, a means of calming and centering myself, replacing the time and space in my Hartford bedroom where I was most content.

Lowering my gaze, I follow an amorphous shadow crossing the surface of the bureau; the long step of the man with clinging charcoal-colored pants comes again to mind. My awareness has grown, but of what I am not certain.

At the window, my fingers press the sill; our third-floor apartment overlooks a small grassy area. Peering out into the morning heat, my gaze settles on Jonas. Below, beneath a willow tree, he sits with his knees raised, his eyes assess the sketchpad resting against his narrow thighs, languidly he fingers the grass, the supple branches loop over him like dangling beads.

Warm air grazes my forehead. The sky is pale, nearly clear. In the mellow light, wisps of white clouds reflect the caressing nature of the morning. Jonas sketches, but then suddenly stops and rests his head against the bark. His mind is off somewhere. And watching how he slightly frowns, it strikes me that the two years and seven months of our marriage have been almost seamless; this thought pricks me like an insect bite, piercing and sweet. My realization of the passing of this time and that I do not feel closer to Jonas causes the initial sting. But there is a subtle pleasure in my recollection as well; I am more fulfilled, more independent than I've ever been.

Now sketching again, his hand moves across the pad, the other one holding down the sheet. Although we had been neighbors for four years, it was not until my eighteenth summer that Jonas and I, over the gate separating our backyards, first spoke. As I approached, he tightened his grip on the art pad in his left hand. Hungry fingers, I thought, and later I would realize whenever he sketched or painted he would do so with a devouring intensity, as if with each stroke in some way he was feeding both the active hand and the passive one.

One cool evening last April, we walked after dinner; the sky was clear, the stars visible between the skyscrapers. Turning onto Seventh Avenue, Jonas, his smile fading, described, as he has in the past, his initial impression of me, his fourteen-year-old new neighbor, sitting in the shade beneath the garage roof in her backyard. How I had reminded him of a young woman in Botticelli's painting *Primavera*. And how, he musingly added, very soon afterward he'd moved out to San Francisco and did not see me again until we first spoke. Then a strong brief wind, reminiscent of March, rattled us, and we stopped walking; he held me close, an expression of anxiety—or was it passion—flickered across his face. I wondered if he prefers the shadowy and painted versions of me.

When we returned to our apartment, he closed the door behind us, and grasped my arm, our mouths and bodies pressing together.

Jonas had misgivings about my marriage to Eric Stram. I know because I understand him, his biases. I also believe he was saddened by Eric's death. Yet there is a part of my past of which Jonas is unaware. In the rushing fog of my first marriage I eventually understood in order for the mist to clear I needed to loosen myself from my relationship with my husband. Jonas was my first choice, though I knew he would not be interested; I was married. But at the time I was determined, more than I consciously realized, to find solace from someone else, even a stranger.

During our years in New York, Eric and I frequented a travel agency on Madison Avenue. The agent we'd worked with was a fatherly looking man with fine red hair and soft green eyes.

When I walked into the agency office last month, a sweltering July afternoon, he was the only one at his desk. It took him a few minutes to recall I was a former customer of his. He asked after my husband; instead of answering, I reached across the desk and presented him with the postcard I'd found in the book. He studied it for a while, then an expression of recognition crossed his face. With confidence he said the hotel straddles the French and Italian Rivieras, and that the colors of the foliage in the area are marvelous. Immediately, I decided this is where we would spend our belated honeymoon, and promptly asked him to book it from August second to the thirtieth. My rationale was that it would be a good place for Jonas to sketch.

When I returned home, I went directly to our bedroom, pulled open the drawer of the night table, and placed the postcard inside.

I now hear Jonas jiggling his key into the lock of the door, and go out to meet him. Unshaven, his expression is dark, studied, and I think of the image of Caravaggio, from a self-portrait, on the cover of the biography. He places his sketchpad on the counter. Then he draws me close. "Have we waited too long?" he asks. There is a tension in his long face; his eyes search mine.

"It is as good a time as any, and the heat in New York is oppressive in August," I answer, my voice sounding strained; I avoid his gaze. "We should start packing," I add, heading toward the bedroom. He comes up behind me and gently tugs my ponytail.

I pull my nightgown up and then over my head. "How I detest packing," I say, tossing the negligee onto the bed.

"Let's try to make it not too dull," he responds, and his voice sounds far away but he is close; his hands, reassuring, cup my breasts.

The taxi arrives outside our building at 5 p.m. Jonas carries the suitcases down the winding stairway. Following him, I hesitate before closing the door of the apartment; turning away, I go back inside the bedroom and pull open the drawer of the night table. I take out the postcard, study the picture, and then Eric's writing on the back. I slip the card inside the front pouch of my tote bag.

Two

The Hotel

From a distance I glimpse the hotel; it is situated on a rocky hill bordering the Italian and French Rivieras. As we drive closer, Jonas abruptly changes gears of the Fiat. The building is a formidable yet odd structure, made more so by how incongruous it appears in contrast to the extraordinarily beautiful surroundings; I gaze up at it with mingled feelings of dread and hope. The road is narrow and winding and after a sharp turn our view is momentarily blocked. Now, directly approaching the hotel, it is evident that the facade is postmodern, veering toward a semicircular shape, with a steel and concrete exterior. Magenta-colored bougainvillea and palm trees cover the lower front of the structure; a short distance away, in its sparkling splendor, lies the deep blue Mediterranean.

We park near the entry. Jonas hands the key of the car to the valet, a thin and energetic man with a deep and solemn tan, and then we carry our suitcases up a circular marble stairway. It's a strikingly hot afternoon, and our climb is slow and uneven. I stop for a moment and hold on to the banister. Jonas has reached the top step. He looks over and our gazes meet; though there is uncertainty in his eyes, his smile is broad and firm.

In a daze from lack of sleep, we step inside the lobby, paved with marble and decorated with bronze and marble sculptures; intricate, richly colored paintings; and tapestries. Brocade sofas and chairs and large gold-framed mirrors adorn the interior. In the far corner is a baby grand piano. I have not been here before, but the interior is remarkably familiar; my thoughts stray to my other honeymoon.

I recall that we did not sleep the night following our wedding; the party after the ceremony had continued until the next morning. In the early afternoon, we said good-bye to our family and friends surrounded by their luggage in the hotel lobby. There was the group from Trieste and another from the United States. Eric was gracious and humble with the departing guests, clearly enunciating each of their names, thanking them for coming. Though I'd not observed this side of him before, I'd been told he had an uncanny ability of remembering people's names, even those he'd met only once and had not seen for five or more years.

Once the guests left, Eric decided to take a walk, and I went up to our suite to shower and change. It was a warm afternoon in early September and from the window I noticed the sky had a golden hue to it; autumn was approaching. After I showered, I went into the bedroom and found Eric lying naked on the bed, sound asleep. I went over to him; there was a hard whiteness to his skin tone I had not before registered. Inwardly I was alarmed; I had no desire to touch him. Then, as if feeling my presence, he opened his eyes and looked over at me, his blue-gray gaze catching mine. Reflexively I stepped back. He patted the side of the bed, raised his brows, and said, "Come lie next to me, Jenny."

Uneasy now, my heart beats rapidly, as if I expect Eric to walk into the lobby, his head slightly lowered. He'd wear a pressed white shirt, short-sleeved, and dark blue pants; the light coming through the open French doors would accentuate his blond-brown hair, unruly despite his overall neat appearance; he'd efficiently shake Jonas's hand, make a comment about my dress—very bright. His expression would be impassive, then he'd smile to signal his words were meant as a compliment.

For a time I fully believed it would not have angered him if I had another love interest, that he might have preferred it.

Now Jonas's sleepy eyes roam the lobby, rest in the direction of a marble sculpture of a white fawn; languidly he moves toward it, soundly bringing me to the present.

From the balcony of our hotel room, there is an expansive view of the Mediterranean. In silence, Jonas and I lean against the railing, stare out, awed by the majesty of the sea. A light breeze ruffles the flags in the courtyard below. After a while, almost in unison as if drunk from beauty, we turn away and pass through the sliding glass door and back into the room. Slowly, as if in a dream, we lift our luggage onto the bed and begin to unpack.

Sunlight streams into the room, illuminating Jonas's high forehead and shoulders, encircling his long waist. His voice, as angular as his face, sounds stilted and tired; opening his suitcase, he says, "The sea—breathtaking—and so is the color of the bougainvillea. The exterior of the building is utilitarian—functional, practical. But our room, the balcony, the view is magnificent." Lowering his head more, he begins to remove his clothing from the case.

Yet I am compelled by the contrast between the ugliness of the exterior structure and the grandeur of the sea, the beauty of the foliage and the sophistication of the finer works of art. The dichotomy allows me to feel settled, confident—perhaps elevated.

In a chaise longue, one arm dangling, my fingertips graze the hot grains of sand; hazily I look out at the Mediterranean. The water appears still, yet sparkles beneath the rays of the sun. Rocks border the sea. It is five in the afternoon. I am a short distance from the shore, surrounded by rows of beach chairs and umbrellas. The sun will not set for a while. Not yet accustomed to the six-hour time change, I find it difficult to accept where I am.

In the distance I spot Jonas on a ledge of rocks, waves cresting a few feet below, a sketchpad resting on his raised knees; with charcoal in hand he frantically draws, perhaps captivated by the movement of the waves or the wings of a seagull. Then he looks upward and stretches out his legs, his head back as if he is soaking up the warmth. His pose is reminiscent of the photo hanging on the wall of his mother's living room; in it, he's lying in the grass, his arm covering his face, as if shielding himself from the warm rays or protecting himself from an onslaught of piercing slashes of rain.

As I try to imagine what Jonas may be thinking, how he might be assessing his work, it occurs to me that I had never attempted to guess what was on Eric's mind, what had intrigued him most about the business he was part of. It would have been impossible to know, I had assumed, because of his experience as a child during the war—horrific, I had gleaned from his nightmares; his thought process to a degree was a disoriented one. I had concluded that what was essential was not what he was thinking about but how he ruminated over what concerned him at any particular moment, and given my paltry knowledge of his past it would have been impossible for me to comprehend, let alone follow.

A child's cry distracts me from my thoughts. Turning in the direction of the sound, I notice a young family, a mother, father, and son lying in beach chairs in the same row as ours, three seats away. The boy, a toddler, is sprawled across the father's naked lean stomach—he has just awakened from a nap and is crying out for a drink. A large beach umbrella open above their chairs protects them from the piercing sun. The mother abruptly sits up, then stands, wiggling her feet inside her sandals; with two fingers of each hand she efficiently adjusts the shoulder straps of her bathing suit and then makes her way to the refreshment stand. As she places her order, her words are not easily audible, but soon I realize she is speaking French.

Wincing, she thrashes through the hot sand toward her family, and then hands the glass bottle to her husband. He sits up in his chair, loosens the child from his chest, pours the liquid into the paper cup he's pulled from a knapsack, and then presses it to his son's mouth. The little boy, his face a feverish red, his dark eyes large and tired, takes quick fast gulps, and then moves his head away to indicate he has had enough. There is something about the mother that is familiar—strong yet wavering, very dark eyes, exotic.

Lying back in the lounge chair, shading my eyes with one hand, I see Jonas approaching. Once our gazes meet, we both half smile. Soon he is lying in the chair next to mine. His eyes are closed, his sketchpad on his lap. I feel his hand reach for mine. Clasping Jonas's hand, I shut my eyes tightly. Searching my memory for the person who resembles the French woman, my thoughts wander from the French and Italian Rivieras and Eric's Mediterranean business trips, while I stayed alone in the summer heat of New York City, to seven years ago, and then almond-shaped brown eyes. I recall her inquisitive and detached look, and how as she introduced herself she vigorously shook my hand. I told her my name was Jenny Stram.

We'd been lingering under a store awning on Madison Avenue. It was a steamy July afternoon, and we were waiting for a heavy downpour to subside. We stood with our arms crossed and listened to the steady rain drum against the top of the awning; at first we spoke sparingly. After five minutes of small talk, we cautiously began to converse.

I guessed she was in her early fifties, close to my mother's age. She wore a sleeveless white dress, an A-line style, that fell three or four inches past her knee. Her arms and face were tanned. She was of average height, her shoulders broad, her ankles slim. Her eyes were an exotic shape, a deep brown color, her chin narrow for her face. She peered at me and asked what type of work I did, her voice both curt and warm. I explained that my husband and I had not been living in New York long, and I was trying to decide on a career, that I was taking courses, hoping to discover a field that would suit me. I added that I had just completed a course in journalism and was considering taking another one in the fall. This was when she enthusiastically shook my hand and introduced herself as Isa Sokolov. She said she had a connection with someone who was a professor of journalism at a small college outside of the city. She said she would call and see if this professor would talk with me, help steer me in a particular direction. Before we parted that afternoon, we agreed to meet two days later, on Saturday morning.

Eric had told me he would return from his business trip on the following Sunday afternoon. Over the nearly three years of our marriage, I had learned to assume that Eric's definition of business could possibly mean personal as well as professional. We were not estranged as a couple but nearly so. He came and went as he pleased and I had not yet decided how I would go about doing so as well. Though I had disliked admitting it, I'd been hoping that we were only experiencing another phase in our marriage and that eventually we would become closer.

A few days later I met Isa at a coffee shop close to our Midtown apartment. She seemed different this day. Two days before she had been wearing a dress and her face had been made up; eyeliner and lipstick had been applied with great care. On this day she was dressed in tight blue jeans and a mauve-colored, V-neck T-shirt. Her manner was different as well. I attributed her casual appearance to the rising heat; it was eleven o'clock in the morning, early to be meeting on a Saturday at the height of summer. But it had been her choice to get together at this time.

In the sharp morning light, her features appeared more harsh, her chin pointy rather than narrow. She seemed unsettled, not composed as she had two days before. We sat outside; although the sun was strong, the temperature had not yet reached its peak. She wore large dark glasses; whenever she questioned me, she would remove her shades, smile abruptly, her eyes squinting, and then put them on again.

My family name was Smila, I told her, and I'd lived in Hartford until I was fourteen. When I asked if she'd ever been there, she shrugged, did not remove her dark glasses, and with a tight smile said she could not keep track of where she'd been.

She lit a cigarette and attempted to speak evenly but there was a hoarseness in her voice, "You are young and beautiful; your life is before you." Her mouth was set, her facial expression was fixed, her lips pursed; tension crossed her forehead.

Continuing, she said, "My hope had been to become a translator—I am fluent in Italian, French, and Russian," she brusquely explained. "But I fell in love with the man who offered to hire me, and decided to decline the position. There were two reasons: the first of course is that we had become involved—I would have felt uncomfortable; there would have been gossip, and secondly, I did not think I would be suited to a career in translation. A few years later I married someone else."

Before I had a chance to respond, a man came up behind her and rested his hands on her shoulders. He was quite tall, even taller than Eric, and I thought he might be five to ten years older than Isa. She turned her face to him, her voice abrupt, and said, "You startled me, darling." But she did not appear surprised to see him. As I got up to leave, she held up her hand as if to stop me. "Jenny Smila Stram, I'd like you to meet Hans, Hans Sokolov." I shook his hand; his fingers were long and thin, more narrow than mine. Then neither of them spoke, but looked away, as if to indicate my time with them was over. There was an evident tension between them. I walked home feeling disoriented by the change in her personality and that she had not mentioned whether or not she had called her contact on my behalf.

When Eric returned the next day I told him about my encounter with Isa and Hans Sokolov. It was another close, hot day. I did not want to ask about his business trip—he'd been in Chicago the past week—for I knew he would not be direct with me; he would evade my questions, speak cryptically about his work. I was in no mood for that. But ever since our wedding three years before, I had begun to put the pieces together and eventually realized it wasn't Eric's own business; he worked for a prominent person whose headquarters, once in Philadelphia, was now in Europe. Eric would travel the world, but mostly throughout the United States, to do his bidding.

Eric sat opposite me, his legs resting on the ottoman; he smiled loosely, listened carefully and with interest to what I was saying. When I finished speaking he responded readily, "Oh, yes, Isa and Hans Sokolov—I met them about five years ago and have seen them from time to time in passing since we have come to New York. But I do not know if they remember me. I was on a business trip, staying at a hotel on the Riviera, the Italian side. I found them to be an interesting couple; yes, she was an interesting woman. It was before you and I became involved, of course." Then he smiled in that haunting way of his, and said, "I believe she may be from Trieste. What a small world it truly is, Jenny."

I still feel Jonas's grip on my hand and soon doze off. When I open my eyes, I am uncertain how long I've been sleeping. There is a light breeze now. My eyes are blurry and I realize Jonas is no longer holding my hand. I feel his absence but hear his voice; following the sound of it, I look over and see he is conversing with the French family. The woman's expression is no longer stern; she throws back her head and laughs at whatever Jonas is saying in his halting French. I look past them to the front of the hotel; from this angle the foliage is not visible, I only see the steel and concrete exterior.

Three

The Guests

Evenings, before dinner, guests drift into the grand lobby to listen to the pianist. Freshly showered after a day spent bathing, sightseeing, or cycling beneath the piercing sun, they lounge on brocade sofas and chairs, dressed in informal yet well-pressed clothing, sitting upright, legs crossed, ears cocked in the direction of the musician. Clutching a glass of chardonnay or Campari, they reach for tiny hors d'oeuvres from the full plates the white-jacketed waiters have placed on low tables before them. Conversations, as they tend to be in the early evening hours, are tempered, almost listless.

The pianist, in his late thirties, dressed in a black tuxedo and cream-colored shirt without a tie, the top button open; his expression is both alert and melancholic, his eyebrows fine semicircles. His shoulders rise gracefully, soulfully as he plays a

Duke Ellington or Johnny Mercer song, occasionally one favored by Sinatra or Bennett. From time to time he'll sing one of these melodies—always in French, yet his name is Italian. He is referred to as Mr. Poldini. At 9:30 p.m., each night, ninety minutes before he is finished for the evening, he'll erupt into a classical piece—Beethoven's *Moonlight Sonata* or a Chopin polonaise. By then some of the guests will have returned to listen. They will have come into the lobby after having enjoyed a satisfying dinner outside on the patio, the Mediterranean not far away, having been serenaded by the swishing sound of the waves while mildly aware of the dim lights in the courtyard surrounding the pristine pool and the flags from various countries on tall poles, colorful, inanimate guards.

Sitting away from the pianist, but with a clear view of him, we listen to his rendition of a series of Ellington's songs. Intermittently I feel the pressure of Jonas's arm against my shoulder. Mr. Poldini plays in a precise almost staccato-like way, never exuberantly, more respectful of the notes and melody.

Jonas's studied gaze wanders over to the other guests and settles on the man and woman sitting next to an antique harp; the instrument is at an angle behind the piano. They appear to be in their late twenties, early thirties. The woman is dressed slightly more casually than the other patrons. They are British—earlier I had walked by the concierge desk and had overheard them inquiring about the afternoon tea hour, adding that they are Londoners. He is dressed in a white short-sleeved shirt and dark pants, he has a narrow face and wide, flat forehead, his small blue eyes following those passing through the foyer. She has short red hair with bangs and is wearing black jeans and high-heeled shoes, a thin gold chain round her left ankle. Her face lights up and she raises her eyebrows in an abstract disbelief whenever Mr. Poldini plays a complicated sequence of chords. She often looks over at her companion with obvious concern—but his demeanor is closed, unreadable. I wonder how Jonas sees them. Maybe he would like to draw the woman, I think, attempt to capture her sense of wonder.

Jonas turns to me; in his eyes I see a look of gratification tinged with irony.

When we go outside to the patio, the maître d', dressed in a dark jacket and pants, approaches us; there is a smoothness in his step, a keen expression in his eyes, a practiced intent to display his confidence, his professionalism. He shows us to a table. As he holds out the chair for me I hear in the distance the lulling sound of lapping waves. There is a very slight breeze, and I draw a light shawl across my shoulders.

After the waiter has taken our order, I ask Jonas if he'd like to sketch the woman who was sitting close to the harp. "No," he says, surprised by my question. Then he smiles. "I would choose to draw the man next to her." Half smiling, he continues, his voice uneasy, "Jenny, there are straightforward people who for the most part are as they appear and there is nothing wrong with that; it actually is refreshing. But there are those who are opposite to what they seem. I never know for certain, but as I sketch, it slowly becomes clear."

He often expresses such thoughts; it is as if he has turned them over in his mind, questioning, then reaffirming his approach. His words reveal his humanness, his humbleness, but there are instances when he is not this way, when he is less accessible; at these moments I am reminded of the haunting image of Caravaggio on the cover of the biography.

I gaze up past a trellis of flowers and see on the closest balcony a woman alone, in her late thirties, wearing a strapless black dress, leaning against the railing, her arms outstretched, her head back, her hair falling long past her shoulders, looking quite comfortable; I wonder if she comes to this hotel every August, and if so had she met or passed Eric in the foyer or walking along the beach. My mind wanders to the postcard he sent twelve years ago. When I discovered it in June, I only glanced at his words. They seemed devoid of any particular meaning, hastily written; perhaps he had felt obliged to send me a note. I was more intrigued by the photo of the hotel on the front of the card. By deciding to come here I may have been hoping to unlock the mystery of Eric in some way, what he refrained from telling me, what I never asked. I believe he was last at this hotel four or more years ago; yet the environment appears as uncomplicated as a person my husband would not be compelled to sketch or paint.

The scraping of chairs disrupts my thoughts. I look across the table but Jonas does not return my gaze; he is absorbed in watching whatever is happening at the table behind me. I hear voices, an argument. A younger woman speaks assertively and then I hear an older woman's voice, hoarse and raspy, her words slurred and loud. Two men respond in cajoling voices as if attempting to calm her. I cannot tell if they are all speaking in French or Italian; they may be going back and forth between the languages.

"Jonas," I say in a low voice. "What is it?" He doesn't respond; his expression is brooding. His comprehension of spoken French is better than mine.

"I am not certain, Jenny."

My curiosity aroused, I turn round swiftly, pretending to look for the waiter, and catch sight of the French family I noticed on the beach the day we arrived—the child is not at the table, but there is an older man, and a woman, perhaps in her late fifties. The older woman's presence is harsh but familiar. I shiver and turn to Jonas.

The waiter moves toward us with grace, yet a concerned expression crosses his face. He places our meals before us. Jonas smiles sheepishly, our gazes lock, and he shrugs his shoulders. And I forget about the party behind us until I hear a loud scream, then a shuffling of feet. Now silence. Jonas leans forward and tells me the two men have escorted the older woman away; they have gone up the path behind me. When I turn round and look, I only see the brick walk and velvet green bushes.

After dinner, instead of going inside the lobby to listen to the pianist, we return to our room and sit out on the balcony. From the patio below, we hear the clatter of plates and the sound of the waves, rushing now, and faint piano music issuing from the grand lobby and through the open doors.

I again ask Jonas about the French family, whether he understood what had happened. He is staring straight out at the sea, his profile straight; yet he sits sideways as if evading any anguish he may feel. Not looking at me, he says calmly, rationally, "The older woman was obviously drunk. She was criticizing Helen, the French woman I met on the beach, telling her she had gained weight, that she was not careful enough with her child, that she should not have left him with a babysitter she did not know. When Helen tried to explain, the woman screamed, drowning out Helen's words. Then Helen's husband and the older man escorted her away."

The lights from below half cover his face, causing him to look sterner on one hand and more mellow on the other. Is he thinking of what occurred between Helen and the older woman, or is he pondering how his life would have been different if he had known his father, if he hadn't died from an illness before being deployed to Europe during the Second World War and Jonas's birth, or is he wondering about my marriage to Eric—which I know is a mystery to him? Though he doesn't readily admit it, he can't quite fathom how the young eighteen-year-old Jenny he had known and had regarded as independent-minded could have married the much older and enigmatic Eric Stram.

"Can you hear the music, Jonas?" I ask.

He smiles and says, "Barely. I do not know what he is playing, not even the style—jazz, classical?"

"Yes," I say, "like something you want to know about a person but can't quite determine."

We sit in silence, the moon a thin crescent in the dark sky, surrounded by a multitude of stars.

We soon go to bed. As if lost in a heavy fog, we make love, groping, then surprised by the hardness of each other's body. Jonas, it seems, is not quite real, more like a shadow with a solid form.

With a start I awake from a horrid dream, the details of it slipping away. Shaken, I strain to recall, but displacing it is the image of the woman with a stain on her lap and the man walking briskly away.

I get up, push aside the long drapes and go out onto the balcony, looking out at the flags in the courtyard, slightly furling from a breeze, then at the Mediterranean, and lastly at the pool below, only partially visible. From the bedroom I hear Jonas's slow and even breathing.

It is quite beautiful, the sky, a pink-gray color. Dawn is beginning to break, and I hear the quiet, morning cries of the gulls. Leaning over the railing, I spot two folded white towels on the bench close to the pool. The sound of a swimmer treading water is nearly inaudible. A tall distinguished man in a white robe walks by the pool. He must be in his seventies but his step appears younger, energetic. Soon he holds out a towel and wraps it around a woman, a woman of average height, strong, robust. I cannot see her face. But now they are out of my view. It strikes me that they may be the couple who was with the French woman, Helen, and her husband last night.

As I step back into the bedroom, I spot my tote bag on a chair, the gold buckle picking up the light from the rising sun. I grasp the bag; my hand reaches inside the front pouch and I pull out Eric's postcard. I sit down and click on the lamp next to the chair and for the first time I read the message closely.

Greetings from the Riviera, Jenny. It is my first time at this hotel, but expect to be coming more often for business meetings. Met a couple who live in New York and are vacationing here—very nice people. Hope you are enjoying your summer.

Cheers, Eric

A chill runs through me. I look up past the raised foot of the bed and see Jonas stirring in his sleep; he reaches out, expecting to touch me, but his arm falls flat onto the mattress. Does he realize I am absent?

Out on the patio we eat breakfast; the weather is changing, the sky streaked with a dull light trickling through a gray mist. After we finish our meal, Jonas and I walk toward the center of town. By the time we reach the main street, the sun has fully disappeared behind the clouds. Inside the tourist office, we recognize the British couple we noticed last night in the grand lobby; they are inquiring about other beaches in the area. Once they leave, Jonas leans over the counter and asks for directions to an old castle that is now an art museum; he read about the collection a few weeks ago.

On the street again, a raindrop falls on my arm. Seeing again Eric's handwriting on the postcard has left me uneasy and restless; I tell Jonas I will look about town while he is at the museum. We agree to meet in two hours at the café on the corner across from the tourist office.

I wander in and out of a few shops, one with a large assortment of cheeses, and two with women's clothing. Outside, I look up at the sky; the clouds are heavier and darker now, rain is imminent. I go into a bookstore nearby, choose a novel, an English translation of *Le blé en herbe* by Colette, and then walk to where Jonas and I have planned to meet.

Stepping inside the café, I hear a distant rumble of thunder. I find a seat away from the door. Avoiding the steady gaze of the proprietress who has come to my table, I order an espresso. Then I begin to read the book, the translation is crisp and evocative.

Soon she again approaches my table, her expression both sensitive and commanding. Her white straight skirt and sleeveless top with a scooped neckline reveal her narrow form and accentuate her deep brown tan. With an elegant turn of her wrist she places the cup of espresso on the table. When I look up to thank her, I notice an older man sitting at a table a few feet from mine. I study him carefully and realize he is the man from the pool this morning. He sits facing at an angle away from me. He appears sad, his posture no longer erect, seeming not as confident as he had earlier. He picks up his cup as if moving in slow motion, takes a few exacting sips before placing it down. The beige pants and light blue short-sleeved shirt he is dressed in are well pressed. His white-gray hair is pushed back from his face, emphasizing his high forehead. The proprietress sits across from him and rests her hands on the table. They speak in Italian and I only can pick up a few words. They do not look at each other as they converse; instead they gaze in the direction of the wide entranceway as if waiting for someone to come in.

Within minutes other customers enter. The proprietress goes over to them and in a prompt yet graceful manner takes their orders. When the four or five people have been served, she returns and sits with the man from the hotel. Again they do not look at each other when they speak. But now they converse in English instead of Italian. I am surprised at how fluent they are, and wonder if they lived in an English-speaking country for a period of time. My guess is they do not want to be overheard by the other customers.

They appear more relaxed now that they are speaking in English, though as fluent as they are, it is apparent that it is not their native language. Their voices are low and I can only pick up certain words, enough to recognize the language they are speaking, but not enough to follow the content of their conversation.

They might be married to each other. Then I think uneasily of the other woman at the table last night, who I believe was with him at the pool this morning.

After some time has passed, I take a pause from reading and look up. The man from the hotel is no longer in the café and the other customers have left. The proprietress and I are alone. There is a stillness, a sense of an impending rainstorm.

She comes to my table and asks, her tone sounding preoccupied, if there is anything else I'd like. I answer in English, and she seems surprised. She has forgotten I ordered in a stumbling Italian, that her language was not mine. A startled expression crosses her face, and she frowns. I realize she may be wondering if I overheard her conversation.

There is a close, loud rumble of thunder and then a downpour of rain ensues. She turns her head to the window and when she looks back at me, she appears worried.

"It should pass soon," I say.

She nods, but her expression still shows concern. And I am surprised as she does not seem to be a woman who worries about much; her show of confidence when I first entered the shop has evaporated.

"Your English is quite good," I say, to divert her.

She smiles and I ask her to join me; no other customers will come in until the rain subsides. She sits down, her back to the street and the rain.

"Where are you from?" she pointedly asks. "Are you an American?"

"Yes," I say. "Your English is very good," I repeat.

She smiles demurely. Her hair is a brown-red color; though she is slim, she is strong-looking. Her eyes are small, close, inward, her brows are dark and full, her lips remain partially open whether or not she is about to speak.

"Yes," she says, "it is because my former husband and I lived in Philadelphia for a while. He is a businessman and in the early days he began his enterprise there. He knew many people who came to America after the war. He is not from this area of Italy; he is from Trieste."

Disconcerted that she's mentioned Trieste, I pause to regain my composure, reminding myself that Eric stayed at the hotel in this town, that it is not unusual he would have heard of it from other natives of that city, like himself. I sit silently and wait, not wanting to say words that may affect her mood. For I see she is pondering, not knowing whether or not to speak more. I listen to the sound of the heavy rain, look around her shop at the dainty pastries in the glass case, at the small, round white tables scattered about the interior, the chairs with pink-and-black-cushioned seats.

She turns her head to glance out the window again. And as if the steadiness of the rain has given her confidence to speak, she looks over at me, her eyes, unreadable, and says, "Whenever there is a storm and I see flashes of lightning, I am reminded of all the mistakes I have made over the years. My life has been interesting, but has deviated in many ways. I do not know if deviated is the right word. What I mean is not direct—I have been down many avenues." Her narrow wrist flexing as she moves her hand forward in a meandering way.

She tells me her life on the Riviera was not a pleasant one. "The war," she adds with a detached resignation. She leans in closer and says the man she was talking to over there—she points to the table as if it is significant in some way—was her husband and is no longer. "He fell in love with someone else after we had been married for many years. Although the affair happened much later, I believe it was because of the war. Like him, she was born in Trieste but grew up in America. But he is a good man and we are still close. I am free now, sad but free. And I must admit, I was not an angel either during our marriage. We lived in many places all over the world. He was very successful; he partially retired not too long ago. He owns the big hotel on the Mediterranean."

"It is where I am staying," I say.

She nods. "Most people from other countries stay there because it is beautiful."

"It is beautiful inside," I answer. "The view of the Mediterranean is lovely too."

She smiles and I know she is thinking beyond my words; it is as if I am missing something.

"My former husband bought this café for me. But I only work the last six weeks of summer. I hire others to take care of the shop while I am away. I stay mostly in Paris, where I have an apartment. But I like to travel to other places too. Although I am away most of the year, this café is what keeps me connected to the life and people I knew when I was young. During the weeks I am at the café, my former husband will come every morning for a cappuccino; we talk, sometimes about our past life together, but today we spoke of the present. We will always be connected in one way or another. We spent too many years together as a couple, experienced much pain and much joy. That was until the woman came into our lives. She was staying at the hotel. She knew he was a very wealthy man, owned the hotel. She was married; it was twelve years ago when she and her husband first came. Her name is Isa; as I said, she was originally from Trieste, but lived in the United States since she was a young girl, before the war—that is where she met her first husband. He was Dutch, but had moved to the United States with his family when he was thirteen or so. When they came to stay at the hotel, I immediately liked him much better than her. He was reserved but kind and she was friendly, spontaneous, restive. I'd stay at the hotel with my husband whenever he hosted a business meeting. Naturally I'd have impressions of the guests, sometimes strong ones."

"Do you remember his name?" I ask, sounding more abrupt than questioning.

"Whose name?" she asks.

"The woman you spoke of, Isa, her first husband."

Appearing compelled by the insistence in my voice, she answers promptly. "Yes, of course. It is Hans. Hans Sokolov."

FOUR

THE SOKOLOVS

My heart beats rapidly; it was Isa Sokolov who created a scene at the restaurant last night and who I spotted by the pool this morning.

The proprietress's deep-set eyes, sharp and inquisitive, meet my gaze. "Do you know him?" she asks; the lone pearl on her gold chain necklace rises and falls with her breaths.

A week after the July Fourth holiday, ten days before I would meet Isa Sokolov, Eric and I drove to an antique show in Westchester. It was a warm day, the trees were close, the leaves on the oaks a bright green color, the sky faint blue and cloudless. In five days Eric would be attending a meeting in Chicago and in three weeks he would leave for a business trip on the Riviera. Adjusting my hands on the steering wheel, my eyes on the road ahead, I asked about joining him on his upcoming trip to Italy. Then I looked over, caught his puzzled expression, his eyes squinting. He leaned his head back against the cushion and said, "Jenny, why would you want to go to a meeting or see people who would bore you? It is only business." I felt a stab of anger, and began to withdraw any feelings I might have for him. Once Eric left for the Rivera, I concluded it was a relief I had not traveled with him.

The day after Eric left for Europe, I went to the public library for a few hours. I left through the main entrance; walking down the front steps I noticed Hans Sokolov on the sidewalk below. The afternoon heat was intense. His shirt sleeves were rolled up; he was pacing back and forth, from the bottom of the steps to the street corner, dragging the toe of his right foot every time he turned round. His forehead was flat, his nose narrow at the top, broadening at the tip, his cheekbones high and broad, his physique was lean and austere. He reminded me of one of Rodin's sculpted Burghers of Calais. I had been struck by the statue when I had seen it at the Rodin Museum in Paris the previous April.

As I moved toward him, he stopped pacing; placing his hands on his slim hips, he looked over at me, not showing any sign of recognition. I observed again how narrow his fingers were and I thought of Isa and meeting him at the café. I was still bothered by the experience. And although Eric had said he had met Hans and Isa at a hotel on the Riviera about five years before and had run into them a few times since we moved to New York, I concluded after questioning Eric further that he did not know much about them and had been only speaking in that generalized provocative way of his, hinting at things that might not have occurred.

Meeting Isa under the store awning that day was pure coincidence and perhaps she had not recognized my last name, Stram; she might not have remembered Eric. But despite my rationalizations I was unsure. My uncertainty led me to feel on edge; I had hoped to keep the encounter from my mind, especially while Eric was away. Recognizing Hans caused my unease to return, for he was a reminder of how much the episode with Isa Sokolov had disturbed me. Eric's remembering their names without truly knowing the couple had made my brief interaction with them seem more disorienting.

Hans stopped pacing and again looked up the steps of the library, his forehead moist from the heat. In his expression there was a hint of expectancy, his eyebrows slightly raised. Passing him, I studied his profile; it was enhanced by his white-blond hair that he wore longer than most men of his age. His tan had deepened since I had met him ten days before. Raising his hand, he pressed one finger to the side of his face, more in a reserved anticipation than contemplation.

Soon his eyes mildly lit up, like a thirsty child given water rather than the preferred soda to drink. I followed his gaze to see who he had noticed. A rush of people were coming down the steps, but soon approaching him was a man in his early twenties, nearly his height, who appeared as if he might be a younger relation of his. They eyed each other, nodded, not quite in unison, and then began to stroll in the direction of the café where I had met Isa.

Walking in the same direction toward my apartment, I kept a short distance away but was close enough to get a sense of their interaction. At first they did not speak. But after five minutes or so, they began to talk in an intense way. I could not hear their words and did not know if they were in enthusiastic agreement or were having a discussion that would lead to an argument. As I drew closer, I gleaned that they were not in accord with whatever they were discussing. There was a mild tension between them. Walking almost in step, both of them would smile ironically from time to time.

Then I heard a sudden loud screech of brakes. Diverted, I lost sight of Hans Sokolov and his companion and began to walk quickly. At the intersection there was a crowd of people clustered together, and I overheard a man with white hair and wire-rimmed sunglasses mention that either a woman had fainted or had been hit by a car. He pointed toward the street. Following the gazes of the other pedestrians, I soon spotted a woman lying prone on the street, a semicircle of onlookers close by.

Hans materialized from nowhere, it seemed; he went over to the woman and crouched next to her, expertly lifting her head onto his lap. With one hand he motioned for the gathered crowd to back away. The man who I thought might be a relative of Hans stood off to the side. Making my way through the crowd, I approached and asked him if he knew what had happened. He didn't take his gaze from Hans, and without looking at me, he pointed to Hans and the woman. He watched closely as Hans administered to her.

When the scene became less frenetic, I caught his attention again and asked if he knew the man who was caring for her.

"It is my father," he said, this time glancing back at me. He shyly caught my gaze.

"He is a doctor?" I asked.

"Yes," he said curtly and turned his gaze back to Hans. I walked away from him but waited until the emergency team arrived and the woman was safely lifted onto the ambulance.

Three days later, walking into the café where I had met Isa, I noticed Hans and his son sitting at a table close to the counter. After Eric had left for the Riviera, I would go once a day to the café, in the late afternoon or early evening; it was relatively close to my apartment. I was not concerned about running into Isa; my intuition was that she would not be there, and if I was wrong, given our last interaction, I was convinced she would ignore me.

I thought Hans's son might be a college student, and assumed he was about twenty years old. I had looked in the telephone book to see what type of doctor Hans was and discovered he had a neurology practice on Park Avenue.

Some time over that summer I had gone to see Jonas at the gallery where he had worked as a portrait artist. Before then, ever since Eric and I had moved to New York, I had seen Jonas four or five times. That day he had appeared more preoccupied with his work than usual; in addition to painting portraits of clients, he was attempting to create his own style of art, which he spoke of at length. Though I believed he was still fond of me, he was more reserved because I had married Eric. I understood it was not possible for Jonas to comprehend my reasons for choosing to do so.

The relentless heat that summer seemed to hover over us, and because of it, the confinement of it, I became more and more intrigued by Hans and his son; they were my sole means of escape. New York was barren, especially during those late weeks of the season. Everything appeared still, my friends were vacationing, and my parents were in Trieste. Though there were tourists, on the whole, the city as it often is during this time of the year was more subdued than usual.

There was no evidence of Isa and that had relaxed me, given me confidence in my ability to assess people. For after a week had passed, I was certain she would not make an appearance—not only because she had not done so, but because her husband and son did not appear to be expecting anyone, and seemed to exist in a private world that only encompassed the two of them.

When Eric returned at the end of the third week of August, he appeared tense. He expressed his anxiety not in an overt way but by withdrawing from any in-depth conversation. He was never unpleasant, just quiet and noncommunicative. This tendency of his would always alarm me; I would be fearful of him surprising me with unpleasant news. But whenever I'd catch a glimpse of myself in a mirror, I'd look calm, unruffled, and, for the most part determined. So I imagine he had no idea how much stress I was feeling about his mood. If I had been older and our relationship had been more of a mature one, I would have spoken directly to him about it.

The evening after his return we went out to dinner. Eric made a reservation at a restaurant neither of us had been to before, and he appeared more at ease. I felt reassured, though my intention that evening had been to speak with him about our marriage, how I thought the age difference between us was becoming more and more of a strain. It had dawned on me that the precocious attitude I had possessed while I was in college and when I married him at twenty had been factitious. Though I had no proof, I was convinced that Eric had affairs and thought nothing of it. Only fleetingly did it cross my mind that he wanted me to believe this about him, that it might have been an attempt on his part to control me.

At dinner that night he was more attentive than usual, and so I suppressed any thoughts I had of leaving him. I believed he understood I was dissatisfied with our marriage. Until then remaining silent had been my way of asserting myself with him.

He comported himself with his usual easy dignity but, closely studying him as he spoke about a bicycle trip he had taken along the Mediterranean coast, I saw that his blue-gray eyes were more dull than shiny. He had been traveling more than usual at the time and although he was only forty-three, I wondered if it was beginning to take a toll on him. Eric ordered champagne and lobster, attempting to do so as always with a subdued flourish. But he appeared uneasy and sounded halfhearted. When he began to eat, I noticed that although he never had had a large appetite, he ate sparingly while encouraging me to enjoy the meal. My heart beat rapidly; I wondered what he planned to reveal. I attributed his lack of appetite not only to a general fatigue but also to an uncertainty in what he was about to say. For the first time it struck me I held some degree of power over him; I was surprised, though more cautious than emboldened.

He lowered his head, his voice sounded weak, no longer even and provocative. What did I think, he asked, of his living in Europe for a few months? He would be back by late November. I looked directly at him and he avoided my gaze. I understood that he had no intention of asking me to accompany him.

It is because of your work, I responded, attempting to sound nonchalant, sensible. He nodded slowly. Then he clarified, saying it mostly had to do with a specific business deal.

I was torn within. I had not wanted to entirely give up on our marriage, though at times I had acknowledged that I needed to leave him. Yet whenever I had attempted to do so, I had been uncertain, frozen. I half hoped the upcoming break would keep the marriage going, but I realized there was a greater chance this imminent separation could very well be the beginning of the end of it.

"Smile, Jenny," he said in his old way, gliding his head forward; the light from the candle on the table flickering, his blue-gray eyes smoky, "and do finish your lobster—succulent, isn't it?"

The restaurant was on Fifty-Fourth Street, walking distance from our apartment. On our way home, Eric attempted to hold my hand but I avoided his touch. I heard the approaching sound of a police car siren, but did not turn to look as had Eric and the other pedestrians.

When we married three years before, I had been mistakenly convinced that I was the most mature, and that my parents, Eric, and his family, because of the pain they had suffered during the war, which still lingered, existed in a purgatory of sorts that had stunted their growth.

Needless to say I did not interfere with Eric's plan to live in Italy through November, though I imagined it would be longer, as life with him was that way, everything took more time than expected. It was as if part of him was moving through life in slow motion and the other part was active and rushed. It was confusing for me and in a way it was much easier to live a relatively calm life without him.

Eric left on the twenty-sixth of August—he had been home for four days. He seemed more confident during the drive to the airport. He was dressed in a navy blue sports jacket, which brought out the blue in his eyes, the gray more diminished, and a light blue shirt. He seemed completely at ease and assured, the heat not affecting him.

Before he left the car, he leaned over and pressed his lips against each of my cheeks. Smiling, he said, "Take care of yourself, Jenny, do take that course in journalism. It might be a good career for you." But I believed he did not know me well enough to understand what might suit me. Because his life had not been easy, harsh you might say, he invariably attempted to overcome it by viewing people in a superficial way, even those closest to him.

I did not wait to watch the plane take off. Instead I drove back to the apartment building, parked the car in the reserved spot, and then went directly to the café, hoping to see either Hans or his son, just for a sense of solace. For that is what they gave to me—they comforted me without knowing me, the reality of them, that was.

Hans was there, sitting alone, reading a newspaper. He didn't seem to be waiting for anyone. As he riffled through the pages, he appeared concerned, yet his crossed legs and relaxed shoulders conveyed a sense of lethargy. The temperature was not as high as it had been when I had driven Eric to the airport. But his shirtsleeves were rolled up as usual.

It was as if a year had passed since Isa had introduced me to Hans Sokolov. Other than the exotic shape of her eyes, I only vaguely recalled her other features and overall physical appearance; it was her personality that was unnerving, open and perhaps deceptive. I assumed her husband and son were different.

Hans folded the newspaper and got up from his seat. He didn't look around. On his way out, he passed my table and our gazes met; he did not show any sign of recognition. Our introduction had been brief and he and Isa had been so eager to be rid of me he probably had not registered it. He had seemed more preoccupied with Isa, hovering over her, not wanting to be distracted by my presence.

After he left, I lowered my head and opened the book to the page I'd left off reading. I became absorbed by the novel and was unaware of what was happening around me. Soon I heard someone clearing his throat. I looked up and met the earnest gaze of Hans's son.

"Do you mind—there are no other seats available," he said. I nodded.

I resumed reading my book, and he opened his as well. Whenever I glanced up I noticed a slight roundness in his face, a sheen to his skin, an intensity in his blue eyes as he studied the text, then wrote notes; I was convinced I was older than him.

I do not remember which one of us got up to leave first, or at what point he told me his name was Caleb Sokolov, and I do not recall how it came about but by the time I left the café, we had agreed to meet in Central Park the following afternoon.

Before I left my apartment the next day, I reached for the doorknob and noticed the wedding ring on my finger. I stared at it, the late August light flowing in from the window picking up the faint yellow color of the diamond and accompanying rubies. Reflexively, I took it off, uncertain whether or not Caleb had noticed it the previous day.

There were not as many people as usual in Central Park that afternoon. I spotted Caleb before he noticed me. Smoking a cigarette, he appeared uneasy, his body erect as if bracing himself for rejection, perhaps thinking I might not show up. Once he recognized me, he threw down his cigarette, crushing it with his foot.

We walked past the entrance to the zoo. Caleb explained to me that in his last year of high school he had been accepted into an accelerated six-year program that included college and medical training, and I was reminded of how I had accelerated my college classes so I could marry Eric at twenty. Caleb was twenty-two, six months younger than I was. I wondered if he had felt as precocious when he had made the decision at eighteen to become a medical doctor as I had in committing to Eric at that age.

Three days later, we went to a movie. Walking toward the cinema, I was energized; it was as if I had been released from a personal prison. I had still neglected to put on my wedding ring, and since Caleb had not asked about it, I assumed he had not noticed it that day at the café.

When we met in front of the theater, Caleb appeared subdued from the heat. It was the thirtieth of August. The air-conditioning inside the cinema was not effective. While we watched the movie, Caleb reached for my hand, his grasp was an anxious one. Though as he gazed at the movie screen, his demeanor revealed confidence. The movie, a French comedy with English subtitles, was one I had suggested. I thought it would be less provocative than a serious drama or a romantic film.

From time to time Eric would come to mind; I'd wonder where he was. It would have been two in the morning in Europe. Was he walking along the beach, or drinking at a café bar? Randomly I thought how people on the Riviera tend to stay up late, as New Yorkers do, especially on the Italian side; the French towns, unlike Paris, close down earlier.

Caleb sensed my attention was wandering; he lowered his head and asked if I liked the movie, I had withdrawn my hand from his. I nodded and focused again on the film.

Later as we walked in the direction of our apartments, I told him I had enjoyed the movie, even though I had not been in the mood to see a comedy.

"But you were the one who chose it," he said, smiling.

Then he gingerly asked if something was bothering me. My heart beating frantically, I explained that I was married, that my husband was much older than I was, that I had married him when I was twenty. It had been a mistake to do so, and that I longed to leave the marriage. I told Caleb that meeting him in Central Park and going to the movie with him had been my first steps in doing so. I said I was unsure and certain, both at the same time.

He smiled, but I sensed his disappointment. He paused, then seemed to collect himself, and said that he was patient; that it would be up to me to decide if we were to see each other again, that he was busy with medical school and that he might be in Europe for a while—his father was arranging for him to do an exchange program in Amsterdam for six months.

We stopped for burgers at an all-night diner. The lights were bright and soon we became animated. To an extent, having told him I was married had freed us.

We discussed the movie and we laughed together over certain scenes, but soon there was agitation in our laughter. Caleb's face was red, almost feverish, and my cheeks were burning.

Caleb spoke warmly of his father, and said, as if it were an afterthought, that his mother was in Italy.

We left the diner at three in the morning. More content now, I was wrapped in feelings of stability and happiness and I did not want the mood between us to change. I was elevated; we had bonded, unexpectedly.

What I recall most about our affair were those long afternoons we spent in the apartment while Eric was away, how the late summer sun, then turning to golden autumn light, flowed through the curtains, resting on Caleb's arms and waist. How young he seemed, and how inexperienced he was, but that was what I had relished most about him. He'd stay with me all night—the following day he'd go either to school or the hospital, and return in the evening. He would not mention our relationship to his father, he had said emphatically—he valued privacy.

One morning, at the end of October, the telephone rang; I was still in bed and Caleb was in the shower. It was Eric. His voice sounded distant and somber; he said that he had to go to a meeting in a few minutes and was checking to see if I was well—he'd had a dream about me the night before. I assured him I was fine, and ended the call before Caleb came into the room. When he did, he sat close, the palms of his hands pressing the mattress on either side of me; he said he would be free most of the day. I met his gaze, his eyes were the same exotic almond-shape as Isa's, yet the color was like his father's, a Chagall blue. It struck me that in a month he would be in Europe and Eric would be home.

I stroked Caleb's arm and told him last July a woman had introduced herself as Isa Sokolov; we'd been standing under the awning of a clothing store in the midst of a rainstorm. He did not respond; he studied me as I described our encounter that day and that I had met her again the following Saturday at the café. As I spoke, his eyes never left mine, his hands still on the bed; he remained silent. When I finished speaking, he stood up, lifted the covers and got into bed. It was the only time during our affair he'd been indifferent.

Caleb left at the end of the third week of November, five days before Eric returned. From time to time, he would send me postcards from Amsterdam, signing them with only his initials. We had not made plans to reconnect. Before parting, Caleb and I had met at the café. It was as cold as winter, and the temperature inside the café was low. He grasped my bare hands to warm them, then lowered his gaze and said I needed to make a decision about my marriage. His voice was insistent and firm. And when, after a few months, I did not write to him to say I had decided to divorce Eric, the postcards stopped coming.

My marriage to Eric continued in its off-balance way. I had a miscarriage in late January, and when I went to the doctor for a follow-up appointment, he told me the pregnancy had been more advanced than he had first thought, three months instead of two. Over dinner that evening, I brazenly told Eric what the doctor had said. He simply shrugged and said, "Medicine is sometimes less accurate than we think." Then later, in silence, we sipped wine in the living room. As we rose to go to bed, Eric began to switch off the lights. He voice low, his face completely in shadow, he said, "Despite what you think, Jenny, I have never been unfaithful to you."

"Do you know him?" The proprietress asks again, more firmly the second time.

My tone cautious, my eyes avoiding hers, I say, "I have heard of Hans Sokolov; he may have been a distant acquaintance of my former husband. He is a doctor, I believe."

I look up, then out the window; it is no longer raining. Within moments Jonas walks into the shop, his hair wet; following him is the proprietress's former husband. And I recall the man wearing charcoal-colored pants walking swiftly past me and the woman sitting in a chair with a red stain on her lap.

FIVE

THE MEMORY

The memory startles, as if you've been doused with an out-pouring of water from a sudden rainstorm. Parts are blurry, extended moments completely flooded, too murky to discern. Yet fragments of it are enlarged and clear, revealing images not visible at first.

The recollection comes when least expected, first on a rainy night driving north, passing an accident, then several days later as your gaze fell on the small wooden statue of a Native American woman you purchased soon after your marriage, the first one. You picked it up, held it to the light, but the memory was lost. Have there been suggestions of this incident in the past that were as innocuous as the gentle recollections of your time in Hartford, memories that did not alarm or confuse, that were accepted as part of your childhood, that were not extraordinary?

You close your eyes and try to think back not only to recall the details of the day, but to exist in the time and season. Were there many in the apartment or just a few? Where was the man coming from when he abruptly walked past you? Had he evoked an aura of smothering heat? There were not many rooms in the apartment. Was he older, middle-aged, or younger?

You close your eyes more tightly, hoping to push past the images, to be there. Why were you, a child, dispassionate? Why did you believe this occurrence would always stay with you? Have there been inklings of this memory over the years, suggestions of it, luring you to recall? Have you refused to do so?

Have you focused on your present life alone, not allowing the past to envelop you? Years ago, needing to accept your parents, how different they were, and then your marriage to a man you felt obliged to accept. Had you so much to cope with? Has your marriage to Jonas freed you to recall a painful memory? Is it real or just a compilation of recollections—perhaps not all occurring on the same day?

Yet you deeply believe it happened in the first Hartford apartment, the fragments of it you recall—standing on a rug in the living room, the woman sitting in a chair against the wall, her legs spread open as a man would sit. Your vision of the memory expands—in the corner diagonally across from you, perched on a dusty table, was the small black-and-white television set—but instantaneously your recollection contracts. Where was your mother? Your father? Were you the lone child in the room?

Your frustration grows; something stops you from reliving it, from recalling more. You feel it in the present but can only view it, ponder it from the distance of your current life, only in the past tense.

Such thoughts run through your mind in a matter of seconds.

SIX

THE CARINIS

The memory, the impression it creates, vanishes. Fully in the present, I press my hands to the table and get up to leave; the proprietress watches me closely. Gently, in the manner of a maternal aunt, she touches my wrist, tells me her name is Mara. "Please come again," she says, her head slightly to the side, a flash of anxiety in her eyes. Then she stands; crossing her arms, she nods in the direction of her former husband who, at the counter, impatiently taps his finger against the glass case covering an array of delicate pastries. She leans toward me and I pick up the scent of Chanel. In an emphatic whisper, she says, "I must go to Roberto—Roberto Carini, he likes to say, " her inflection a blend of pride and irony.

Jonas, approaching, meets my gaze, then lowers his eyes. I sense he is uneasy. Walking with him to the doorway, I steal a glance at Mara and Roberto. In the presence of her former husband she exudes a combination of the relaxed attitude of people who reside on the Riviera as well as an inherent practicality. Roberto is animated, his cheeks flushed. Hastily he eyes me then looks away. He and Mara speak rapidly in Italian; he is giving her news of some sort. His eyes are hawk-like; hers are fixed on his. Though not touching, their bodies, his more forceful like a bird of prey and hers as deft as a sparrow, are distinctly synchronous.

After the rain, in the emerging sunlight, the pavement glistens. As we walk back to the hotel, Jonas is quiet, meditative, his steps languorous, his lips pursed.

Roberto Carini—there is a sound of familiarity to the name, but too vague, a strain to recall; soon I no longer try. Jonas, pensive, but with an edge to his words, tells me about his time at the museum, the art he finds interesting, especially a Klimt he'd not been familiar with. He is surprised that this small town holds an extensive collection. Then before we reach the incline to the hotel, he stops walking; he turns to me, rests his hands warmly, steadily on each of my arms. With a forced clarity, he says that the man at the café, the one standing at the counter, had asked as they were going into the shop if his family name was Stram. "How did you answer?" I reflexively ask. He shrugs, replying that he simply ignored the question, pretended he did not hear it. I tell Jonas I find it odd, that maybe someone recognized me. I add that the person who made a scene at the restaurant last night may have been a woman named Isa Sokolov, whom I had met very briefly in New York. I thought she had seemed familiar.

"Have you been to this town before?" he asks.

"No. I have been to the Riviera a few times, but not here."

Jonas studies me, his expression intensely curious. Then suddenly he smiles broadly, with no trace of irony. "You expect a certain amount of anonymity in a small town in another country," he pointedly says as we walk up the incline to the hotel. The sun, now very strong, beats down on us; with each step I feel more and more disoriented, not knowing whether or not to tell him about the other Sokolovs, Hans and Caleb, or about the postcard.

A few days pass before I recall Roberto Carini. Jonas and I are tasting hors d'oeuvres and drinking wine in the lobby. No one else has come down yet this evening. When we speak, there is a slight echo. Though shadows cross the sofas and tables, the sun will not set for a while.

Because of the heat over these past few days, Jonas has put aside sketching. Mostly we have spent our time lounging by the sea beneath an umbrella. The Sokolovs seem distant now, as undefinable as figures in the background of an impressionist painting. As Jonas takes a sip of wine, I notice how his deep tan affirms both his earnestness and his mild sense of irony.

A clacking sound—high heels over marble—deflects my attention. I look up toward the reception desk and recognize the woman I noticed standing alone on the balcony the night of the disturbance at the restaurant. She walks hurriedly toward the exit. She appears to be older than I first thought, maybe in her mid- to late forties, and is quite thin. Her movements suggest she may be late for an engagement. The off-the-shoulder turquoise dress she wears, a straight cut, falls just past her knees. Johanna, my mother, is much more physically solid than this woman, yet is invariably rushing off in a frenzied manner. I recall the turquoise-and-brown dress she hastily stitched for me on her new sewing machine for my thirteenth birthday. Then coming to mind is the turquoise dress she purchased for an occasion she and my father attended in New York. I was sixteen years old and though I did not attend the event, I had driven into the city with them.

But what preceded the trip to New York is what I recall; connecting it to our time spent in the city is like piecing together a mosaic. Though my memory—flashes of various conversations at the time—may not be exact, I am able to imagine from both my recollection of how I would converse with my parents at that age and the information I have learned since coming to the Riviera, what could have occurred, what might have been said.

It would have begun on an afternoon in late fall. Upon catching sight of the invitation I would have been drawn to the swirling dark letters forming the name on the return address: Roberto Carini. Having just returned home from school, I would have noticed the card on the shelf next to the front door. I would have been encouraged—my parents rarely received an invitation. As I picked up the card, I would have felt a deep sense of anticipation, and would have pensively traced the letters of his name with my finger. Delighted for my parents—since their move to Massachusetts they had regarded themselves as outsiders and were rarely invited to an event—I also would have been anxious that they might not attend. I would have felt my mother's presence as she stood behind me looking over my shoulder, a large shadow covering me, protective and at the same time creating a chill.

"I did not know you were home," she said, easily extracting the card from my hand. She wore a brown-and-gray plaid poncho; the fringe on the wide hem grazing my arm as she loosened the invitation from my grasp.

"It's an invitation," I said evenly, meeting her gaze.

She looked deep into my eyes and said, her voice edgy, "Jenny, darling, some invitations are hopeful and social, and I know you want this for your father and me, but this one is not a happy one for us; we will go because you might say we are obliged to attend."

"But you haven't opened it," I insisted, feeling discouraged.

"I don't need to open it, Jenny; it is because of who it is from. He is a rich and impervious entrepreneur from Trieste who has lived for some years in America," she said, placing the invitation back on the shelf. "Attending his event will be a reminder of sad days."

"You don't have to go," I answered, deeply disappointed.

"That is not true, Jenny," she said, opening the door.

I watched as she walked down the front steps, a breeze ruffling her poncho, the outline of her shoulders appearing more erect than usual, her movements more stiff.

Once she had driven away, I picked up the card and went to the large front window; holding the invitation up to the fading afternoon light, I pressed it against the cool glass. Slowly a smattering of words became evident. What I determined was that the event would be the first Saturday in January. It would be in New York but I could not make out the name of the hotel. After moving the envelope farther up against the glass, I understood that the event had to do with an opening of an office in Manhattan.

At dinner that night, hearing determination in my voice, I asked my mother if she had read the invitation. My father did not respond; he had always been slow to react as well as adept at hiding his thoughts.

Rising from her seat to go into the kitchen, she said, "I don't need to. I know when and where it is."

"You know everything about it?" I asked, my curiosity piqued.

She nodded, and then I lost sight of her.

"Is Roberto Carini from Trieste?" I called out to her, then looked steadily at my father.

"We only know people from there," he answered with unabashed frankness.

"Roberto Carini is from Trieste," my mother said, coming through the doorway, carrying a large bowl of salad. She tossed back her head and said, "His wife, I believe, is from the Riviera—she had encouraged him to bring the small business he had opened in Italy to the United States." With a sense of finality she placed the bowl on the table. I looked at my parents and noticed how my father gazed down at his salad, his eyeglasses, which he had recently begun to wear on occasion, sliding forward; he intently studied what was before him, his cupped hands resting on the table, on either side of the bowl, as if he were about to attempt an experiment. My mother waited a minute or two before picking up her fork. She looked straight ahead, her posture erect, inhaling and exhaling, her expression softer than usual. Outside the window, it was pitch dark.

What I next recall is accompanying my mother to a shop on Newbury Street to help her choose a dress for the occasion. Impatiently, she tried on each dress the salesman had suggested, then she'd study herself in the three-way mirror, her expression exacting, pensive and highly critical. She intended to look her best but I sensed her uneasiness and doubted she would find the appropriate dress. After an hour or so, she chose a turquoise-colored evening dress that suited her, causing her to look younger. The sleeves of the dress flared at her wrists, and the A-line shape of it softened her form. She was about forty-six at the time. She had studied to become an opera singer and, like most opera singers, the older she became, the less attractive her body; once curvy and voluptuous, it had become dense and strong looking.

When we left the dress shop, she said, "I've done my duty—or I should say almost so." I remember her words and although I was accustomed to my mother's use of language, her syntax, her emphatic and often unexpected way of expressing herself, I was not accustomed to her reining in her nature—she mostly did as she pleased. But this event was different. I was uneasy about it.

About two weeks later, on a warmer than usual day in early December, my mother and I drove into the city to look at the holiday lights on Boston Common. I was slightly melancholic; it struck me that in a few years I would be in college and would not be available to visit the city with her at this time of year. But she was happy that day; she was not frequently cheerful and soon I became caught up in her spirited mood and less guarded about what I said to her. I had always been careful not to use words that would affect my mother's frame of mind. Her mood easily changed and it was pleasant to be with her when she was more optimistic. For she had a dark side to her; she could become brooding, cynical.

After viewing the lights, we stopped to have a cup of tea at a shop across the street. It was growing dark earlier with each passing day. Sitting close to a window framed with silver tinsel, we looked out at the blue-black evening and how the lights shone brightly in contrast, casting a reflection and shadow across my mother's face. She looked content. Her eyes seemed less on guard, more relaxed.

"Who is Roberto Carini?" I asked, eyeing her as I took a sip of tea.

Although she seemed surprised by my question she did not appear suspicious or questioning.

"You are talking about the name on the invitation, aren't you, Jenny dear?"

"Yes, you never do what doesn't please you, and now you feel obligated to go to this event. If you were happy about it I would not be curious; you are uncertain about attending—but you are going."

"It doesn't often happen that you must do something you truly don't want to do," she began. "Usually this occurs only in very sad situations. Yet this event is not in the least meant to be sad."

"Why go, Mother?" I asked, hearing alarm and defiance in my voice.

She leaned forward in her seat and patted my hand with her warm, round one. "Jenny," she said, "Roberto Carini has been good to many people from Trieste. He has helped the community rise and restore itself. And yet he has many sides to him. He is a very successful businessman. In a way it is an honor to have received the invitation. And there will be other people from Trieste at the event; some were very good to us, and so we must go." Her eyes were suddenly melancholic. And I recalled how soon after our move to Massachusetts I had come home early from school and had found her wearing a kimono, haltingly singing what I would later learn is "Vien, diletto, è in ciel la luna," from Bellini's opera *The Puritans*. Crossing her face was the same expression. She now looked out at the darkening evening, her reflection an older and more solemn version of herself. When she turned toward me I saw in her eyes both a sense of pride and one of hurt. I looked down at the table, at the pale pink-and-yellow linen cloth covering it. "Look, Jenny," she said suddenly, her voice hoarse and wistful. "It is snowing."

The only recollections I hold of that weekend are of my mother rendering a detailed and detached description of a woman's dress—perhaps it was Roberto's wife—and my father suggesting we say good-bye to Roberto as we checked out of the hotel. I do not know if they did speak to Roberto that afternoon or whether or not I had been introduced to him. For in memory a curtain has been drawn.

Now I feel Jonas's hand on mine. "Are you okay, Jenny? You seem far away." I nod and study his hopeful eyes and how the lines of his mouth now suggest a subtle irony. Then I reach out and press my finger to his lips, hoping to silence his doubts.

After dinner and a long walk by the sea, we go up into our room. Our bed is covered in a pool of moonlight, beckoning us to submerge ourselves.

The next morning Jonas awakens, sprawled on his back with his arms outstretched. His forehead is hot and moist. A summer flu, I think. He looks at me, he appears pale and weary. Soon he drifts off. Once I am assured he is sleeping I open the sliding glass door and go out onto the balcony.

The day is sunny, with no breeze. But there is a haze in the sky muting the bright light. The ocean is calm and mellow this morning. Below and off to the side I see part of the pool. From what I can determine no one is in it; I do not hear splashing or voices.

I think of my conversation with Mara and long to go back and speak with her, hear more of her story. I wonder what she knows of Hans or maybe even Caleb. Again, the memory of the woman with a red stain on her lap and the man with the charcoal-colored pants comes to mind—I am more distraught by it than before.

While Jonas sleeps I take the elevator down to the outdoor restaurant near the pool for a late breakfast. I see the French family at the table next to mine. The husband picks up the child from his seat, then holds him in his lap and feeds him with his fork. Aware I am sitting not far from her, Helen turns to me. She's wearing a white floppy hat and dark glasses. I cannot see her eyes. "Your husband, is he away?" Her strong French accent is disarming.

"He might have a flu, but I am certain he will be better if not tomorrow, then in the next few days," I say. Reflexively, I ask about the woman at her table, some nights ago, was she not well?

"That is my aunt," she answers and sighs. "Sometimes she is well and sometimes she is not. She is in Tuscany now and will spend the remainder of the summer there. Her husband owns this hotel. They live in a beautiful home down the road," she says, pointing in no particular direction. Her lips are thin; she smiles slightly. “She is my mother’s sister; both were born in Trieste. Their parents separated before the war. My mother went with their mother to France. And my aunt went to America with their father.” She shrugs, and before turning away, she adds, “My father, of course, is French.”

I bring Jonas a cup of hot tea. I sit close to him; he drinks from the cup. He is only able to take a few sips, then drops his head back onto the pillow. Once he is asleep, I go out to the balcony.

But soon, his voice weak, Jonas calls out for me. Leaving the balcony door open, I go back into the room. But I realize he is asleep; he is dreaming. I lean close to him. “Stram,” he says clearly, then he mumbles nonsensical syllables, turning his body slightly to the left and then to the right. His expression is pained. I wait. Soon he is still and sleeping, his demeanor now calm.

Out on the balcony, I hear the sound of the waves, the clattering of the dishes below, the waiters clearing up the breakfast plates and cups. From the bedroom comes Jonas’s breathing, alternately even then staggered. In a lounge chair, I close my eyes and drift off to sleep. In my dream Eric and I are out on a patio, overlooking the sea, but we are not on the Riviera. The environment is not as restful as the Mediterranean. Uncertain where we are, I am uneasy; fearful of the answer, I do not ask him. There is a strong, cool breeze. Maybe it is Bar Harbor in early fall, or south Florida on a cool day in January. Certainly it is the Atlantic Ocean; it is because of the dampness, the harshness of the breaking waves, the chill in the air that I have never felt on the

Mediterranean. Eric wears dark glasses. I lean forward, attempt to read past his shades and into his eyes, hoping to comprehend his mood; I cannot penetrate his thoughts, who he is. I press him with questions and he doesn't respond. The pain caused by his silence is unbearable. When I open my eyes, the Mediterranean is before me, the warm air caressing—I have escaped my dream. Yet I recall the last time I was with Eric. We were driving to the airport. It was a cool day in November, and the air was damp. "You are sick, Eric. You shouldn't be going."

"It's business," he answered.

"You mean the business you help someone else run."

"I can't disappoint him, Jenny."

"If he were as nice as you say, he would understand you are too sick to go to Key West."

He looked over at me and smiled. "You'd like him, I should introduce you."

"It is surprising, Eric, that you have not done so. I don't even know his name, only that you refer to him as Il Capo."

I do not recall what I last said to him, I can't remember him leaving the car. Did we lightly kiss good-bye? I have no recollection of our parting and do not believe I went into the airport with him. What I do remember is parking the car in front of the terminal, and Eric gingerly running his fingers through my hair, and lightly touching my face, my neck as if for the first time. Then he was no longer with me.

Looking out at the Mediterranean and then over to the side, I spot Roberto Carini in his bathing trunks facing the pool, his arms crossed—fourteen years ago my mother and father attended an event hosted by him. I imagine that was where they reconnected with Eric and his parents after some years. People I have not seen since we lived in Hartford will be there, most from Trieste, my mother had said, her eyes sorrowful. Yes, Trieste, where she had studied opera. I think again of that day I had come upon her wearing a white-and-red kimono, her arms extended, her voice hesitant, wistful, as she sang from the score of *The Puritans*.

SEVEN

THE COUSINS

Not until Jonas is fully recovered and sketching with his usual intensity will I realize what should have been obvious. It will dawn on me as if, sitting in a dark theater, I am startled by a flood of lights at the conclusion of the movie. After the effect of sudden illumination subsides, in silence and from within, I experience my vulnerability, my loss, a dimming of insight.

On the beach on a Friday afternoon, I have neglected to bring my dark glasses, and the sun is blinding. A trace of a breeze carries with it the prickly smell of salt and sea. The sand is hot and loose. Next to me is the French woman, Helen. While Jonas was recovering from the flu, in a casual way we became friendly.

A short distance away, Jonas is perched on a small hill of rocks overlooking the Mediterranean; a piece of charcoal in his grasp, he moves his hand across the art pad, a sudden, abbreviated wind ruffles the short sleeves of his T-shirt. At the water's edge, Helen's husband Marc plays with their son Remy. As a wave breaks against the rocky shore, he lifts the boy with his sturdy hands. Above the swirling water, the child moves his feet as if bicycling, the dark wet sand and a scattering of pebbles cling to his feet. Marc seems more of a maternal figure than Helen; though I like her, her directness, her honesty.

The more I speak with Helen, the more I glean how different she is from Isa. Whenever she raises her head from what she's been reading, she'll slide her sunglasses to the end of her nose and I'll note again and again how her eyes are the same shape and dark brown as Isa's, but her forehead is narrower and her chin round instead of pointy like her aunt's. There is a frankness in her gaze unlike the impetuous avoidance I found in her aunt's eyes, as if Isa lacked a center, an identity. But I was younger then and wasn't seeking wholeness.

Now Helen closes the book and leans her head back against her lounge chair, her wide-brimmed hat casting a shadow across the side of her face. She tells me that she and Marc are deciding whether or not to have another child—she is inclined not to, but she isn't certain if she wants Remy not to have a brother or a sister. She doesn't want him to be alone; yet she is still not convinced. "What about you, Jenny? You and Jonas have no children?" With her index finger she pushes up her sunglasses; I no longer see her eyes. She is providing me with a sense of privacy, an option not to respond. She does not open her book. Glancing at the cover, I see it is by the French writer, Céline. With only a vague knowledge of the author and a sparse understanding of French, I translate the title as *Journey to the End of the Night*. She gazes away, in the direction of her son and husband, a breeze flapping up the towel at the foot of her chair.

I explain that Jonas is my second husband, and then briefly describe my uneven marriage to Eric, his death, how he had been most likely swept off or had fallen from a yacht in Key West. He'd had a severe flu and had been taking a good deal of medicine. He was disoriented. I pause, wait for her to absorb what I have told her, then add that I have not yet considered having a child. Jonas and I have discussed it only in passing, in theory, never with intent, I say. I tell her that I miscarried during my first marriage.

Helen lowers her glasses, turns toward me, smiling kindly. "I am sorry about your miscarriage," she responds thoughtfully. She is quiet for a moment, then says, "You are young to have been married twice. It is very sad to hear of your first husband's tragic death. You say you were not compatible; because of this it must have been devastating for you."

There is something in her openness, her warmth, the expression in her discerning gaze, that is familiar. But I recall the eyes as blue, not brown like Helen's, and it now strikes me that she and Caleb are cousins. Startled, I draw away, from my initial perception of her, and study Helen closely. She returns my look as straightforwardly as Caleb would have. Thoughts of Caleb, his earnestness, his quick, strong energy evoke distant memories of pain and joy.

"What is it, Jenny?" Helen asks. "Have I upset you? I should not have spoken to you in a familiar way?"

"No, Helen, not at all. Eric's passing is very tragic and painful, and I think more so, as you say, because we did not get along."

"But you are fortunate to know Jonas. He is, I believe, not superficial and very loyal." She smiles encouragingly.

"Yes, I have known him for a long time, since I was eighteen. He was at first my neighbor, later my friend," I say, feeling a sense of dislocation, and ask her if she has any siblings.

"Yes, two sisters, one older, one younger—you see, I am the middle child. My mother's sister had only one child, and we would visit America once a year and my aunt and her family would come to France once a year. And so we knew our cousin. But he was an only child and I always thought he seemed lonely. Yet you are an only child, didn't you say, Jenny, and so is your husband? Or was it Jonas who told me? You do not seem lonely, nor does your husband, but I guess that is my assumption."

"I have never felt lonely. My mother had two miscarriages, I've been told, one in Trieste and one when she lived in Connecticut. Your mother was born in Trieste too, you said the other day. I wonder if they know of each other."

"So many coincidences," Helen says, appearing puzzled.

"It is not really surprising," I answer. Then I tell her how a few months ago I discovered the postcard my first husband, had sent, with the hotel on the front. "It is not unusual I would meet people from Trieste here; your aunt's husband is from Trieste and so was Eric."

Her voice drops, more sensitive now, and she asks what Eric was like. I feel a sense of panic; I was never certain. "Eric was much older than me—twenty years, in fact—and as I said he too was born in Trieste. His parents helped mine during the war, shielded them as my father was a member of an anti-fascist group. And during all the turbulence of that time, my mother had desperately longed to become an opera singer. Eric was a young boy during the war; naturally it was traumatic for him."

"What was his family name?"

"Stram. I believe they were well known in the city, but came to the United States after the war, returning to Trieste before Eric and I married. I felt obliged to marry him in a way. But it was my decision to do so. I was overwhelmed by him, by the attention he gave me, and I thought I was more mature than I was. I was under an illusion." I hear my voice sounding factual and distant, shielding my emotions which are swirling, muddling my recollections of my marriage to Eric and my affair with Caleb.

"Stram—the name is familiar, but I can't quite place it," she says. I see she is somewhat uneasy.

Her husband is coming up from the shore, their son Remy walking beside him, holding his hand, tugging at it, wanting to go back to the sea. Marc looks down at the little boy, who is jumping up and down, kicking sand; soon they are going toward the small café behind us. Helen nods at them and smiles as they pass us. She says something very quickly in French to them.

Now as she turns to me I say, "You mentioned your aunt is in Tuscany. Will you see her again before you go back to France?"

"Yes, Aunt Isa will be mostly alone until the end of the month; her husband needs to remain on the Riviera because of his business interests. He is not completely retired. He has meetings at the hotel with partners of his, but he will go in early September to join my aunt. We will travel to Tuscany to see her after we leave here in a week; her son will be visiting her, as well as my two sisters and their families and my mother. My father is too busy with his work, he says, but he has never been fond of my aunt. We will have a reunion weekend of sorts. Her first husband may come too; they still communicate. He may come with her son."

As Helen speaks in her matter-of-fact and unerringly honest way, I am startled—though she does not speak their names—by her innocent reference to Hans and Caleb. I lower my head to avoid her gaze. Hearing her mention them in this way is disquieting—for naturally she does not realize my past intimacy with her cousin and my knowledge of Hans and Isa. Yet what I find most disconcerting is that my connection to them is severed; they are strangers.

On the table next to her chair I notice Orwell's novel 1984. "You read in English, too, Helen?"

"Yes, I am a translator, you see. I think it will be good to read this book as it is the same year as now."

"Our lives are not like that at all," I counter. "There is no big brother watching over us."

"Yes, but it could occur at another time, maybe not too far away," she says in an even and thoughtful way.

Helen lowers her head and begins to read again from the Céline novel, and I lie back in the chaise longue. After a while I look over at her; she grasps the book in two hands, her expression focused as if she is deriving something essential from it, as if she is being fed by the contents of the book. I recall how in the past my mother would often say that serious novelists from Europe touch your soul. Americans do not want their souls to be touched, I have concluded; they want them to be free, uncluttered.

In the distance I see Jonas waving at me and guess he wants me to come and look at his sketches. Walking toward him, I feel the heat from the sand through my thin sandals. I remove my shoes, then climb up the warm hill of rocks. Once I reach him, he turns his pad over and places a stone on it. He moves close and puts his arm around me. I look out at the beauty of the Mediterranean; it is as if we are miles from the shore, the beach a good distance away. I feel a fine breeze and the pressure of Jonas's arm across my shoulders. When I look over at him, his eyes avert from my gaze. "Jenny," he begins, and I look straight ahead, feeling a stab of anxiety within.

Up ahead, a few yards from us, I catch sight of the British couple swimming in the sea. I have not seen them since that rainy day at the tourist office in the town center, asking about different beaches in the area. I am surprised they are here. They are frolicking, splashing water at each other.

I look over at Jonas; his expression reveals frustration more than anger. "What are you thinking?" I ask, urging him to speak.

"Why would that man have asked if my name was Stram? Do you know him, Jenny?"

"I had no recollection of him when we came to the hotel," I say, my words muffled by the overwhelming strength of the sun. "But I remembered him soon after his name was mentioned by his former wife; she is the one who is the proprietress at the café. Her name is Mara, and his is Roberto Carini. He purchased the shop for her after their divorce." And I fill in the details about the event in New York my parents attended long ago and how I had not heard his name again until Mara spoke of him that day in the café. I add that he may have been the business mogul Eric had worked for. He might have been the one who had instructed Eric to go to Key West—maybe he did not know how poorly Eric had been feeling, but for some reason Eric could not refuse his request. Then I tell Jonas that Roberto Carini owns the hotel we are staying in.

"Stram," he says, "maybe in some convoluted way he associates us with Eric." He smiles. "But it isn't so convoluted, is it, Jenny?"

Warily, I smile at his humor, a blend of warmth and dry sarcasm.

As I walk over the hot sand back to the lounge chair, the grains sieving into my sandals, burning my heels, the memory strikes me again. It is in a different way this time. What comes to mind is not the woman, but the man, his feet, how narrow they were, so narrow for his size. But then I am shaken out of it by the sight of Helen bent over her book, and again I see her resemblance to Caleb.

I lie down in the lounge chair and close my eyes, feel the piercing rays on my eyelids. As I inhale the sea air, I hear the waves breaking and the water sloshing onto the shore. When I open my eyes and look over at Helen, I see she has stopped reading and is looking away. She is not bothered by the heat; it energizes her. She turns to look over at her son and husband who are now in the chair next to her. Remy has fallen asleep across his father's stomach.

I look out at Jonas on the rocks, wondering if he wants to go inside, if the sun is too strong now, but he seems to be sketching more intently than before. And I feel a sense of anticipation, the heavy sand, the intensity of the sun, and the sound of the sea, mostly soothing, but thunderous whenever a huge wave hits the shore.

Soon I hear Helen's voice, crinkly now, "Jenny, it is a lovely day, isn't it? Your husband relishes it—look at how he sketches, with joy."

I gaze in the distance at Jonas and smile.

"It is too bad we will be leaving in a week," she says, her voice pensive.

"Your family reunion in Tuscany is something you might enjoy, though; Tuscany is beautiful too."

"Yes, it is true. But I do not know how relaxing it will be. I am concerned about my aunt. When I think of her behavior that night, I realize she has never been this unwell. My mother will be upset by her condition. Both her former husband and son are doctors; they have a better understanding of why she is this way. She is erratic. Roberto's approach to Isa is practical. He only stays with her when she is well; when she isn't, he sends her to their home in Tuscany and he goes off to speak to his ex-wife—if she isn't working at her café, then he'll take a short flight and visit her at her Paris apartment. I don't know her well; her name is Mara, but she is the reason my aunt and her husband divorced. They had an affair—Aunt Isa's first husband and Mara. Isa couldn't forgive him. It was good Roberto was there to support Aunt Isa at the time—they comforted each other." Listening to her, I conclude her words about Mara, though not judgmental, are not fully accurate; she has been exposed only to Isa's point of view. There is more, I surmise.

An echoing distant scream interrupts our talk. Helen and I look toward the sea; in water up to her neck, the English woman is waving her arms, crying out for help.

Eight

The Lovers

"They are lovers," Helen tells us, her voice hushed, then she lowers her eyes as if troubled by her words. It is twilight; she and Marc, Jonas and I are out on the patio, sipping wine. Our dinner plates have been cleared away. During the meal, we refrained from talking about the incident, which, I believe, struck us at different moments, as if in concert with the rotating light surrounding the pool, spotting the back of the hotel, then the water in the pool, the flattened stone floor of the patio, and lastly and individually, each of us at the table.

Quiet and awed by the near drowning and rescue we witnessed only hours before, we look away as she speaks; Marc fixedly stares up at the hotel, toward the room, where Remy sleeps; his sitter is a sixteen-year-old girl from the town. Jonas's eyes wander in the direction of the ocean, not far away, and I gaze across the pool and watch the pianist behind the glass doors, his shoulders gracefully rising and falling, his music barely audible. Helen's straw hat is on the table next to her glass; with one finger she taps the brim where there is a slight tear; her motion is lulling, like the now-muted sound of the ocean.

From a distance, it seems, Jonas asks, "Aren't we all?" I turn, expecting to see irony in his eyes, but instead his gaze is direct; he studies each of us.

Helen explains what she means is that they are married, but not to each other. While she speaks an image flashes across my mind: Jonas diving off the hill of rocks and swimming rapidly toward the woman, his swift, surreal strokes, the sun burnishing the red color of her hair, her desperate cries for help. At first I was filled with pride and hope, but soon I felt a sense of devastation, remembering Eric's death. And the frenzied motion of Jonas's arms awakened the memory of the man in charcoal-gray pants walking quickly by. Then, almost instantaneously, I was freed by the sight of the lifeguard in a small boat motoring out to save her and the man I had believed was her husband, rescuing the couple before Jonas reached them.

"You were brave, Jonas," Helen says, looking over at him, her expression sincere.

"Not really—I don't think I would have reached them in time."

Marc, who is more inclined to listen than speak, says, "You were brave, Jonas; it was your instinct, your humanity that compelled you to save them. You are not like the average person, you are better, *auguste*—in English, 'august,' what you call this month. You would do the same again, I think. For you, it is natural."

Jonas, not accustomed to flattery, looks away, toward the ocean; his expression tightening, his face appearing more angular now. I interject, "You are very kind, but I believe either of you would have done the same."

"Yes, I agree," Jonas says, facing us now. "If you were perched where I was, most anyone would have done the same."

"But I am a poor swimmer," Helen says, emphatically. With one swift movement she thrusts the hat on top of her head, as if covering her ineptitude.

Marc responds, "Though I am an adequate swimmer, I do not know if I would have had Jonas's instinct. I would have been fearful of not possessing the strength to bring them in." He looks over at me and asks, "Jenny, can you swim?"

"Only moderately well, not well enough to rescue anyone, unfortunately. I do not know if I would have jumped in as reflexively as Jonas. On second thought, it does take a certain type of person to extend him or herself in such a way, a selfless person, I think." I ramble on, but when I look around the table I see the others are focusing on my words. And so I change the subject. Looking at Helen, I ask, "How do you know they are married to other people?"

Carefully she removes her hat and places it on the table. "My aunt Isa's husband Roberto told me. He isn't certain if the man will survive—he has been hospitalized—but the woman will be fine. She was crying out to save him; apparently she is a better swimmer than he is."

As Helen speaks in her precise and honest way, relaying only the facts she is aware of, not wanting to pass judgment, she again taps the brim of her hat with her finger. But suddenly she looks up, and I follow her gaze. Roberto is approaching our table, his walk slow and purposeful. I feel a sense of anxiety, attempting to imagine him as a younger man, how he and Eric might have interacted. Eric would have been respectful, would have deferred to what I surmised would have been Roberto's instructions, his exacting demands.

"Any news, Roberto?" Helen asks in English.

"The woman is on a plane back to London, and the man's wife has arrived and is on her way to the hospital. His condition is very serious."

After he finishes speaking, he sits down in the empty seat and crosses his legs; his gaze fixed on me, he says in a direct voice, "You are Eric Stram's widow. My wife, who is now in Tuscany, recognized you; she said she met you once."

Reflectively I introduce Jonas as my husband.

Roberto nods at Jonas but does not extend his hand.

"Your parents," Roberto asks, "are they well?"

"Yes," I say, wondering if I met him that weekend in New York years ago.

Helen looks at me, her expression startled, and says, "I did not realize you had met my aunt Isa."

"It was a quick meeting, and the night I noticed her at

dinner, I wasn't certain if she was the same woman I had met in New York."

Helen doesn't say anything but a puzzled expression crosses her face. She turns to her uncle and asks again about the couple. But Roberto doesn't respond, apparently wanting to move on, past that situation, on to another topic. He looks over again at me, meeting my gaze. His eyes are a steel gray color, framed by his bushy brows, his skin is a dark olive and his stare is sharp and inquisitive, experienced, and I feel a sense of familiarity. Jonas clasps my hand, resting on my lap.

Roberto raises his finger, not in a hostile way, but warmly, as if he knows me. A half smile crossing his lips, he says, "Eric Stram, I first knew him as a young boy in Trieste. He was quiet, shy. He didn't speak for a few years. People thought it was because of the war. It was a mystery. Why did young Eric Stram stop talking? It would have been more of a mystery if it hadn't been for the war, but from time to time people did wonder. His mother Alma is a woman who is both intelligent and beautiful in that you ask yourself if she is more intelligent than beautiful, or vice versa."

"Can't a woman or man be both?" Helen chimes in, and we all laugh.

Roberto calls over the waiter, ordering everyone another round of drinks. We neither decline nor accept his offer. When the wine comes, we sit and drink as if to still our nerves, not knowing what he will say next. For Roberto's presence is commanding, not easy to escape.

By the time he speaks more, it is dark, the rotating light around the pool brighter now in contrast. The ocean appears more distant; it is nearly impossible to discern the steady rise and fall of the waves.

After a long silence, Roberto says, "I was partial to little Eric. Maybe he was shy because his parents were so well-known in Trieste. His father was a wealthy banker and his mother was involved in volunteer work. She would go to the homes of those who were most ill and read to them. His parents took in yours, Mrs. Stram; your father was solidly against fascism, was rumored to have taken part in actions against the government. He needed to be protected and the Strams took it upon themselves to do so. Eric's older brother had died at the beginning of the war in an unfortunate accident—I can't remember the details but it was because of a foolish act on the part of one of his friends. It was more tragic because of the idiocy of it all."

Roberto crosses his legs, leans back in his chair, and closes his eyes. I wonder if he has fallen asleep. I grasp the narrow arms of my chair and begin to rise, ready now to leave. I am filled with anguish, remembering only Eric's death, not his life. But Jonas touches my wrist to stop me, and I sit down; he whispers in my ear, "It is better to stay, to listen, he may say more."

I look over at Helen and then Marc, across the table from each other; they seem quite still, half-intoxicated, half under the spell of Roberto. Marc winks nervously at Helen; she tightly closes her eyes, suddenly opening them as if startled. The reflection of the rotating light surrounding the pool crosses her face and

I see another side of Helen, one more like Isa, a stark and stoic expression, but once the light passes, she again seems her straightforward self.

Roberto, his eyes now open, studies us one by one, nodding as he does so, as if reading a book he is in accord with. Marc sits directly to his left, his narrow shoulders hunched slightly forward, his pointy face, his even expression. Then next to him is Jonas, sitting back in his chair, his expression a complex mix of irony and aspiration, his hands loosely clasping the narrow arms of the chair, very much in the present as well as thinking about other things that may cross his mind, how the ocean is barely visible, how the rotating light strikes the hotel. And when Roberto looks over at me I sense he is thinking not of me, but only of Eric, not Eric the man, but Eric the boy, who was unable to speak, the mysterious Eric, who Roberto eventually took under his hawkish wing. Lastly his gaze meets Helen's; she is to my left, his right, the niece of his second wife. I wonder if he wishes he and Mara had not divorced, and I remember how Helen told me earlier in the day of Mara and Hans's affair. I think of my affair with Caleb, something that hasn't been real to me for a while; yet the events of this day are hazy as well.

Roberto continues, "Most will never know for certain why young Eric did not speak—was he traumatized by the war or was it something else, another reason? I needed to understand his silence. After his parents moved to America, I invited him to join my business. He was in college at the time. Eric had an uncanny ability to recall people, their faces and names, and so he was good for my business. Clients were relaxed with him, not because he was particularly warm and inviting, but because he remembered who they were."

Surprisingly I hear Helen's voice, as muted as the sound of the lapping waves, asking Roberto, "Did you ever discover why Eric did not speak?" Her words are slurred, as if she has had too much wine. Then she turns to me and says, "Maybe you know, Jenny, maybe you know," but though I hear in her words a yearning for truth, I wonder how much she is aware of what she is saying. It is as if she is speaking in her sleep.

Before I have a chance to respond, Roberto interjects, sounding baffled, which seems antithetical to his nature, "How would Mrs. Stram know? She wasn't in Trieste at the time; it was before her parents came to America, where she was born. No, she does not know why, and may not know that Eric did not speak during the war."

"No, I did not know," I say. "He was not very forthcoming; his tendency was to hide things. He did not like to talk about himself. I always thought he regarded himself as ordinary."

"But he had an uncanny memory for faces and names," Roberto says, shaking his head. "Eric was not ordinary."

"Yes," I say. "It was as if he knew certain people well, people who seemed not to recognize him, as if they were celebrities who naturally do not know their admiring fans." And I think of Isa and Hans Sokolov and how their names had come so easily to Eric's lips even though Isa may not have recalled him at the time, perhaps did not know of him until she married Roberto.

But I glean how with Isa things are not as they seem—even her loyal niece has acknowledged her erratic behavior.

"Eric was important to my business because of his reticence as well. His growth—emotional, I guess you could say—was stunted because of his experiences as a young boy. It isn't surprising he married a much younger woman," he says musingly.

I think of the anguish Eric caused during our marriage, the uncertainty I experienced, and I am pained and angry with Roberto's presentation of my former husband as innocent and naïve, perhaps exceptional. Needing to leave, I look over at Jonas. Just as we stand, Helen says, her voice pensive and dazed, "What possibly could have happened to young Eric?" Jonas takes my hand and we nod good-bye to those round the table, who are enclosed now in near darkness. We walk toward the hotel, and as Jonas opens the door to let us inside, I vaguely hear Roberto's voice, his words like scattered, floating notes from a saxophone being played in the distance—rumors . . . rape . . .

Nine

The Proprietress

"He survived. His wife arrived yesterday evening—he is weak—and the woman, the other one, has returned to London, to her husband, I imagine," Mara says, leaning forward in her seat. There's a seductive note in her tone; an indistinct marbly look in her gaze. She has interrupted our conversation with these words, which have nothing to do with what we've been discussing; they are as dissonant as if, having been immersed in a discussion of impressionism, she deviates to politics.

"You are speaking of the couple at the hotel who nearly drowned. Roberto told you?" She eyes me and nods, the late morning light flows through the open front of the café grazing her red-brown hair and narrow shoulders. She takes a sip of cappuccino, an unlit cigarette dangling between her fingers. She appears more subdued today.

Awakening early from a hazy dream of Roberto and Mara entwined like branches of a century-old banyan, I felt compelled to speak with her this day.

Over breakfast, I told Jonas that I needed to walk to the town center to buy some incidentals at the pharmacy. He was motioning for the waiter, who immediately came to our table. After ordering more hot coffee and steamed milk, Jonas looked at me, nodded and smiled loosely. Jonas speaks less and less—no more in-depth discussions about line and shadow in Picasso's *Blue Nude* or *The Old Guitarist*. Though he does not talk of it, I gather Jonas is focused on his own work, what he is producing.

Thirty minutes ago I walked into Mara's shop and ordered a cappuccino at the counter; she seemed to vaguely recognize me. I realized she may be accustomed to speaking with customers in an open-ended and confidential way; I was no different from the others. As she prepared my drink, I told her I was in the café ten days before and mentioned our conversation about the Sokolovs. Nodding, she did not respond. I sat at a table close by, and four or five children, escorted by two women, came in to the café, asking for gelatos. With a distracted smile Mara served the children. Once they left, she approached my table.

Our conversation began awkwardly. It was more on my part than hers; Italians, particularly those I've observed on the Riviera, do not possess a sense of hesitancy. I gleaned from the time she had served the children and had come to join me, she had mostly recalled our previous conversation, but soon I understood it was more because of what her ex-husband had told her.

Placing her cup on the table, her expression thoughtful, she said that Roberto had noticed me as he was leaving the café the last time I was there, and that I was Jenny Stram, Eric's wife. Mara's speech was more circumspect than I recalled; she seemed to be piecing together our last conversation with Roberto's words.

My pulse quickening, I asked, "You knew Eric?" How familiar of a presence he is here, how uncanny, I thought. But apparently he was a different Eric at the time than I had known, a docile Eric, more aware of others, and even more magnanimous, perhaps.

"Of course I knew Eric," she said, her eyes concerned. "I was married to Roberto for many years—how could I not know Eric? His death was a tragedy for us all. Roberto respected Eric. He knew him as a young boy in Trieste. Although he was not part of Eric's family's milieu—Roberto was quite poor—he would notice young Eric enjoying a cookie at the pastry shop, accompanied by the woman who took care of him. Roberto has always had a good understanding of people; it is why he's been very successful in business." She turned her head while speaking to see, it seemed, if there was anyone in hearing distance; except for the two of us, the shop was empty.

She then explained in a staccato-like way, her English less fluid, her Italian inflection more obvious than it was the last time we spoke. Her expression was more contemplative, less wistful. She said that most people in Trieste knew of Eric's family, the Strams. But Roberto was perceptive; he understood that Eric was unlike his family. She continued, saying that on occasion Roberto would deliver packages to the homes of the wealthy, and from time to time he would go to Eric's home. Roberto had known that Eric's older brother had died in an unfortunate accident and, though his parents had been stoic, he thought Eric carried this sadness with him. One day when he brought a package to the Strams—Eric opened the door and whispered something to Roberto, but Roberto could not hear his words. When the maid came to the door Eric ran away. "Of course this is what Roberto told me, how he remembers it," Mara said confidently.

"How old was Eric at the time?" I asked, attempting to organize in my mind the events of my previous husband's life. My heart beat rapidly, I clasped my hands together nervously. Mara eyed my discomfort.

"Roberto must have been in his late twenties," she said offhandedly—"Eric may have been seven or eight."

And it is now that she leans forward and speaks about the man and woman who nearly drowned yesterday afternoon. After asking if Roberto had told her, I add, "My husband and I were on the beach at the time. It is good to know he has survived."

Yet she continues to speak about the couple, deftly diverting me from my intense curiosity about the young Eric.

"Of course Roberto was concerned for their safety, but if either of them had been seriously harmed, it would have severely hurt the reputation of the hotel—it is what Roberto is most proud of."

Finished with her cappuccino, Mara leans back in the chair and lights her cigarette. She alertly eyes the entrance. My back is to the front of the café, but I know by her satisfied and relaxed expression that no one is coming in.

"I first met Eric when he was nineteen years old, " Mara begins, her gaze distant, focused. "It was in America. Roberto and I lived in Philadelphia at the time. It was before his business became successful. When Roberto discovered through a mutual friend that Eric's family had moved to the United States and that he was attending college in Philadelphia, he called him and invited him to dinner at our home."

As she speaks, I grow more and more apprehensive, fearful of my memory of Eric; it is only a silhouette of him, but it is more intrusive, more daunting than ever was his presence.

Relaxing more in her seat, Mara continues, describes how Eric appeared startled, those blue-gray eyes of his, uncertain as he came into their home awkwardly holding a bouquet of flowers, each one wilting. Promptly she took them from him, buried her face in the bouquet, inhaling, then reached out, touching his shoulder, assuring him how lovely they were. Intuitively she understood how important Eric was to Roberto. She also felt sorry for Eric, how confused he seemed. He was hesitant in this environment, this new country, she gathered. As she speaks, I picture her with Eric: Mara smaller, more confident. Eric, wanting to please her, would have tried to appear less, so she could seem more. Then Mara adds that naturally Eric reminded her husband of those years in Trieste, before the war. To Roberto, although he was quite poor, those were idyllic times. Money wasn't important to him. The simple life was rich and plentiful, the beauty of dawn, the sound of children playing in the large square, the Adriatic, the quietude of the evening hours. Mara extends her arms as she speaks.

Then she lowers her voice and leans forward, "After Eric left our home that night, Roberto told me that during the war there had been rumors that the Strams were protecting a couple, the husband, Henri Smila, an anti-fascist, had taken part in risky activities, the Smilas, your parents. Your father was very brave, Jenny. We may have visited them once when your parents lived in Hartford and Roberto and I had a home in Philadelphia but I am not certain—it was years ago."

Upon hearing her words, my heart pounds.

She continues, "This rumor added to Roberto's curiosity about the Strams; he had assumed they were not people who would have involved themselves in a perilous situation—they were not brave or fearless, he had believed, and so at first he discounted the rumor, but later he discovered it to be true.

"The night Eric visited, Roberto questioned him lightly about college—he was, I believe, in his first year—and then spoke to him of his business, how it had started slowly on the Riviera and now in America he wanted it to grow more; his dream was that it would expand throughout the world. He was hoping to draw Eric out of himself."

She says that Eric had not communicated much about school; he had given basically yes and no answers but seemed intrigued when Roberto spoke of his work. Eric's interest had spurred Roberto to describe how he had conceived of his business and in what direction he wanted to take it; as he spoke it struck him that maybe he should hire Eric to work for him—maybe he would discover more about this inscrutable young man.

Roberto soon forgot about the child Eric, as the nearly twenty-year-old Eric had taken to the business adroitly. He left college within the year. Roberto became friendly with Eric's family and the families the Strams were acquainted with in Trieste. They all admired Roberto because Roberto was successful. His financial holdings had grown significantly while theirs had dwindled.

Roberto sent Eric around the world to speak with potential clients. Eric remembered people well, and never revealed too much; he had a natural discipline with words. Roberto trusted his impression of people; Eric was accurate in the way he naturally understood clients, how to assess their interests, their needs. Roberto's business grew, and he always attributed it in part to Eric.

Eventually, Mara says, Roberto opened an office in New York as well, but they continued to live mostly in Philadelphia. After twenty years in America, she and Roberto returned to Italy, mostly living on the Riviera. Roberto did not see Eric as much as before, though they spoke often on the telephone. And they spent some time together during meetings at the hotel, maybe once or twice a year.

"We did not attend your wedding," Mara adds. "An emergency had come up with one of Roberto's interests in Hong Kong;

we happened to be there at the time and could not leave." She pauses, then says, "Roberto did not attend Eric's funeral—it would have been too painful for him, and he did not tell me of your first husband's passing until a month later." Inhaling from her cigarette, she tosses back her head and continues, "It is not surprising Eric never mentioned Roberto to you. I think your former husband may have desired to appear more independent than he actually was. And you were young, most likely not curious about the details of Eric's work, more interested in your own career, I imagine." She sighs. "At that time Roberto wondered less and less about the young Eric. But now with your appearance, Roberto seems intrigued again; it brings back memories to him. Now that he is mostly retired, he has more time to reflect."

"And he shares his thoughts, his concerns with you," I say, and feel myself smiling, thinking how, as confident as her words sound, I do not know if they are entirely true; I understand how foggy memory can be.

"Yes, it is as if we are still married. I blamed myself for the failure of our marriage. I had slipped into an affair with Hans Sokolov, the man we spoke of the last time you were here. We were both unhappy in our marriages. Roberto was very irascible at the time, preoccupied with his business, and Hans's wife, Isa, a flighty personality, appeared not to be interested in her husband any longer. But eventually, I realized Isa had needed us to become involved. She understood we were lonely and flawed, but Hans was less flawed than me. And though I must admit I made the decision as an adult, to go forward with the affair, I wonder how much free will I was exerting—or was it the will of Isa and perhaps even Roberto? I was weak—not defiant; I succumbed to Isa's will. If I hadn't, I believe I would not have become involved with Hans and would still be married to Roberto."

My relationship with Caleb comes to mind. "Does anyone ever have free will?" I ask. I think of the memory that has become a shadow I live with every day, no longer startling and unexpected but more and more a part of my life. The child is still alive within me, the young girl who watched dispassionately as a man with charcoal-colored pants rushed by while a woman sat in a chair, a red stain covering her lap.

"I do not know, Jenny. You are young, life must seem very straightforward to you, I imagine. Yet there is something about you; I think you may have had a lover while you were married to Eric. He was much older than you and was often away because of Roberto's business." She lowers her gaze. When she raises her head, she looks past me; her eyes startled, her posture more erect. I turn round; standing in the entrance way, the rays from the noon sun outlining his form, is a slightly older Hans Sokolov. His gaze rests on Mara, and I recall him looking upon his son in the same way, seven years ago, as Caleb walked down the steps of the public library.

TEN

THE LETTER

All the doors are propped open, and the soft morning air flows through the foyer. Coming in from an early walk, I stop at the front desk. *Un momento, prego*, the clerk says and turns away. Smiling, he then hands me a letter along with the key to my room. It is disconcerting to see Helen's name on the return address; I was not expecting her to write until she returned to Paris. Uncertain whether or not to read it now, I hold it loosely, weighing the pros and cons of opening it immediately. I hesitate, and then decide to wait until late afternoon—Jonas will be sketching then, and, as usual, I'll be drinking tea out on the patio before dressing for the cocktail hour.

There is only one person, a young girl, swimming in the pool, lightly, playfully slapping the water. I glance at the plate of petit fours the waiter has placed on the table, but decide I will only drink tea, black, as I like it at this time of day. The white shorts and pale blue halter top I wear feel crisp and clean, constraining. Once the tray with teapot and cup is before me, I cross my legs and take a few sips. I rest the cup in the saucer and then intently open the letter; with a strange sense of excitement I peer down at Helen's fine, circular writing.

I read the first few paragraphs, studying each sentence. Then I stop and skim through the letter, intending to go back and read it more thoroughly a second time. Soon I have a sense of the gist of the letter; most importantly how much Helen has discerned about my relationship with the Sokolovs. Now, with care, I again read her words.

Tuscany
August 25

Dear Jenny,
I imagine you are surprised to hear from me—Helen, of all people, you think—or possibly not; maybe you have been expecting to receive news from Tuscany. Most who meet and share confidences while on holiday form a friendship during their short time together and agree to write once separated, but few do. We will be one of the exceptions, I trust. I often think of our parting ten days ago—you stood outside the hotel in the midday heat as Jonas helped Marc pack the car with our luggage. After you and I buckled Remy snugly into his car seat, you seemed faint from the strong sun

but readily and graciously hugged me. I felt there was a sense of detachment in your warmth, or maybe "detachment" is the wrong word—perhaps "evasiveness" is better. Did you not want me to perceive something about you, or, maybe, in a subtle way, you did?

With the exception of a few cool evenings, the heat has been stifling since I have come to Roberto and Aunt Isa's Tuscan home, fertile ground for the imagination. I wonder if I should start at the beginning of my stay in Tuscany or work backward. I believe it is always best to write in an orderly way and then things will be more clear to you; knowing who I think you are, I believe you will prefer it this way.

We arrived at Roberto and Isa's home in Tuscany about six hours after we'd said good-bye to you and Jonas. Remy slept most of the journey, and awoke with a start once Marc turned into the long driveway of their home. Cypress trees stood on either side of the path; riding over the dirt driveway, we could see in the distance a succession of green hills with spots of brown. The air was warm and soothing. Their stucco home is large with flower boxes in the front windows. I was surprised to see Aunt Isa sitting outside at a long table on the front side of the house. She wore a floppy white hat and an A-line white cotton dress. Just as we got out of the car my mother came to the front door. She ran down the steps to greet us, encircling the three of us in her arms, her glasses slipping to the end of her nose. Her movements are much quicker than Aunt Isa's, more svelte. Then after embracing us again, individually this time, and asking about our trip, she took Remy by the hand and led him up the front steps.

As I wiped my face with a handkerchief, Marc went over to speak with my aunt; she was reading a magazine. Looking up, she squinted and waved hello to him. When she saw me coming toward her she smiled curtly, but at the same time seemed pleased to see the two of us. She did not say much, responding nonchalantly to our small talk. I thought she might have been embarrassed by her behavior at the hotel. She told us she didn't expect Roberto to come for another three weeks and by then we would have left for our home in Paris. I responded that we had seen a good deal of Roberto at the hotel and I knew he was looking forward to coming to Tuscany once he had finished with his business meetings there. "Oh," she said, "Roberto, all business, all the time." Then in her hasty way, she instructed us to go inside, and said that Cira, my mother, would show us which rooms we would be staying in this time. As we began to turn away, she added that her son Caleb and Hans, his father, had driven to Florence and would not return until later in the evening. I felt less apprehensive after hearing her speak, and although she was not as welcoming as she was when we were children, she seemed more steady than she had at the hotel a few weeks before. I was relieved, hoping the visit would be more pleasant than expected.

Over dinner Aunt Isa was more talkative, and my mother was quiet; she had prepared dinner and had spent much time engaging Remy with food and a game of hide-and-seek while Marc and I had slipped off for a nap after our drive from the Riviera.

That evening Aunt Isa was fussy about what she ate and drank, and I don't know if now she was adhering to her doctor's orders. For not only do I not know what ails her, I do not know what she needs to do to protect her health. But she appeared more even-tempered than she had on the Riviera, where she had been tense and had been drinking too much, acting out in ways that had been extreme, even for her.

As we enjoyed dessert, mille-feuille, my mother's specialty, Aunt Isa spoke of those years when my sisters and I were young and would come to visit America, how we had been awed by New York and the tall buildings. She said it had struck her as curious each time we had come, as she had thought Paris to be quite sophisticated; we'd acted like girls who never before had been within miles of a city. It was then I noticed she was not wearing her wedding ring; I supposed it was because Caleb would soon return. He does not like ostentatious jewelry, and since her marriage to Roberto, Aunt Isa tries to appease Caleb.

Caleb has a closer relationship with his father than he does with his mother; Uncle Hans and he are more compatible—it is not surprising that Caleb has chosen the same profession as his father. I understand that Caleb, despite his awareness of Aunt Isa's flaws, her unpredictable personality, which became more and more evident to him the older he grew, feels a deep warmth toward his mother at certain times and on other occasions appears annoyed with her. As an adult he will be happy to see her when they have been apart for a while, and then after too many days together he will appear resolute in leaving her until the next visit. He has not acknowledged this to me but I have closely observed Caleb—as I am the older cousin I have felt protective of him and because of this I think I know him quite well. I am confident Caleb would wholeheartedly agree with what I am relaying to you, Jenny.

Although Aunt Isa was talkative during the meal, the rest of us were more subdued than usual. Remy sat next to my mother and she helped him eat and spoke to him gently, asking him questions about our vacation on the Riviera. My sisters and their husbands and daughters had not yet arrived, and were expected to come early the next morning. Even though Marc and I had taken a nap, we were still weary from the drive. It was pleasant to see Aunt Isa in good spirits, telling story after story of the people who lived in this small Tuscan village and how American she felt in their company. Wasn't it ironic, she said, that she had been born in Trieste?

"America is compelling," she added, "the culture is transformative." But I think Aunt Isa must have always been comfortable in the United States, for she had seemed very American to me—no different in this way from her first husband and son. But now she was married to Roberto, I thought, who, like herself, had been born in Trieste.

Even at a young age I had wondered how stable Aunt Isa was. I had never liked being alone with her, as she could say something unexpected and jarring. Or she'd be suddenly alarmed about an occurrence that even as a child I understood was innocuous, but then at the next moment she'd be calm and practical and continue on with her plans for the day. She was different from most other adults I knew, and sometimes I would look over at Caleb and wonder what it was like for him. Yet he seemed indifferent, apparently accustomed to her behavior, and when I was young I accepted his response. But eventually, I realized how difficult it must be for him.

Out of the blue, Aunt Isa sighed, her expression more melancholic. She put down her fork and said emphatically, "Roberto is angry with me; he said I was too boisterous the last night I was at the hotel, but I don't think so. Perhaps I had too much wine, though I was not intoxicated, simply ebullient."

My mother turned to her and said, "You become much too excited, Isa, over meaningless things. Situations and people in general are not always how you imagine them to be. It is as if you are looking at life through a mirror that causes a person to appear misshapen. Hans has always been kind but you envisioned him differently; in your head you invented images of him that were not true. He is a much better person than you believe him to be—or maybe you wanted him to become a negative force in your life because you needed to divorce him so you could marry Roberto."

I have heard my mother express such thoughts before, especially during dinners with only my aunt and herself and Marc and me. She does not speak to Aunt Isa in this way when my father or sisters and their husbands are present. When Aunt Isa is in Paris or when we visit her, my sisters never pay as much attention to her as Marc and I do. For some reason we are more drawn to her than are other family members. Roberto, I gather, detests Aunt Isa's unpleasant moods, but when she is bright and spirited, he relishes her.

Over coffee, we were mostly silent, weary from a long day, but soon heard the shutting of car doors, then steps in the foyer, and shortly Caleb and Uncle Hans came into the dining room. I had not seen Caleb in two years, and now that he would be thirty in a few months, he appeared more like Hans than before. His expression was more serious than I remembered and he was thinner, his face more narrow and defined; he had grown a faint mustache. I was curious to know what his life had been like these past few years.

Uncle Hans appeared the same as always; he never seems to change very much. Aunt Isa waved to him briefly, as if shooing him away. Although she had invited Uncle Hans to her and Roberto's home in Tuscany, she did so to ensure that Caleb would visit.

My mother offered to serve them dinner. They were appreciative, as they had come upon traffic driving back from Florence, where they had met a former colleague of Uncle Hans's, and then had spent some time at the Uffizi Gallery. Florence suits them; according to Caleb, it is where in Europe they are most at ease, especially since Uncle Hans and Aunt Isa's divorce.

Over the osso buco that my mother had adroitly placed before them, they spoke about a painting at the gallery, attributed to Francesco Furini, Portrait of a Young Girl, *saying that although it was dated 1650, her expression is surprisingly modern. Aunt Isa looked at them quizzically, as if she could not understand their interest in the work—or was it that she found their description of the painting too frank and uninspired?*

It was close to midnight when we got up from the table. As we were leaving the room, Aunt Isa approached Caleb and put her arms around him. From the hallway I heard her ask if he would stay with her for a while so that they could catch up. Her tone was more subdued than usual but she sounded motherly and sincere. I looked back and saw him smile uncertainly. I could see his fondness for her and at the same time there was a subtle wariness in his look. But I saw and heard no more; soon we had reached the top of the stairway. Marc was carrying Remy, who was sleeping, in his arms, and I went ahead to open the door of our bedroom.

The next day I came upon Uncle Hans in the study. He would be staying until Monday, and Caleb would be leaving two days later, on Wednesday. It was early afternoon, a Saturday, and my sisters and their husbands and daughters had arrived that morning. I had just come inside; reverberating through my mind and body were the sounds of the girls splashing water in the pool and their screams of joy. Remy had been sitting on Marc's lap, gleefully watching his older cousins frolicking. When I walked into the study, Uncle Hans was lounging on the sofa. He immediately stood and greeted me. He appeared distracted and I believed he was lost in thought about something that was disturbing him. I know how dedicated he is to his work and guessed he was concerned about patients of his. He asked how I was, and together we tried to determine when it was we had last met. I addressed him as Uncle Hans as I always had—for was he not the father of my dear cousin Caleb? We concluded we had last seen each other in Paris two years before. He and Caleb had been attending a con-

ference and I had invited them to dinner at our apartment. Remy had not yet begun to walk. We sat across from each other; the curtains were open and light flooded the room. In the distance I could see a small group of people walking toward the grassy hills.

Uncle Hans mentioned he had been to Roberto's hotel on the Riviera. "I heard you and Marc were there at the time. My stay was brief—one night. I was meeting friends in Genoa the next day. I did not have a chance to contact you, but knew I would see you in Tuscany. I heard a couple nearly drowned the night before."

As he spoke, it struck me that his purpose in going there might have been to see Mara. I have always found Uncle Hans to be a person who keeps his feelings at a distance. I don't think he would have wanted to be questioned about her. Instead I spoke of Aunt Isa, telling him she appeared more stable in Tuscany, and explained her behavior at the hotel, how she had erupted at dinner. And then I told him about you, Jenny. What might have contributed to Aunt Isa's behavior that night—according to what she had told Roberto—was that at the next table she recognized a woman her husband refers to as Jenny Stram, her maiden name, Smila.

Uncle Hans smiled and said, "The name Smila is familiar." Then he crossed his legs, leaned his head back as if searching his memory. After a few moments, he said, "I know of her through her mother, who once was a patient of mine. I probably should not reveal this, but it has been so many years. She would come with her mother to New York to see me—they lived in Connecticut,

Hartford, I recall, but when they moved away I lost touch with them. The young daughter would stay in the waiting room while her mother would come in to see me. I don't believe she would recognize me—a nurse would accompany her mother into my office. Her mother would tell me that her young daughter was in the waiting room. I remember more clearly now. Often we would talk about Caleb and her daughter once we realized they were the same age. From my office window I would see them climbing up the front steps of the brownstone. Her mother was born in Trieste like your mother and aunt, and that is why I remember her—because of that coincidence. And even before she was my patient, Isa and I may have gone to a party at their apartment in Hartford, a party mostly for immigrants from Trieste, but that was too long ago to remember for certain; it is very vague and it may be that Isa only talked of herself going. And now that you say she is staying at the hotel, I may have seen her on the Riviera. I knew I had seen her somewhere before; she carries herself as she did as a twelve- or thirteen-year-old girl. Even though she was quite young, there was something old about her. And the same expression—it is haunting. It is coming back to me now. Maybe it is why Isa, who tends to respond emotionally rather than thinking first, reacted to seeing her in that way. I think Isa tried to befriend her once and I had advised her against doing so because of my past professional contact with her mother, but I did so more because I was concerned that Isa would not be a good influence on her. But I probably did not need to say anything to Isa; you know she is not the most consistent of friends and she was much older than her. And so I may have seen her again in New York when she was in her early twenties."

At that moment Remy ran into the room, soaking wet from having been in the pool, and jumped onto my lap, clutching at me in a wet hug.

Uncle Hans left a few days later, and I did not have another chance to speak with him alone. Coming upon him following our talk, he would seem preoccupied and distant as if we had not had conversed that day, but whenever he caught my eye he would smile thoughtfully. His time in Tuscany was spent mostly with Caleb; they would swim in the evening and speak alone together in the study after dinner. Uncle Hans left Tuscany on Monday, midday. Caleb drove him to the airport.

I did not have a chance to talk alone with Caleb until the night before he left. During most of his stay he had enjoyed playing with my sisters' daughters and with Remy. I had not seen that side of Caleb before and wondered if he were considering having children of his own. He seemed more delighted by his second cousins than he had in the past. They all called him Uncle Caleb.

The windows remained open and throughout the house there was a sense of early autumn. Remy had fallen asleep over dessert. Marc held him in his arms for most of the dinner, and after we finished our meal, he carried him upstairs to our room. When Marc did not reappear, I assumed he had fallen asleep alongside our son.

After dinner I went in to the study to look for a book to read. Although the others were tired from the change in the weather,

I was restless and needed to occupy my mind. As I was looking through the shelves, I heard footsteps. Turning, I saw that Caleb had come into the room, a glass of wine in his hand. He offered to get me one as well. And soon we were sitting across from each other, lounging in big stuffy chairs, my legs tucked beneath me. We had always enjoyed talking with each other, and it was easy to take up where we had left off two years before. I told him I had noticed his sudden interest in the children and hadn't seen that side of him before. "Is there something more to it?" I asked.

He shrugged. "I am not involved with anyone now, Helen, if that is what you are asking," he said, smiling.

"You will be thirty in October; that is how old I was when Marc and I married. Maybe there is someone you are interested in but you do not realize it yet," I said, teasing him.

What I gathered from Caleb was that he had been overworking lately, and seeing the children and enjoying time with them had been his way of unwinding, diverting himself from the burdens of his career. Both he and Uncle Hans only treat trauma cases; that has always been Uncle Hans's specialty. I can only imagine how exhausting it must be. They are both in practice together now. I asked him about his father, if he thought he would remarry at some point. Caleb then told me that Uncle Hans had stopped by to visit Mara when he was on the Riviera, and although they were happy to see each other, his father had said that there was a distance between them. Caleb closed his eyes and told me this was because they blamed each other for the failure of their respective marriages.

"Yes, Caleb," I said, "people like to blame themselves; ironically it makes them feel less guilty. I met a woman on the beach at the hotel, her name is Jenny, and I thought she blamed herself for her first husband's death—he died tragically, in a yachting accident—his name was Eric Stram. He was from Trieste; he had worked for Roberto—that was how she had known about the hotel."

Caleb's gaze met mine, and there was silence. I was surprised and uncomfortable. After a while, he simply said, "There was a time when I knew her well." At that moment the tension between us lessened some.

"She is married to an artist now, a talented one, I think, who is also kind and surprisingly brave," I answered, and Caleb seemed pleased, but then we discussed other things.

I am not certain what your relationship was with my cousin, or the year or years you were in contact with each other; you now have both moved on—haven't you?

Your friend,
Helen

Eleven

The Response

I do not reflect much on Helen's letter, realizing I need to respond while still in the surroundings in which she and I met and exchanged confidences. For once we each return to our respective homes, our day-to-day lives will resume, and the mystique of our vacation on the Riviera will fade away.

Early the next morning, while sipping coffee at the patio café, I watch Jonas swimming in the pool close by. The water is an aqua color; his strokes are even and strong, the movement of his head, left, right, left, right. Then I look out a short distance at the Mediterranean, the glinting sunlight crossing its breadth. I pick up my pen and close my eyes; I need to write the truth. What I glean most from Helen's words is not that I did not reveal to her the depth of my relationship with her cousin Caleb, but that I neglected to mention I had known of him. My intention was not to be deceptive, just protective of Caleb's privacy and mine. But after reading her letter, I realize I was mistaken; I should have told her. Secondly I was disoriented by the news that for a time, while we lived in Hartford, Hans Sokolov had been my mother's physician. Eighteen hours later, I am still puzzled by this information. My instinct is the friendship Helen and I have begun to develop will not survive.

Jonas now is the only one in the pool, and as I begin to write, I hear the sound of his arms slapping water.

The Riviera
August 28

Dear Helen,
I realize you must be home in Paris by now—perhaps you have just returned and are still under the warm spell of your summer trip.

I was not surprised to receive your letter, but disturbed by its contents. You are very perceptive, Helen—I understood this about you when we first spoke on the beach, and I noticed you were reading Céline's Journey to the End of the Night, *a novel, I believe, that is enjoyed by those who tend to be contemplative, questioning, and responsive to life.*

And as I attempt to imagine the light in which you may view what I say, I weigh in my mind what to reveal about my relationship with your cousin Caleb. I realize what is most important is that you continue to think well of him. What I write will be with that purpose in mind. It is not helpful, I think, for you to have too many unanswered questions about your cousin, questions that may arouse doubts that affect your genuine appreciation of him. And although you see each other every so often, maybe once every two years, it is enough, it sounds, to maintain a close relationship.

I met Caleb seven years ago; it was a transitional time for each of us, or at least for me—I will not speak for him. That summer I became enthralled with the Sokolov family. The months of July and August were extremely hot and I was feeling listless and uncertain about my life, the choices I had made. My husband Eric was away for many of those weeks.

I met your aunt Isa first. It was during a heavy downpour; we stood beneath the awning of a clothing store on Madison Avenue, waiting for the rain to subside. After a while, to help pass the time, we began to converse. When she discovered I was thinking of a career in journalism, she offered to introduce me to an acquaintance of hers, who was a professor in the field. I was surprised by her openness and desire to assist, and since I was lonely in New York and unhappy in my marriage, I was hopeful and pleased by the idea of seeing her again to discuss this possibility. However, my next meeting with your aunt, two days later, a Saturday morning, turned out to be an abrupt and disorienting encounter. Her personality was very different when we first met. Her husband Hans soon joined us and he was indifferent to me as well. I had no idea he had been my mother's doctor. I remember when I was young and we were living in Hartford, I would often take the train with my mother to New York and accompany her to medical appointments. But I do not remember Hans. My mother has always been inclined to visit doctors, specialists, even for minor health issues. However, it is true that seven years ago I was drawn to Hans. Hans was the Sokolov I found most compelling. Maybe it was because unknowingly I had seen him at one point when I was young, and memories I was unaware of had been in some way reawakened, evoking a sense of familiarity. I found there was something both warm and mysterious about Hans and Caleb—their relationship, I mean.

You write that Hans's specialty has always been trauma, but I know of no personal trauma my mother might have experienced, nor am I aware of any apparent neurological deficit she might have had. I was young at the time and not very observant of either of my parents. I tended to focus primarily on my future, what would happen once we left Hartford; my parents would often speak of moving away. This was what was foremost in my mind; I was both excited and apprehensive about leaving Hartford, the only place I had known.

My mother is and always has been a complicated person. My father has been called heroic. As I mentioned to you on the beach he was an anti-fascist; he had taken part in dangerous activities—in opposition to Mussolini—in Trieste, which I had not been aware of until Eric informed me. My mother has never been straightforward about any matter, and once I was mature enough to understand her behavior, I attributed it to her experience during the war. I can only imagine how difficult the time must have been for those living in Europe. I do not know if your mother has spoken of those years.

I did not see my parents during the months I knew Caleb—they had spent a good deal of time in Trieste that summer and remained there through the fall. Although Eric had encouraged me to go with them, I had decided against doing so; I had not wanted them to know our marriage was an unsuccessful one. Naturally they would have realized this if I had visited Trieste with them and had not planned to see my husband later while he at the time was in Italy on business. For Eric had led me to believe he did not want to meet in Europe that summer, that he intended to keep his distance.

Caleb had completed his medical school coursework the previous spring. Hans was attempting to set him up in an exchange program in Amsterdam. I do not believe Hans was aware of my relationship with Caleb. It might have been a difficult time for him as well—for I gathered that Isa had begun to spend much time away from Hans and Caleb. It was a time of uneasiness for all, and as I said, the heat was relentless, seemingly inescapable, our limitations both practical and psychological preventing us from exiting the city.

When Caleb and I first spoke, he did not realize I was married, and by the time I told him it was too late; we had become close very soon after meeting. Before he left for Europe, he told me I needed to make a decision about my marriage. I would have preferred to have continued on in secret, but Caleb did not agree. While he was in Amsterdam he wrote and asked several times if I had made a decision. As I repeatedly avoided his question, he eventually stopped contacting me. And so your cousin Caleb remained honest and ethical; he always wanted to do what was right and fair and I wish him only the best, as I had put him in an untenable position from the start. But you must understand I did not do so in a calculated way or willingly. I simply could not leave Eric; I felt bound to him and it was an awful feeling. It was as if I were in a jail of sorts, a self-imposed one—for I could have walked away; no one would have stopped me. Maybe it was related to Eric's nightmares; he had horrible dreams because of the war and I felt responsible for him in that way. He had been harmed because of what he had witnessed, I believed. As Roberto asked, "Why did little Eric not speak?" After some thought, I now wonder if Roberto may know the answer.

Eric never spoke of his experiences as a child during the war, and whenever I questioned him about those years, he would not answer; he'd become angry—not openly, but I could feel hostility brewing within him. I was never frightened of Eric but I was frightened for him, what he might do that would cause him to become more flawed, more withdrawn. For I had gathered that we would eventually part—we had not been intimate in over a year—things could not go on as they were.

When I miscarried, it was, of course, Caleb's baby. Eric did not ask questions, pretending it was his when both of us knew it was impossible. I do not think it disturbed him that I had been involved with someone else—I think he was that confused. How was it possible for me to leave someone who was lost? I was waiting until he found himself in some way—then I would be able to go on with my life, then I could leave. But I was compelled; I could not separate from Eric until this began to happen. At the time I could not explain this to Caleb, as I had not fully realized it myself.

You must be convinced I treated your cousin terribly, but I did not purposely do so. Caleb was searching for some sort of comfort that summer. He was disillusioned with his mother—he eventually told me he was vaguely aware she was having an affair with someone on the Riviera—and he was angry with his father for his lack of assertiveness, allowing Isa to leave the both of them for long periods of time. And Caleb was looking, I believe, for a distraction, a way to soothe himself, and I was there and I was good to him—that was, until he left for Amsterdam.

I believe Caleb was right to end our relationship, and I made the correct decision to stay with my husband. My regret is that I was not able to help Eric.

I never told Caleb about the miscarriage. Would he have wanted to know? I find it painful that you speak of his playing with the children. If my pregnancy had continued, would not our child have been six years old now? Close to the age of one of your sisters' daughters? But the pregnancy ceased and Eric died three years later. And so in essence nothing of significance had been gained.

Although I knew Jonas was in New York at the time, and had seen him occasionally at the gallery where he worked, he was simply a friend. Before I met Caleb I had hoped to have a relationship with Jonas; he wasn't interested because I was married. I did not see him with any regularity until after Eric's passing. He had come to me to extend his sympathy. And eventually and slowly we became involved. He encouraged me not to feel guilty about Eric's death and coaxed me out of my mourning. Of the two of us, I was the one who was looking for a romantic relationship. Jonas was hesitant because he was only beginning to feel confident as an artist and wasn't certain how successful he would be financially. He also was unsure about becoming involved in a committed relationship; his father had died before he was born, and Cora, his mother, had kept him from knowing her lover—and for those reasons he believed marriage was beyond him; he had not witnessed a mature relationship.

I did not tell Jonas about Caleb. I do not think he would have wanted to know. Though I believe he would have been understanding and would be today if I told him about my involvement with your cousin. Jonas was always aware that Eric and I were not compatible; as a friend and neighbor he accepted my decision to marry Eric and never caused me to question it. I trusted Jonas because I had known him longer than the other men I was acquainted with; he had never been dishonest with me, nor had he ever attempted to intrude in my life.

It has taken me this long to realize that Eric would never have been happy—it had to do with his temperament, I think. But I am not certain, I do not know what he experienced during the war. As his wife all I was aware of was how he would cry out from his nightmares. I would awaken and try to soothe him. Only when he was half-conscious would he let me do so.

If I had not been so young when we met and married, I would have asked him directly about his dreams and maybe he would have been more forthcoming about his past. Perhaps he would have revealed what he had experienced and I could have helped him resolve it in some way. I simply do not know and will never know—it is something I will live with always, but as the years pass, the burden is lighter; time allows you to see that one person cannot solve all problems or be everything to any one, even one's spouse. We all have a responsibility to improve our lives. It is up to the individual, I think. Yet I understand I will always believe that to a certain extent I contributed to Eric's sadness. Living with an unhappy person causes you to become melancholic and then you act in ways you would not have before you met him.

I have enjoyed speaking to Mara the few times I have gone to her shop. She has given me a perspective on my own life, one that was needed, and to a degree, she has helped me sort things out.

As I told you on the beach, Jonas and I came to Roberto's hotel because of the postcard I discovered this past June, one that Eric had sent me before we became involved. There was nothing of significance in his words, but the picture on the front of the card was of the hotel. In coming to the Riviera I was hoping to find some justification in my marriage to Eric—it has been my way of mourning him—but this visit has only unearthed more questions than answers. I brought the postcard with me, but I have misplaced it, which is probably for the best.

I hope my letter has eased your doubts.

Your loyal friend,
Jenny

Twelve

The Dream

On the thirtieth of August, Jonas and I motor toward the Nice airport; the drive is easy, the car windows fully open, the morning breeze soft, caressing. I look back and take a last glimpse; once we turn the next corner the hotel will no longer be in sight. What comes to mind as it has many times over this month is how the exterior of the building, utilitarian in concept and odd in structure, is markedly inconsequential in contrast to the exquisite foliage and the all-encompassing vista of the glistening Mediterranean.

We will take a quick flight to Paris and from there we'll board a plane to New York. It is early and there are only a few other cars on the road. Off to the right we pass a series of stone walls and an abundance of magenta-colored bougainvillea.

As we near the airport, I am stricken with a sense of loss.

Many questions linger; I understand that I may never fully comprehend the memory that has become part of me, haunting me; it may never cease doing so.

I did not say good-bye to Mara and have not seen her since the day Hans walked into her café. I had slipped away before she realized I'd left. I strain to keep in memory that image of her—the moment her eyes fastened on Hans, her lips parted, the contours of her face, accentuated, hardened, reflecting her passion for him, her eyes expressing her fear of it.

Six hours have passed since we left the hotel. At the Paris airport now, about to board the plane to New York, we wait in line, our shoulders touching. Jonas takes my arm and I turn to him, his eyes set; he asks if I am happy about having come to the Riviera. There is a yearning tone in his voice, which confuses me. I nod. And then to deflect his serious mood, I tease him, tell him I am surprised he has not shown me his sketches. Grinning briefly, he shrugs. As we file onto the plane, I sense his unease.

An hour into the flight we drink wine, a red musky liquid, lingering in the throat. When I ask Jonas to describe his drawings, he speaks evasively, vaguely referring to the Mediterranean, the foliage. He does not say which ones, if any, will become paintings, which works he will discard, or just keep as sketches. In his shirt pocket there is a small box filled with sticks of pastels. When I ask about them, he says he purchased the pastels because they remind him of the colors of the Riviera.

Feeling loosened from the wine, in exaggerated detail I begin to describe the memory that has been haunting me. Fervently, I say it has become a part of me; it burdens me, prevents me from being completely free.

He takes my hand but does not speak of my memory; instead, he responds, "Jenny, I encouraged you not to mourn for Eric, I hoped to distance you from that feeling—you were too young to be sad."

As he speaks, I watch him closely. Although there may be truth in what he is saying, I do not reflect on his words, more on his demeanor. How he raises his brows when he speaks, the turn of his head, revealing the sharp angle of his face, his high forehead, his hand clutching mine, long fingers, wiry, active hands, not passive, but he is mostly calm and assured, how he rests his shoulders against the chair, how he spaces his words.

Then he turns away as if to gather his thoughts. When he again faces me, he says, "This memory you have been speaking of—is it real? Or is it a conflation of bits and pieces of occurrences in your life from many years ago and perhaps even from the recent past? Maybe they have all fused in your mind to create this memory. Maybe it did not happen in the way you recall; perhaps it is a dream, a recurring one you had when you were a child—or, could it have to do with . . ." He pauses and then says, "Eric."

I look directly at him and say honestly, "But Jonas, I never think of Eric, unless I am forced to."

His voice is caressing, yet I hear a touch of irritation in it.

I know he does not want to sound mean or hurtful, "Who forces you, Jenny?"

"I force myself, Jonas, whenever I am reminded of him, who else would?"

"Roberto?" he asks.

"Roberto doesn't faze me. I do not believe him, his words. I think he invents what he says; he is unreliable," I say flippantly.

"Roberto is complex," Jonas answers.

Then he smiles as he does whenever he intends to change the subject. He tells me about one of the waiters at the hotel, how he had asked him if he'd like to buy a watch. Understanding it was a joke, he went along with him—I do not need a watch, Jonas told him. But you will when you are home, the waiter said, pointing to me as I approached the table. You will need to watch her when you go back to America. I laugh. We laugh together at the silly joke. Soon, drowsy from the wine and the hum of the engines, I turn away, and before I fall asleep, I look over at Jonas and my gaze catches the box of pastels in his shirt pocket. Reflexively, I lower the flap of material to cover them, my fingers graze the powdery sticks; my eyelids heavy, lowering against my will.

The box of pastels is larger now, the size of a window. You reach over to touch it as if it were a pane, but the sticks begin to melt from the strong sunlight. The colors pour out, staining the glass. A hand presses your shoulder, but when you turn round no one is there. You become fearful. In the distance you see Hans coming toward you. You are on the street now. He stays at a distance, does not look at you. As he approaches, you realize it is not Hans but Caleb, and suddenly he seems more at a distance, and disappears. Did he go inside a house? There are many homes—you do not know which one it is; you feel discouraged. Tears flow down your face. As you begin to walk home, you bump into Helen—or is it Mara? They appear similar in every way, even age, though you know Mara is more than twenty years older. Your dispiritedness turns to frustration. You look upward and see the window that was Jonas's box of pastels; the pane is now red. Someone is opening it—Eric sticks out his head and nods at you; he does not wave but nods. You stand on your toes and wave, but looking up, you see he is no longer there. Instead it is Roberto, staring out with his hawklike gaze, and behind him is Mara—or is it Isa? Now you find yourself in New York—your apartment, but no, it is another apartment, the one in Hartford maybe, and you are alone, no one else is here. You hear your mother crying out for you. It is very cold, no more sun. You are shivering and alone in the apartment; there is no heat. There is no furniture other than one chair against the wall. You go and sit on it, crossing your arms, rubbing them with your hands to keep yourself warm. Eric walks by in a rush, does not see you. You cry out, tell him you are cold. He is gone. Hans and Caleb walk in attached at the shoulder; they are naked and their expressions are in opposition, as if one is wearing a mask of tragedy and the other of comedy, but you cannot determine who is wearing which one. Jonas comes in; he stands in front of a gate. You are outdoors now; it is warm but you are still in the chair. He opens the gate and swiftly approaches Hans and Caleb, placing one hand on each of their shoulders, and attempts to pull them apart. You watch without feeling. You know Jonas but not as much as you will know him. Soon he disappears and so do Hans and Caleb.

Inside the room again, you are more cold than you were. You shiver; still sitting in the chair, you realize you are glued to it. But looking out the window across the room you see it is warm and sunny. Your parents come to the window and wave from outside, your mother blowing kisses in that stolid way of hers, your father subtly smiling. He is pleased with your mother, with you, with himself, but it is not obvious; people do not realize, do not know him. He is more confident than he seems. But suddenly it becomes dark as if night has come. You no longer see your parents. You do not know if they are still outside the window or if they have left. But soon you realize you are alone, as if you have been alone the entire time; you feel separate from those you have seen—they have not made an impression on you.

Slowly coming into consciousness, you are unable to raise your eyelids; they are glued to your sockets as you are to the chair. For you are still half in your dream, one you cannot leave. Caleb returns, but not Hans. He is not alone; he is holding something in his arms, a baby with blond hair. Abruptly Caleb and the infant vanish. Not able to move from the chair, still stuck to it, you look down; at your feet is a pool of blood.

~

My lashes wet, I open my eyes and hear the uneven sound of Jonas's voice as if he's been roused from his sleep, telling me we have almost arrived; over the intercom I hear a voice telling us to straighten our seats. As I press the button to do so, I look down and smile, but then I am uneasy—for what I thought I lost has been found; on my lap is the postcard from Eric.

Thirteen

The Return

The day after our return, the last of August, the heat is dry and piercing, no hint of a breeze. In the grassy area behind the apartment building, we rest beneath the shade of the willow tree. Jonas presses his head against the trunk; I lie across his lap, my back against his shifting knees. Surrounding us are clusters of daisies, limp and spaced apart, nearly hidden by the overgrown grass. Weary from traveling, we are mostly silent.

A streak of light passing through an opening in the fine branches is blinding. I shield my eyes with one hand and slightly lift my head; Jonas comes close, anticipating my words. A ray crosses the side of his face, revealing a glint of green in his dark-eyed gaze, a suggestion of mild sarcasm at the corner of his mouth, a purposefulness in the line of his jaw.

"Jenny?" he asks promptly, willing me to speak.

I lie back again, my head touching the dry grass, my heart beats rapidly. Flushed from the warmth of the sun, I eye the drifting, wispy clouds, and then raise my head, bringing my face near his. "You want to know about the postcard," I say, peering into his eyes.

Blinking, his lashes long and sparse, his words measured, "How long have you had it?"

"Only a few months." I sit up, now facing him, empowered by my need to reveal. "I found it in my parents' home, in my bedroom, in a book, one that I read a few times the summer I met you, months before I became involved with Eric. I had used the postcard as a bookmark, I suppose. When I discovered it in June, I did not recall having received it—it drew a blank in my memory. And I thought the hotel might be interesting to go to. I was not aware that once there on the Riviera, figures would emerge from the past."

"You really did not know Roberto's second wife," Jonas says, his voice edgy, "and his ex-wife is from Eric's past, not yours. You had heard of Roberto but did not know him, did not even remember his name."

I take a breath; avoiding his gaze, I say, "There is more, Jonas."

He lowers his head, does not raise it; I speak candidly about Isa and Hans and Caleb and Helen—I add that I had not met Helen until this summer; I had not known that Caleb had a cousin who lived in Paris. He had only vaguely mentioned cousins in Europe—not naming a particular country—and said he would stop by and visit with them once he finished with the exchange program in Amsterdam.

Jonas's head remains lowered, I cannot read his expression, do not know how he comprehends or interprets what I am telling him. He's wearing khaki shorts, his legs slightly open, his knees up, his palms on the grass. An ant circling his shin is nearly camouflaged by the hair on his legs. I cannot intuit what he is thinking, feeling—he doesn't want me to—I continue on as it is what he desires; he needs to hear, to know.

When I speak of my affair with Caleb, I wonder if Jonas is uncertain—will I be disloyal to him too? This is important to him—Jonas lives by a strict ethical code. My guess is he will surmise that if I believed I was unhappy in my marriage I should have left, perhaps even married Caleb, been honest about it with Eric, with myself—but these are only guesses. I continue, sometimes hesitantly, sometimes warmly, sometimes uncertainly, but invariably honestly.

The more I explain, the stronger I feel, the more compassion I have for Jonas, and at the same time, the more angry I am with him for not having realized what may have occurred during my marriage to Eric.

When I finish, there is silence, not an empty silence, but one filled with apprehension, frustration, anger, and passion—each of us inwardly experiencing these emotions, maybe not in the same order, but with the same intensity. Yet there is an ironic side to Jonas, which he may very well express momentarily. But I am older now, accepting of his flaws, my own, and those of others, understanding that I come face to face with one or more of them every time I converse with a person or eye myself in the mirror.

Jonas speaks first. He does not raise his head and I am reminded of when I first met him that summer, my eighteenth, the August I received Eric's postcard, that when I approached Jonas, his head had remained lowered, and that he had not raised it until after he had introduced himself. Then when he lifted his gaze, I had been struck by the complexity in his penetrating dark eyes and, as young and inexperienced as I was, I understood he possessed a perspective and knowledge of the world that was quite foreign to me, one that I might never desire to comprehend. At that moment, I was endeared to him. Though I had realized all this about him on that day, I never could have foreseen our evolution as friends, lovers, and eventually a married couple.

"Jenny," he now says, and in his tone I hear concern, hurt, and longing, but not distrust or irony, the way he may sound at his darkest moments. "You did not need to say everything; it wasn't necessary." But when our gazes meet, I see he is uncomfortable about what I have revealed to him, uncertain whether or not it will bother him in the long term. Yet I believe he is relieved I have been this forthcoming. Maybe he knows he can trust me now. Though I am not looking for his trust or acceptance.

Because of our jet lag, we go to bed early. In the middle of the night Jonas calls out in his sleep. I sit up and lean close to him, hoping to hear what he is saying—it is a muddle of words: Eric, Cora, Caleb—as if he's speaking of one person.

I lie down again and try to sleep. I glance at the clock. It is 2 a.m., a new day, a new month, September, realizing summer is slipping away; with a slight feeling of melancholy, I already miss the intensity of August. Different thoughts wander through my mind, fleeting images—Mara, sitting in her shop, an unlit cigarette dangling between two fingers, her expression enigmatic, or Helen, her head lowered, fingering the edges of her floppy hat. I envision Hans, his expression a blend of wistfulness and dispassion as he came into Mara's shop, as well as Roberto lifting his chin and asking, "Why did young Eric not speak?" his hawk-like eyes evading my gaze. But I am not thinking of the memory that dominated most of the summer, that passionately clung to me, haunting me—the man in the charcoal-colored pants swiftly passing me, a woman sitting in a chair with a red stain on her lap. For it strikes me now that it has lost its significance; it is not important anymore. I do not know if it was real or imagined or pieces of my past life from different experiences, out of sequence, folded into one memory. All I know is it no longer resonates within me; it is no longer there as a warning, or a burden I carry. There is no depth or mystery to the image I have broken apart and played over and over in my mind.

FOURTEEN

THE SKETCHES

Ten years have passed since the August we spent at Roberto's hotel. Although Jonas and I have not returned, we have visited other places on the Riviera, pointedly avoiding the French-Italian border area and any city or town in close proximity to Mr. Carini's establishment.

I have not heard from or seen Roberto or Mara, or Helen and Marc; neither have I come across Hans or Caleb in New York, which is not surprising given the size and sprawling geography of the city, and how many of its inhabitants yearn for anonymity. Yet every year since that summer of ten years ago, some time in the heat of August, I have recalled our visit to the hotel. In certain years I have done so thoughtfully and on others, when I've been preoccupied with work or busy with practical matters, I have only fleetingly remembered the people I met and who in one way or another afforded me insight into my first husband, and also, though less significantly, the Sokolov family. In those years when my focus was contemplative, I arrived at different conclusions, each with the same intensity. The summers that my interest was superficial, my analysis was swift, equal to the short amount of time I spent thinking of them. The mystery or confusion of that August, I decided, had to do with the fact that I was not aware that Hans Sokolov had been my mother's doctor and that she had gone to him for behavioral neurological therapy—for that is what I have surmised. Given that her husband, my father, had worked in opposition to the government during the 1940s, the stress of it may have caused an assault on her nervous system, and naturally Eric, a child at the time, must have been scarred by events surrounding the war. In terms of Roberto, I concluded he was simply an aging man attempting to arrange the past in his mind, more for practical, cognitive reasons than with any depth.

On those August days when I thought more deeply about the summer of 1984, I'd replay in my mind the details that have stayed with me—my conversation with Helen on the beach, the novel she was reading, how tightly she gripped it, her mouth tense and awed, the magenta-colored bougainvillea surrounding the front of the hotel, Roberto standing next to the pool in the early morning hours, his fixed expression. What had he been contemplating? What had he experienced? How much did he know about my parents, how much did he know of Eric? As the years have passed, more and more I have believed he understood very well why little Eric did not speak, and that asking the question had been his way of gauging my knowledge.

After we returned to New York, our life together took its natural course. Jonas submerged himself in his work, and gradually his paintings garnered recognition from his colleagues. Once critics became interested in his work, art dealers did so as well. It was a slow process, but then suddenly, about three years ago, his name became recognized in that world.

The spring following that summer on the Riviera, I completed my master's degree in journalism—seven and a half years after I'd first contemplated doing so. After two years of freelance journalism, I found a job with a magazine that suited me.

The name of the magazine is *Life and Times*; it presents a cultural and psychological look at the world we live in today. It has a small but consistent following and I am not paid very much for the articles I write, but I am content with my work. I meet interesting people and have enjoyed interviewing each one of them, discovering their purpose in life, why they have chosen to do what they do. I have traveled to different parts of the country as well as to various nations.

Jonas and I have often been apart; I need to be away a good amount of time—occasionally he'll accompany me, especially if there is a particular landscape or site he wants to see or if it is a place he has never been. One time he came with me because there was an art exhibit he wanted to view in London, where I would be interviewing an antique dealer—it was about seven years ago, the first year I began writing for the magazine.

The dealer had red hair cut short and styled—Jonas and I saw her through the front window before walking into her store, we looked at each other, silently wondering if she was the woman on the beach Jonas had attempted to save from drowning. She appeared eerily like her. And during the interview, whenever I questioned her about her work or one of her items, the way she raised her eyebrows with surprise yet absence was hauntingly familiar. Jonas had been looking about her shop while she and I sat at her desk in the back. When we walked out, Jonas and I shook our heads, not knowing if it was more our imagination than reality.

The interview that has affected me most was with an articulate and talented ninety-year-old woman. Her life had been simple, she said, smiling effortlessly. She lived in Cleveland and for the previous twenty years she had been a sketch artist for certain newspapers and magazines. It had happened inadvertently, she added, shrugging her narrow shoulders, seemingly unimpressed with her success. She had been visiting the Cleveland Museum and had been struck by one of the paintings, a Sargent, *Portrait of Mrs. Ralph Curtis (Lisa de Wolfe Colt)*, and though she had seen it before, this time she was struck by profound sadness in the woman's expression. She took out her pad and began to sketch—she would do so from time to time with paintings she found compelling. As she spoke I pictured her standing before the Sargent with one leg forward—her stance when she had opened the door to greet me—looking up thoughtfully at the work then lowering her head to draw. An editor who worked for a city newspaper had walked by and had come over to look at her sketch. He nodded and suggested she come to his office the next day. That was the beginning, she said, crossing her hands on her lap.

She had one son who lived in California, the wine country, and her husband had been an exuberant person. Their relationship, she said, had been complicated—in some ways they had been opposites, had had different interests, but in other ways they had been very much alike.

A few weeks later, she sent a sketch of herself, a self-portrait so that I would remember her, and there was also a sketch of me, a smaller one—she apologized and said she tried to remember me as best she could, but the Sargent at the museum that had launched her career kept coming to mind instead. In the sketch of herself she appears as unimpressed with herself as she had in person, but her gaze is more focused, more penetrating than I remembered, and in her rendition of me I was surprised by my slightly lowered head, the furrow in my forehead, the intent expression and subdued sadness in my eyes. I have framed the sketch of her and it is in my small office; I look at it every day for inspiration and affirmation. She possessed no illusions; she was content.

Five months after we returned from the Riviera, a Saturday in mid-January—the first storm of the winter season, I believe—I had awakened late and Jonas had offered to make me breakfast in bed. As he generally did not like the snow, I was surprised by his animated mood. The window was clouded with white patches, sunlight piercing through; I was happy to stay in bed, and remain beneath the warmth from the covering layers of blankets.

Jonas brought in the tray, smiling openly, no trace of irony. The aroma of bacon mingled with that of warm maple syrup was intoxicating. The snow was falling heavily now. I ate wholeheartedly; he sat on the edge of the mattress next to me, not saying a word, watching me closely.

When I finished eating, I lay back against the pillow and studied Jonas as if observing him through a different lens: his high forehead suggesting concern, his eyes small and brown, his lashes long, yet sparse, his face angular, his expression fixed. I fully understood how much of an enigma he was to me.

He took the tray away and left the room. Soon he was standing in the threshold; he instructed me to close my eyes, his expression steadfast, half boy, half man. And I did so, firmly covering my lids with the palms of my hands, waiting in anticipation. I heard him call out, his voice hoarse with anticipation, telling me to wait, he wasn't quite ready. Finally he cried out, "Open!" I lifted my hands, and at first my gaze was blurred; but as my sight became clearer, I saw spread apart and taped on the wall across from the bed seven sketches—the ones I believed he had done in August, on the Riviera.

The first sketch was of bougainvillea, only bougainvillea, as if bursting from the wall, not the inspiring, richly colorful bougainvillea we admired each day, but now sketched in charcoal, mostly in black and white—hauntingly devoid of color. The starkness of this rendition was eerie to behold, more intricate and narrow, without bloom.

The second drawing was of Roberto Carini, sitting at a round white table, a smaller one, at the café part of the restaurant. One elbow on the table, his hand raised almost in a salute; he looks outward in profile, a hint of the sea in the distance, his expression is pensive, yet decisive.

The third one was of the man who nearly drowned, sitting on a small towel on a beach, in a bathing suit, his legs spread open, his wet hair pressed to his head like a skullcap. There is a sense of isolation in his demeanor and posture, his arms close, his shoulders, drooping.

The one next to it was a sketch of the Mediterranean Sea. Touches of gray throughout, and a narrow strip of sand outlines the shore, pebbles and rocks nearly covering it. Shadows darken the rocks and sand, the frothing waves overwhelmingly white.

The fifth work was of a lone palm tree, only the sky in the background, more white than gray. The dark fronds and even darker trunk appear ominous in contrast to the sky.

Next to it was one of Remy, Helen and Marc's child. He is dressed in the clothes he wore whenever he came down to dinner, a pressed short-sleeved shirt and shorts. In both hands he holds a small globe, cupping it as if fearful he may drop it, it seems. Behind him, in the distance, the sun is rising. His feet are bare.

The last one was of a young woman leaning forward against the railing of a balcony. The face is not visible. The nightgown she wears reveals much of her back. Her hair is in a French braid, falling to the middle of her spine. The sea is in the distance, and her arms are extended across the railing, her head is tilted to the left. Dangling from her right hand is what appears to be a postcard.

From time to time I will recall the winter morning Jonas presented me with the sketches. I understood it to be an affirmation of our relationship, an acceptance of himself, of me, of each of our flaws, ultimately of our marriage. He was exposing himself to me in a way he had not before. The sketches were piercing and revelatory. For in each work there was something of Jonas—his deep sense of irony in the sketches of the bougainvillea and the palm tree, his sense of fear in the one of Remy, his anguish that I had chosen the hotel on Eric's postcard for our honeymoon in the sketch of the young woman on the balcony, and that I had held on to the card. But it was clear we would go forward with our lives and not look back. At the same time I comprehended our path would not be smooth and easy, more prickly, not unlike the beaches of the Riviera.

It took me some time to summon my resolve—I prefer the word resolve to courage—to speak with my parents about their years in Trieste during the war. Five years after our return from our honeymoon on the Riviera, on a November day, with this purpose in mind, I went alone to visit them. I had been writing for the magazine for three years and had become adept at interviewing people. In my mid-thirties at the time, I was confident in my ability to ask questions subtly, yet thoroughly—I had honed my skills to a certain degree as an interviewer and journalist. Though I had not yet developed the necessary empathy, a professional empathy, you could say.

Jonas was busy with an upcoming exhibit, deciding which of his paintings he would choose, wanting to be true to the theme of what would be a broader showing of works by other artists as well. I told him I needed to see my parents as my father was not feeling well and it was difficult for my mother to care for him. He had had a virus and had not yet recovered from it. Although he was thin, he had a strong constitution so I was not concerned; yet he had recently turned seventy-five. I wanted to be certain he was not ignoring my mother's requests to consult his doctor if necessary.

When I arrived I was weary from the three-hour drive but not overly so, and spoke with my mother for a few minutes before going in to see my father. He was lying on his bed, watching the television. The Berlin Wall was coming down and he seemed amazed by it and appeared fully satisfied. I understood that he saw himself as a part of what had been accomplished. He was smiling steadily and I was reassured. In a way, given his past anti-fascist work, it was a gift to him, a reaffirmation of his beliefs, his hatred of oppression, his courage and selflessness.

I sat on the chair next to his bed and together we viewed the footage of the dismantling of the wall. Young men with large picks, chipping away at the wall, appearing lighthearted, more likely stunned by their newfound freedom. My mother soon came into the room; she sat on the bed and crossed her arms. She looked more tired than my father.

"Was it worth it?" she asked musingly.

My father looked sharply at her, and said, "Johanna, it is always worth it." She nodded and I noticed her eyes watering, but soon she composed herself.

She stood up and said she would start dinner.

I followed her out of the room and into the kitchen. I sat down at the table and crossed my legs, preparing myself to ask a question, one I'd most wanted an answer to since meeting Roberto Carini five years before.

At the stove, her back to me, my mother began to hum and when I offered to help her, she firmly shook her head. I went up to her and placed my hands on her shoulders; she was crying. I guided her to a chair, then I pulled my seat close to hers, and leaned forward, looking directly into her eyes. I may have lacked the empathy I should have had, my gaze was perhaps too penetrating, but I needed to know the truth. "Why did Eric not speak when he was a child?" I asked, hearing a certain directness in my tone, one I had never used with her before. She was surprised by my question, taken aback; her defensiveness evaporated.

At first she spoke haltingly, searching for words, her eyes tear-filled, but soon her innate stoicism prevailed; her speech became succinct, her expression guarded. "He was with his sitter, they were walking down a dark street and heard screams; a woman Eric knew was being raped by two men who were angry with your father; they viewed him as a traitor, working for the other side. Eventually it was understood that Eric was mute for a few years because of what he had witnessed."

I was silent, stunned by her sense of dissociation. Then suddenly, overcome with emotion, I reached out, my arms shaking, and drew her close. She did not resist, accepted my tears and her own.

The day before I left, my mother had driven to the store to pick up an item she had forgotten to purchase. It was the first time I had been alone with my father. He was much better by then, and was now watching the television in the living room, sitting in his favorite chair. He had been viewing the news almost continuously since the beginning of the fall of the wall. Growing up, I had known of no other person who was as humble and flexible as my father, and at the same time I realized that no one I had encountered could be more inscrutable or resolute than he.

Once my mother had walked out the door, I went over to the front window and watched her drive away. I felt chilled and hurt, fully comprehending that because of my father's heroism our lives had been formed by the violent actions of two unknown men. My mother and Eric had been most wounded, an understanding that has become the basis of my compassion for Eric as well as for my parents.

I soon determined that the memory that had haunted me that summer and then suddenly lost its resonance, that eventually became insignificant, symbolized the underlying anguish of my mother and father during my youth. The memory lessened in strength not because it wasn't in one way or another true, figuratively or literally, but because I needed it to weaken in order to fully live.

Epilogue

A late August day, the kind that occurs sporadically over the last few weeks of the month; the sky is clear, the color of lapis, the leaves of a hickory are a resounding green, and the blue hydrangea in hue and form, at the height of its beauty, reflects the stately perfection of summer.

She decides to visit a gallery where one of her second husband's works is on display, a painting that evolved from a sketch he had done on the Riviera twelve years ago. When Jenny walks in, the owner, a woman wearing black-framed glasses, her dark hair in a bun at the nape of her neck, is showing the painting to two customers, men in their mid-thirties. As she studies a painting nearby, an abstract one with spurts of color, she overhears her words, her voice imbued with a dry fervency:

"The painting is by Jonas Smila-Hoffman. His work is a marriage of postmodernism and traditionalism, though he says he does not like applying such labels to his paintings or to those of other artists. He is an interesting person, eclectic, in that he is not what he seems, though eventually one discovers most people are not. His paintings, muted in tone and color, are surprising;

stoked, perhaps, by the artist's deep sense of the unknown, for they are essentially emotional and passionate, as is evidenced in this work, The Postcard. *How does he achieve this? It is his talent, I believe."*

Moving on to study another painting, she no longer hears her words, only the lull of her voice, followed by the questioning tones of the two men who are viewing it with her. Jenny's mind wanders to the trip on the Riviera twelve years ago; she envisions Jonas swimming fiercely and assertively, attempting to rescue the British couple. But after all this time, she has come to realize what he was doing was not trying to save the memory of her first husband in her imagination as she first believed; instead he was hoping in some way to rescue Eric, a fragment of his life itself, as if in doing so, the person he believed was complex, whom he admired and thought resembled the young woman in Botticelli's Primavera, *would return to him. No matter his reason, he had been brave to do so. For in the heat of a hazy August day, his motions were firm and clear. She recalls what Helen's husband Marc later said, that Jonas was different than most.*

Though a circumstance may occur when many have the ability to be clear-eyed in the face of a seemingly impossible situation, rising above the heat and haze of it, reflecting the same sort of majesty that prevails on certain days in the last full month of summer. For in the midst of your deepest challenge, you may be selfless in choice or action, or, with all the strength you need to muster, walk away—whichever course you decide, at that moment, you are august.

www.ingramcontent.com/pod-product-compliance
Lightning Source LLC
LaVergne TN
LVHW040826090826
845145LV00001BA/208

* 9 7 8 1 7 3 6 0 5 3 6 7 6 *